HIGHLAND RECKONING

WILLA BLAIR

OLIVER
HEBER
BOOKS

To all the supportive, protective, and fair men in our lives. May there be many more of you.

1

At a shout from the Aerie's gate guard, Drummond Lathan looked up and narrowly missed losing his head to his sparring partner's attack. He dropped to his backside as his younger brother, Tavish, wrenched his blade from its arc and drove it into the sod between them.

"Christ, Drum! I expected ye to block that."

Drummond collapsed to his back. "My fault," he admitted. He took a moment to rid his gut of the sinking sensation his close call left behind, then rolled to his feet. "'Tis lucky ye were paying attention." He pointed to the gate at the far end of the Lathan keep's bailey, where a rider he didn't recognize was dismounting. "I let *him* distract me."

Drummond glanced at his brother as Tavish rubbed his shoulder. "Are ye hurt?"

"Strained it, I think," Tavish answered with a grimace. "Trying to avoid killing ye."

Drummond clasped his other shoulder. "Thank ye for that."

"I'll live," Tavish added with a shrug and a wince. "And so will ye, no thanks to him."

Drummond studied the rider. He didn't recognize him.

But all of the clans that signed the Lathan's treaty over the last twenty years were coming to attend a gathering in two months' time. Perhaps this man had come early to make arrangements for his laird, or to deliver a message to the Lathan laird. While Drummond and Tavish watched, the man spoke at length to the Lathan's chief guard. Once the man stopped speaking, Bhaltair turned his gaze to meet Drummond's and lifted his chin toward the keep, then escorted the visitor inside. Drummond's sense of anticipation deflated.

"Sorry, damn it," he groused, turning back to his brother. "The messenger must bring trouble, or Bhaltair wouldna summon me. Any idea what kind?" Did Tavish seem aware of anything about the man?

Tavish pulled his blade from the dirt, shrugged, and grimaced again. "Nay, not a hint," he answered with a frown. "Ye had me focused on keeping ye alive. If I'd had a vision, yer head would be on the ground and I'd be the heir. God forbid."

Tavish did not want the job—and was not suited for it. He'd already said he dreaded the upcoming gathering. Drummond was looking forward to the event. "Could ye?"

"Could I what?"

"Could ye have a vision while we're sparring?" Drummond glanced at Tavish when he hesitated to answer.

Finally, Tavish said, "I dinna think so."

"Ye dinna sound certain."

"How can I be? 'Tis not in my control, not yet, but of late, they seem confined to dreams."

"Get Eilidh to look at yer shoulder." Drummond clapped him on the back. Tavish's twin sister could quickly heal whatever he'd strained in his effort to save Drummond's neck. "Duty calls, little brother."

He headed into the great hall. When he didn't see Bhaltair and the stranger, he pivoted and went down the short hallway to his father's solar. The door was open, and Toran's voice was audible as Drummond approached.

"I'm sorry to hear ye are having such problems," Toran said. His tone made it clear he hadn't expected this visitor either. He wouldn't be so polite with a visitor he knew was coming, especially if the visitor was an old friend. Rather than voicing sympathy, he'd be in full problem-solving mode, telling the visitor what to do, or what Lathan was willing to do to help.

Drummond leaned on the doorframe and turned his attention to the man. Gray threaded his dark hair. A slight paunch to his belly made Drummond think he was middle-aged. Older than usual to serve as ghillie and carry messages for his chief, but perhaps his news was too dire to entrust to a younger lad.

Toran finally noticed Drummond and beckoned him in. He didn't seem concerned to have this stranger inside the Lathan keep, so perhaps he knew him. Still, Bhaltair stood guard at the back of the chamber, massive arms crossed, relaxed but watchful. Drummond knew him well enough to be confident that, though silent, he was alert—and fast. He'd be between his laird and any threat before a man could blink. Drummond gave Bhaltair a nod as he stepped into the room. The three Lathans could handle any threat, but this man did not appear to offer any.

"My son and heir, Drummond," Toran said to the visitor, then gestured his eldest son to a seat. "Angus is from the village near our Moncreiffe border. Reivers are raiding their outlying crofts." He gestured to their visitor. "Go on, Angus."

Angus nodded to Drummond, then turned his attention back to the Lathan laird before resuming his tale. "It started last year. We drove them away and thought we had ended the trouble. This spring, they came back."

"Do ye ken who they are? What do they take?"

"We havena caught one, so we canna be certain, but they ken the area verra well. Still, I doubt they're any of ours."

He rubbed his chin and Drummond heard the *skritch* of days-old whiskers.

"They dinna take much. A cow, or a couple of sheep at a time, this and that from a garden plot," Angus related, frowning. "Like, as they finish the last, they're only taking what they need to survive. No big raids such as ye might expect if they was to run the beasts down to Crieff for the cattle market."

Something didn't make sense to Drummond. He glanced at Toran for permission to speak, then lifted a hand to catch Angus's attention. "So if they're doing nay more, why are ye here?"

"Over time, they're takin' enough to keep us from gettin' through the comin' winter." A touch of color suffused his face as he turned back to Toran. "Men from our village fought with yer da and brothers at Flodden Field. Many died. We pay ye rent each year. 'Tis time for ye to earn it."

Toran showed remarkable restraint at Angus's criticism. He crossed his arms, bulging muscles the only sign of his sudden tension.

Drummond fought the urge to lean forward, expecting his father to throw Angus out of the solar. Instead, Toran continued to question their visitor. "Ye've sought them... "

"We've searched after each raid and havena found 'em. I've sent out patrols, but the reivers have evaded them. Like ghosts, they are. They strike at night, silent as a wraith, then disappear into the hills."

Toran frowned. "Yet ye must keep looking for them. What do ye need from us?"

Drummond knew his father felt strongly that any crofts or villages in Lathan territory could appeal to him for aid. Based on what Angus described, Drummond feared Lathans would soon spend days, weeks, or even months searching for these raiders.

"Men, Laird. Trackers, men trained to search out—to *find*—those who dinna wish to be found."

Drummond bit back a groan as his father's gaze shifted to him. As far as they knew, Drummond was the only one of Toran and Aileanna's children who did not inherit any form of her uncommon talent. Yet, he was good at finding things—in the keep, at least. Things people set aside and forgot. Things he noticed. He prided himself on his power of observation. His memory. Those were his strengths, his only powers, save his position as heir, that could compete with his siblings' special abilities. He'd seen the toll those took, and counted himself lucky to be without them.

And he didn't see how his knack for finding a lost brooch or eating knife would apply to searching for reivers near a village at the edge of Lathan territory. But he had no doubt what his father would say in response to Angus's request.

"Drummond, this sounds like a problem ye could solve more quickly than most."

His father's voice snatched him back from his woolgathering, and his words, though expected, made Drummond's jaw clench. But he knew better than to argue, certainly not in front of their visitor. He'd have words with his father when they were alone. For now, all he said was, "I'll need men."

"Ye shall have them." Toran turned back to Angus. "Ye dinna ken how many raiders have been stealing from ye?"

"Nay." Angus opened a hand, then clenched it into a fist. "A handful, mayhap. Not many at a time, but they may hold men back to guard their encampment."

"Women and children?"

Angus shook his head. "I dinna ken. 'Tis possible, I suppose, given that they take more than cattle and sheep."

Toran turned back to Drummond. "Fifty men should be enough to clean out a reiver encampment."

"Laird—nay," Angus interrupted. "We're already stretched thin. I canna support so many... "

So Angus was the village's chief? And came himself to appeal for help? Judging by Toran's raised eyebrows as he glanced toward Bhaltair, he had not been aware of that fact, either.

Drummond could see Bhaltair out of the corner of his eye. The big man gave his head a slight shake. He hadn't known either.

"A dozen, then," Toran amended with a nod. "With supplies. They willna strain yer larder any more than needful." He looked at Drummond. "They'll do the job, then leave ye be, as quickly as is possible."

"Thank ye, Laird," Angus said, and stood. "'Tis a long ride I've made—too long. I would appreciate—"

"Of course," Toran said, cutting him off. "I ken ye are eager to return, but ye must enjoy my hospitality this night. Ye will leave with my men in the morning."

AFTER THE STEWARD took charge of their visitor, Bhaltair closed the solar door. Toran waited while he took a seat next to Drummond.

"This could take far longer than Angus believes," Drummond began, hoping to convince his father not to send him away from the Aerie. Drummond felt that as the heir, his place was here. He needed to be at the upcoming clan chiefs' gathering, making himself known to those lairds he'd yet to meet, and staying on top of their discussions and decisions. Hieing off to the borders of Lathan land to chase ghosts seemed a poor use of his time.

"Aye, and I ken why ye dinna wish to go," Toran told him. "I, too, want ye at the gathering. But ye are the best at finding lost things. And ye'll have enough men with ye to cover a lot of ground."

"Fifty would be better," Bhaltair spoke up then, his voice a deep rumble that matched his size. He was one of the largest Lathan men. "But supplies for so many would slow us down."

"I havena decided ye are going," Toran told him.

"If yer heir is going, I should go with him," Bhaltair argued.

"All the more reason to keep both of us here," Drummond said, driving home the point he wanted to make. "Ye will need us when the other lairds arrive. Many may come early, for private discussions. And ye canna be certain whether Angus has told us all he kens about these raiders."

Toran shook his head. "That doesna matter," he said, decision apparently made. "Drummond, ye will go for a sennight." He held up a hand as Bhaltair cleared his throat. "I need ye here, Bhaltair." Then he turned back to his son. "If ye havena cleaned out the raiders by then, ye will return. Ye will be home well before the lairds begin to arrive. I'll send more men to reinforce the ones ye leave behind with Angus."

"If there's trouble here, ye'll want yer men at the Aerie, not days away," Drummond commented.

"There willna be any trouble—none that we canna handle. The lairds' men will camp in the glen. If need be, we can close the Aerie's gates and lock them out."

"With their leaders inside?" Drummond glanced at the Aerie's defensive walls, visible through the solar window. "We'll be under siege. Possibly from within as well as without."

"We have been besieged and survived. The prospect doesna fash me."

Drummond had heard all the tales of how his parents met during the lowlanders' invasion and ensuing siege. There hadn't been another since. "It should," Drummond argued. "How many of those lairds ken the Aerie's secrets?"

"None ken save yer uncle Jamie and Donal MacNabb."

Toran's answer rang out, terse and edging toward angry. "We've kept that information close."

"Da, think. How many lads have we fostered with those lairds? Lads who ken all there is to ken about this tor? How many of their lads fostered here?"

"Fewer than one a year, in either direction. Ours are sworn to secrecy, and theirs are kept from the kenning."

Bhaltair shifted uncomfortably in his seat.

Toran eyed him, giving Drummond a moment to enjoy having his father's attention off of him.

"What are ye not saying?" Toran's brow had drawn down at Bhaltair's movement.

"Only, Laird, that we canna be certain. Lads are not always the most reliable at keeping their silence. 'Tis one reason why we guard the hidden way as carefully as we do the front gate. As we always have."

"And always will." Toran stood and gestured to Drummond. "Get yer gear. And Bhaltair, pick among yer men to go with Drummond, including someone to leave in charge if 'tis time for him to return—with an escort."

Bhaltair got to his feet, Drummond rising next to him. His father's mind was made up. "How far away is Angus's village?"

"More than a day's ride," Toran told him. "Maybe longer, with supply wagons slowing ye."

Drummond nodded, caught Bhaltair's gaze, and left the solar, the big man on his heels.

"See to yer men," Drummond told him once the solar door closed behind them and they were alone in the hallway. "I'll have Cook assemble what we'll take with us. Tell the lads to ready two wagons—nay, three—and camping gear for a dozen men for a fortnight, maybe more." His father had said a sennight, but they both knew how plans could change. He'd rather be over-prepared.

"And medical supplies," Bhaltair advised.

"Of course. My mother and sister will be too far away to help."

Bhaltair nodded and left him to his own preparations.

MORVEN MACCOMAS PAUSED at her loom, leaned back and took a breath. Where was Rory? She'd heard him playing outside a short time ago, but now he was quiet. Too quiet. She'd long ago learned the first rule of mothering a young lad—silence meant trouble—and unfortunately, she didn't know how long he'd been quiet. The noise from the loom had covered the sounds he made.

She set aside the shuttle and stood, stretched her arms overhead and leaned first one way, then the other, to ease her back. Then she moved to the open door and peered out into the sunshine. "Rory?"

When her six-year-old son didn't answer, she frowned. Had he wandered off again? The lad loved to roam the glen and into the woods. She worried that someday he wouldn't come back. When he was younger, she'd search for hours, only to find him curled up under a shady tree, fast asleep. They'd had a dog who roamed with him and kept him safe, but that dog had gone this spring. It wandered off and did not return. She feared a pack of wolves had gotten him. Or someone in another glen who could feed him better than she could had won him over. No one in their village had seen him. Not that she'd tell Rory, but she feared he'd met his fate with wolves.

Rory still missed him and often said he still searched for the dog. Or his bones. So far, he hadn't found either.

Should she look for her son? The day was waning, but there were still a few hours of sunlight left. He always came back before dark. Almost always. The one time he hadn't was the day after the dog didn't come home. He'd searched as long and as

far away as his short legs would carry him, and had come home
in tears not long after the sun set, when the full moon also set.
She'd thought to punish him for scaring her so, but in the end,
his grief tore at her, too. She fed him a late supper and sent him
to bed, but only after extracting a promise that he would never
stay out after dark again.

She stepped out into the front garden, where she grew a few
flowers and flowering vines she used to make dyes, and called
again. "Rory, lad. Where are ye?"

"Here, Mam." His piping, childish voice came from the back
of the cottage. She walked around their small home's structure,
noting as she went where the wall needed repair, or the thatch
on the roof looked frayed by the wind. Something always
needed her attention. Or she needed to barter with someone in
the village to keep the rain and wind out of their small home, to
repair a rusted kettle, or carve a piece for the loom her father
had built for her mother. She never got ahead, never made
enough cloth to sell and set aside funds for their future.

She rounded the cottage to find Rory in a hole up to his
knees, digging with their one small spade she used for garden-
ing. "What are ye doin', lad?" She put her hands on her hips. If
he broke the spade, it would be expensive to fix or replace.

"Digging for treasure, Mam. I was told there was treasure
here."

"Ye were? Who told ye such a tale?"

"My friends, Kieran and Rabbie." He went back to scooping
rich, black dirt from the hole.

Kieran and Rabbie were no friends, though they were as
close as Rory had in his life. They teased him unmercifully, and
now they'd set him to wasting his energy on this task. He was
getting his clothes filthy, too, though he did that well enough
without their encouragement. It was a good thing that she
could make his clothes, from weaving the cloth to sewing each
garment. He was growing fast. As he turned, she noticed he'd

split a seam along his side. Aye, time for a larger set. She wondered how long new clothes would last before he outgrew them, too.

The loom that kept her trapped here was her only source of income and of keeping herself and her boy clothed. Without it, she would have been able to follow her handfasted husband to his clan, and perhaps her life would have turned out differently. Her son would have a father. Rodrick would ken he had a son, instead of disappearing from her village when their year-and-a-day ended. She'd sent word to his clan when she found, after all, she was pregnant with his bairn, and again when his son was born, but he'd never replied. Never returned. He'd forgotten her and cared not at all for the bairn they had created. He'd left her to face her village's censure for an unwed woman with a child. To be looked down upon by some as a failure, a lass who could not keep a man, even when she gave him a son.

She crossed her arms and watched Rory dig. She'd sworn when he was born that he would be the only man she'd ever love. So far, no one had tested her resolve. After six years of living on the edge of the village and the edge of village life, she knew that would never change.

E ven with Angus leading the way, the lack of notice by the people in the village surprised Drummond. He thought more of them would greet Angus and ask about the visitors. Those who didn't wave or nod simply went about their business as if more than a dozen mounted men riding with their chief toward their tower house keep was an everyday occurrence.

After Angus halted them, Drummond and Eduard, Bhaltair's second-in-command, exchanged a glance as they dismounted. Perhaps everyone in the village knew why Angus had been away, so they were able to guess why he returned with a small army.

"Yer men will have to camp out on the edge of the village," Angus told them and pointed to where he wanted them to go. "They can take meals here in the great hall when they're not riding patrols. Get those supplies ye brought to the Cook. She'll take care of the rest."

"Thank ye," Drummond answered. He turned to his men. "Do as Angus says and get the camp set up while Eduard and I go with him." He watched for a moment as the men led their horses and the wagons in the direction Angus had indicated, then followed Angus and Eduard into the keep and mounted the stairs to the great hall. There, Angus gestured to another man to join them and led them to his solar, waved them to a seat, and closed the door.

"This is my guard captain, Archibald."

"Archie will do," the man interjected.

Angus introduced the Lathans to him. "As we rode in, ye saw the lay of the land around the village," he continued, as he moved to his desk and sat facing them, leaning his elbows on its surface. "The glen to one side, aye, but on the other, plenty of tree cover for the raiders to appear suddenly and disappear into. Forest higher up. Mountains all around, of course, that make pursuit difficult, as well. There are many ways to come to disaster if ye dinna ken where ye are going. I strongly suggest yer men spend as much daylight as is left today getting familiar with the trails hereabouts. There are cliffs that willna be apparent in the dark, rocky burns, and other hazards to man and beast."

"Which implies yer raiders have done much the same and scouted the area."

"Aye, they ken how to disappear, and quickly. Ye need to learn to do the same. Archie," he added, turning to his guard captain, "assign a man of ours with each group. Take care to pick the men from among yer best. That should help keep the Lathans alive."

Archie crossed his arms and dipped his head. "Aye."

Drummond nodded. "What else do ye need?"

"That ye dinna cause trouble with the neighbors. Clan Moncreiffe. The last time we spoke, their laird told me they'd suffered some raids, as we have. But he's had more men available to help drive the trouble in our direction."

"Thoughtful of him," Drummond commented.

"Aye, well, in his place, I'd do the same."

"How long ago did ye talk with him?"

Angus leaned back. "Now that I think on it, longer than I realized. It must be two years gone. He'd had some trouble within the clan a year or so before, and suspected the reivers were lost men he'd banished, and a few who'd escaped his justice." He drew a finger across this throat, sat forward and placed his hands, palms down, on the surface of his desk. "Now, I've been gone nearly a sennight, fetching ye. I must get a report from my men. Go on and get yer patrols organized. Archie will join ye and pair up yer men with some of ours when I'm done with him."

Drummond's hackles went up at the abrupt dismissal, but he held his temper. Better he save his energy for finding and fighting the raiders. He summoned Eduard to him with a glance and left the solar. He sent Eduard out to organize their men, then stopped by the kitchen to speak to the cook about the supplies they brought and to request food be prepared for the men who would go out first on patrol. His mind stayed on their mission. How could they fight ghosts in the mountains who raided in the dark? At home, he was always good at finding things, but he doubted he would have the same luck here.

Morven MacComas, arms laden with cloth she'd made for the chief's wife, approached the keep from her cottage at the edge of the village. Her son, Rory, had insisted on keeping her company, as though the walk across the village was a trek into the mountains. For his short legs, she reasoned, perhaps it seemed so.

She eyed a group of lads playing with a stick and a feather-stuffed leather ball. "Stay away from those lads," she warned Rory. "They're too big for ye." Rory was small for his age, and the older boys were playing rough. His so-called friends, Kieran and Rabbie, were not among them.

He gave her a disappointed frown from under his favorite blue cap, but nodded agreement. She felt bad that the circumstances of his birth made both of them ostracized by some in the village. If not for her skill and her loom, they might not have a home at all. She hesitated, considering for a moment taking him into the keep with her, but Lady MacComas would not approve of an unsupervised child in the keep, so she gave Rory a last stern look and turned to enter. Instead of the handle to the thick oaken door, her hand encountered a solid, warm, leather-covered surface. Surprised, heart thumping, she glanced up.

A stranger! He must have opened the door and stepped out at the same time she reached for it, while her attention was on Rory or the lads she feared might harass him.

"Pardon me, my lady." He reached out to help her as she stepped back and juggled the folded fabric lying across her arms. Once it was secure, he nodded. "I am Drummond Lathan."

She'd heard Angus was back with reinforcements. This man was the first she'd seen. "Ye are one of the men Angus brought."

"Aye, I am. We've come to put a stop to the raiding."

"Thank ye. I hope ye do—and soon." She tipped her head and glanced toward the cloth in her arms. "I'm the MacComas weaver, Morven," she replied, looking back up at him. She was tall for a woman, but this Lathan was taller, broader, with muscular shoulders and arms that left no doubt he could handle himself in a fight. His eyes were the color of the forest loam outside the village, or old honey. His hair, a warm auburn touched with copper in the sunlight, covered the nape of his neck, framing his strong throat, but didn't reach his shoulders. Her gaze dropped to his muscular chest and flat belly, outlined by the travel-worn fabric of his shirt, then landed on the cloth in her arms, recalling her to the reason she was here. Not to acquaint herself with the attractive features of the handsome man before her. She had business with the clan's Lady. She tore her gaze away from him and nodded at the door. "If ye would?"

"Of course." He opened it and gestured her inside, but did not follow. Inside, before the door closed behind her, she glanced around to thank him again. He looked her up and down, then gave her a smile that froze her in place. For a moment, her breath caught in her chest.

"I'm pleased to meet ye. I hope to see ye again," he told her, before he closed the door firmly between them.

Morven became aware she was staring at the oak door, heart pounding. She took a breath that filled her cramped lungs. How dare he inspect her like a prize mare! What was it about that man? Handsome, surely, with a muscular build that made her fingers itch to trace each strong curve. He'd looked at her as if he wanted to do much the same, like she was a sweet, and he a starving man.

She forced herself into motion. She had to deliver the fabric in her arms, not stand here holding it to her chest and dreaming about a stranger who attracted and irritated her at the same time. No matter how much she liked his looks, she knew nothing about him, and her priority was Rory. The one and only love of her life.

She headed back toward the Lady's chambers. This time of the morning, she knew she'd find Ilise there. The door was closed, so she knocked softly and waited, her mind returning to the man she'd just met. Drummond Lathan resembled Rory's father. Was that why she was attracted?

She hardly thought about Rodrick any more. Her hand-fasted husband had been mysterious, handsome, and most of the time, kind to her. At the time, she'd thought she could have done much worse in her choice of mate, even though she knew little about him save that he came from Clan Moncreiffe, their nearest neighbors. They'd met at a Beltane fair held in a nearby village. He'd said he was an apprentice smith looking for his own place in the world. Their attraction had been instantaneous, and he'd followed her home to speak to the chief about blacksmithing for MacComas. Since her father, the clan's blacksmith, had recently become too beset with painful joints to work, Angus offered him a place. Before long he'd asked her father about marriage to her. Since they barely knew each other, her father had been reluctant. They'd compromised on the handfasting.

She'd had a rough time of it after he disappeared—and ever since. She'd lost him, then she'd lost her parents to a fever that swept through the clan. She'd never seen him again, despite her attempts to let him know she was carrying his bairn, and then again after his son was born. Rory looked like him, though, so she couldn't forget him completely. She shook her head as she knocked again and listened for an invitation to enter.

Her son came first. No matter how long that man remained in the village, she would keep him at arm's length. A weaver had no need to interact with a strange warrior.

Resolved, she turned her thoughts from him to the reason she was here. She was not eager to have strangers, especially big, handsome strangers, find out about her disgrace.

A serving lass admitted her to Lady MacComas's chamber.

"Ah, Morven, thank ye for coming to me. I fear I'm not at my best this morning."

Morven gave her a cheerful smile, though her heart broke for the woman sitting in a padded chair, a blanket draped over her legs. Months ago, she'd been injured in a fall from her horse, and had yet to recover fully. Some days were better than others. Some days, she could barely walk, which is why she had a chamber on the ground floor of the keep rather than joining her husband upstairs. She'd furnished it with a bed, table and chairs, rugs—one of which Morven recognized as her own work—and a chest for her clothes. Simple, but comfortable, it was clearly meant to be temporary. It didn't compare to the chamber she shared with Angus before she was hurt, but she bore the change in her circumstance with as much grace as anyone could muster.

This appeared to be one of the bad days. The strain was aging her, turning her dark blonde hair gray, making her skin wan and sallow, the constant pain she was in stealing the flesh from her face, etching lines of pain around her mouth and the corners of her eyes. Despite that, she kept an amiable air about her. Morven knew she was conscious of her position as the clan's Lady and didn't want her troubles to disturb anyone else.

"I'm sorry to hear that, Ilise. Perhaps after ye see what I brought, ye will feel better."

"I'm sure I will. The cloth ye weave is always the best and most beautiful." She glanced aside. "Could ye open that window? I'd like more light."

"Of course." Morven stepped toward it, but the serving girl got there first and drew aside the fur covering.

"Ah, good. That is better. Now, Morven, show me what ye brought." She reached out a hand, an eager smile lighting her face.

Morven laid the fabric in her lap, making sure to place it gently, then opened a few folds.

Ilise ran a hand over the surface, picked up a layer and turned it over. "'Tis lovely. Thank ye, Morven. I'm pleased."

"I'm so glad."

Ilise nodded to the serving girl, who brought Morven a small pouch. It clinked when she took it.

"Thank ye," Morven said to Ilise, and slipped the pouch into her skirt's pocket.

"Now, lass, how is that lad of yers? I havena seen him in days."

Which likely meant she hadn't been out of this room in days. How sad to be trapped in a body that suddenly would not do what it once did.

"He is much the same. Curious, full of mischief, as is any lad at that age. I'm sure ye'll see him the next time ye come outside."

"I hope so. I'm sorry to bar him from the keep, but since I'm forced to live on the ground floor, the clan's bairns would add to the noise of the adults going upstairs and back down again. There are times when I canna tolerate the noise, and as it is, I sometimes hear them playing outside."

"Yer own lads—"

"Can be a trial, but at least they are mine to discipline, and they generally will obey." Her quick smile was almost a grimace.

Morven felt all the more sorry for her. Likely she knew her lads needed a stronger hand to control them, but she was not up to it, and Angus was consumed with the village's troubles.

Ilise raised a hand. "Now, Angus tells me he brought back a dozen of the best Lathan warriors to deal with our wee problem. Have ye seen them?"

Morven laughed and settled into the chair Ilise pointed her to. "I have met one of them." She described the chance meeting at the door to the keep.

"What does he look like?" Ilise demanded. "We havena had any new men around here in months. "Is he handsome?"

Morven felt the heat of a blush bloom on her face. "Och, aye, I think so. And I think ye would, too."

"Damn, and here I sit, while a dozen handsome men invade us."

"I'm sure ye will feel better tomorrow. Ye will be able to see them for yerself."

"I'll hold ye to that," Ilise threatened with a grin. "Ah, something to look forward to. We've little enough of that lately. Save for yer lovely work." She ran her hand across the fabric's surface again.

"I'm glad ye are pleased." Morven paused, gauging Ilise's mood. The woman seemed more tired than usual. It was time to leave her in peace. Morven lifted a hand to her chest. "I really should go. I left Rory outside the keep, waiting for me."

"Ach, of course. Go on with ye. I'll visit with ye and that wee man outside tomorrow."

"We will look forward to it," Morven promised, as she stood and moved to the door. "Perhaps by then, ye can tell me what ye will make from the cloth."

"I'll think on it. Ach, I nearly forgot, I will want something for the Martinmas feast. The cloth ye made last year for Yule was beautiful. Can ye outdo yerself for this year for Martinmas?"

"Ye must tell me what color ye would like, and I'll do my best."

"Ye ken what I favor. Surprise me! I'll make something with a gathered skirt that will swing around me when I dance with my husband."

"That sounds perfect," Morven told her, and summoned her best eager smile. Wouldn't it be wonderful if by then, Ilise was well enough to dance?

Smiling to himself, bemused by the lovely woman he met at the keep's door, Drummond walked through the village toward where his men were setting up camp. He couldn't get her out of his mind. Her blonde hair fell in soft ripples to her slender waist. When she turned her head, he saw it was bound behind her shoulders with a simple clip. Her full curves pleased his eye

—and the rest of him. The village's weaver, she'd said. He paused by the well and looked to the edges of the village below him, wondering which cottage was hers and whether she lived alone.

He had a great deal of respect for women with special skills, a respect he'd learned at his mother's knee, and his sisters', as well as from others at the Aerie, such as the women who spun, dyed, and wove yarn; the cook, the alewife, the falconer, and others. He knew from Ferelith, the Lathan's weaver, that producing fine fabrics took a lot of work, skill and, to some extent, an artist's eye. The fabric Morven MacComas held to her chest had been exquisite. As he'd helped her right her burden in her arms, the material he touched was soft, almost slippery, with a deep, rich, dark wine color. Angus's wife was a lucky woman to have such a skilled craftswoman making cloth for her clan. The weaver was a beautiful woman, too, and his age, he guessed, or very near it.

He pursed his lips. Given the weaver's age, she was probably married, and he didn't consort with married women. He'd have no reason to spend time with her—with Morven—again.

As he moved across the open area surrounding the keep, a leather ball hit him in the side. He managed to catch it before it bounced away, and tossed it to the boys he'd noticed kicking it around the open space before he entered the keep. One of the lads caught it and waved. Drummond paused to watch their game for a moment, but a couple emerging from between the keep and another building caught his eye.

The lass carried a large basket in front of her, and wore a worried frown. The man paced beside her, leaning close to her ear and speaking to her in low tones. Each time he did, she leaned away from him and stepped to the side. He followed, crowding her.

Reluctant to cause trouble, Drummond watched the pair. Perhaps they were a husband and wife, having an argument, or she had displeased him in some way and he was berating her for it. Villages were full of couples like this one, angry one minute, and, he hoped, in accord the next. So far, the man hadn't touched his companion. But he hadn't taken the basket to carry it for her, and her expression made Drummond pay attention.

The lass noticed Drummond and met his gaze. She glanced aside at the man with her and grimaced, then looked back to Drummond. Her meaning couldn't be more clear. She wanted him to intervene. Should he?

He was a stranger here. He didn't know these people. The lads playing ball ignored them. Perhaps he should, too.

The man grasped her forearm.

She twisted and failed to escape his hold. "Let go of me." Her voice rang out sharp and clear.

"Not until ye give me a kiss," the man coaxed and leaned toward her again.

Drummond couldn't let the lass suffer unwanted attentions. His sisters had told him tales they'd heard from friends of how quickly a situation like this could escalate—and rarely ended well for the lass. He walked toward the couple, unhurried, as if on his way back to the keep.

"I willna. Not now, not ever," she said, and tried again to pull away.

"Do ye need something?" Drummond phrased his question to the man. As he expected, the man released the lass and rounded on him.

"Nay, naught. Who are ye?"

"It seemed to me the lass wasna interested in whatever ye told her," Drummond continued smoothly, keeping his gaze on the man and ignoring his question.

The lass gave Drummond a smile and took the opportunity he offered to slip away from her companion.

"Come back! I wasna finished with ye," the man yelled as she walked away.

She didn't look back.

"I think *she* was finished with *ye*," Drummond observed with his mildest tone. "She didna appear to enjoy yer company. I suggest ye leave her be from now on." He laid a hand on his dirk.

The man's eyes widened and he stepped back. "Ye are one of those men Angus brought. What's between me and her is none of yer business." He cut his gaze to follow the retreating lass.

"Is she yer wife?"

The man looked back to Drummond and shook his head.

"Betrothed?"

"Nay."

"Have ye asked her?"

"What? Nay."

"Then ye shouldna be restraining her and demanding a kiss. And in such a public place. Ye frightened her, and likely embarrassed her, as well. Is that how ye treat the lasses? What is yer name?"

Going red in the face, the man told him, "My name is none of yer business, just as that lass is none of yer business."

Drummond shook his head. This lad was stubborn enough to get himself killed someday. "Ye made her my business when ye accosted her," he said, letting his voice go gruff and angry. "Dinna do it again. The next time, I willna be so polite."

A smattering of applause startled him. He'd been so focused on the miscreant, he hadn't realized the lads had stopped their game to watch, and they'd been joined by a much smaller, younger lad, a few lasses, and an older couple.

"Ye'd best listen to him, Harlan," one of the lasses called. "He looks like he could make sure ye never bother another of us again."

Harlan paled, turned, and stomped away.

"Thank ye, milord, for Glenna's sake, and the rest of us, too," the lass continued, approaching Drummond. "Harlan doesna like to be told nay." The rest followed her and surrounded him.

He spent a few minutes answering questions about who he was and where he came from, then excused himself, happy that the situation had ended as well as it had.

It was time to focus on the reason he was here. He forced the weaver and the other villagers from his mind as he approached the Lathan camp being set up on the village outskirts.

It took the rest of the afternoon to get his men organized, some riding patrol with a MacComas man to familiarize them with the area, others resting and eating. Eduard went out with that first patrol, or Drummond would have consulted with him. He would have preferred to keep the size of his force hidden from raiders, but the village had no place to hide so many horses and men. So they'd done the opposite. Perhaps the show of force would encourage the raiders to go elsewhere for bounty. If not, he and his men would make sure they never bothered this village—or any other—again.

3

By the time Morven finished with the clan's Lady and stepped outside to collect her son, two older boys chased him. She didn't care if they were Angus's lads. They were ruffians who'd cornered Rory twice in the past. They stopped when she called Rory to come to her, the glare in her eyes fearsome enough, or so she hoped, to freeze them in their tracks and remind them they didn't want to endure what she'd dish out to them if they ever harmed her son again. To her, they were bullies, wild animals who preyed on younger, smaller lads. If she hadn't been so dependent on their mother's goodwill and purchase of the fabric she made, she'd knock their heads together, then go tell their father why.

Instead, she headed home through the village, coins clinking in her pocket.

Rory ambled along as only a six-year-old could do, from one interesting bug to another interesting dog and back to her, then off again, and chattering about a man rescuing her friend, Glenna, right before his eyes.

The lad liked to make up stories. Keeping an eye on him, she turned her attention to Ilise's request. If only her marriage had survived the end of the handfasting, she wouldn't be dependent on these commissions. She was thankful her mother's training still stood her in good stead. She'd been the village weaver and taught Morven everything she knew. Morven and Rory still had a roof over their heads because her father built their cottage when he married her mother. He was the village blacksmith until his joints gave out. From him, she learned patience and strength. She'd needed those lessons, too.

Something for the Martinmas celebration, Ilise had said. Something even finer than she'd created last year for Yule. Such a project would take planning to set up her loom. She wasn't certain whether there was enough spun and dyed wool in the village for what Ilise had in mind.

She was so deep into ideas of what to make, suitable for the clan's Lady, that she stumbled into a solid wall of male shoulder and muscled arm before the man's feet in front of her downcast gaze registered.

Damn it, she'd run into the handsome stranger again. Or he into her, she realized as her gaze tracked up his body to his shoulders and head. Drummond had bumped into her while looking back at one of his men. She took small comfort in that, as he twisted around. "Lady Weaver! Are ye harmed?"

"Nay, I'm well. And 'tis just Morven."

"I'm sorry, Morven. I wasna watching where I was going."

"Nor, I fear, was I, since I ran into ye."

"I think it more my fault."

"Nay. Had ye run into me, I'd be on the ground." The glint in his gaze told her he was amused at the idea of her falling flat on her back after colliding with him. Suddenly, she didn't appreciate that at all. "Do ye find that funny, Drummond Lathan?"

"Nay, 'tisna. I apologize again." He looked honestly remorseful and confused by her ire, his expression mimicking Rory's when he'd been caught at something he shouldn't be doing. "I will be more careful and less of an impediment to ye in the future." He waited for her nod of acceptance.

Rory ran up, shouting. "'Tis him! He saved Glenna."

Morven frowned at her son. What? Had something really happened to her friend?

"Now," Drummond said, turning to Rory, who had stood by while the adults sorted themselves out. "Who is this young lad?"

"My son, Rory." She turned her gaze to address him. "Rory, meet Drummond Lathan."

"Ye have come to rid us of the raiders," Rory said with the calm conviction of a much older lad. "And ye saved Glenna from Harlan."

Ah, now she understood. The village lasses considered Harlan a pest, always trying to steal a kiss. As far as she knew, he'd collected more slaps to his face than kisses.

Drummond raised an eyebrow and glanced her way. "A wise lad, and well informed," he told her, then knelt to put himself on Rory's eye level. "I have. I and my men. Ye needna fear trouble from any of us. Well, perhaps only yer mam does, if we continue to pay no attention to where we're going and run into each other again."

"But ye must pay attention," Rory admonished, "or ye will fall off a cliff."

"A cliff, indeed?"

"Aye, up there," he said, and pointed toward the mountain peaks, now painted gold by the setting sun.

"And how would ye ken that, my lad?"

To Morven, Drummond seemed partly amused, partly impressed. Rory looked younger than he was, yet he was smart, and in some ways, older than his years. With her neighbor Kelso's help, she'd spent hours tutoring him, proud of his agile mind. But he had a wanderlust she couldna control. Hearing him speak of falling over cliffs made her wish he was old enough for her to trust that he could take care of himself.

"Ye havena fallen, have ye, son?" She lifted her hand to her throat, waiting for his answer, grateful that every time he wandered off, he'd come home safe and sound.

"Nay, Mam. But I heard the other lads saying these newcomers wouldna be with us for long. That they'd all go over a cliff in the dark."

"Nay! Rory, ye mustna repeat such as that." Relief made her tone sharper than she intended. "These men are here to help us."

"Aye," he said, nodding. "I'm sorry," he added, and cast down his gaze.

Morven was stuck again by the resemblance between her contrite son and the expression on Drummond Lathan's face only moments ago.

"'Tis all right, lad. I ken ye didna mean anything by it. Ye were just repeating what ye heard. Thank ye for telling me. My men and I will be most careful."

Rory's head popped up, his eyes bright and a grin stretching his mouth. "Ye will? So I helped ye?"

"Ye did. Thank ye."

"Rory, lad, 'tis time to go home. Yer new friend has much to do, I'm certain. Come along." Morven had heard as much of falling over cliffs as she could bear.

"Aye, Mam." Rory sighed, then his eyes widened. He reached a hand to his head. "My cap!"

"Have ye lost it again? Rory! Ye had it on the way to the keep. Where have ye been since then?"

Rory studied his feet, then lifted his hands in surrender. "I dinna ken. Everywhere."

"Tell me, lad, is it blue, the color of yer mam's eyes?"

Drummond's question startled her. and her heart beat a little dance in her chest. He'd noticed the color of her eyes?

"Aye, 'tis."

"Then I believe I saw it behind those trees, over there," Drummond said, and pointed.

Rory ran over to the stand of trees Drummond indicated, then circled behind it and let out a whoop. "'Tis here!" He reappeared holding it high and waving it as he ran back to them. "Thank ye!"

"Ye are most welcome, lad."

"How did ye ken it was there?" Morven hadn't seen it from where they were standing.

"I passed by there earlier and noticed the color. I left it so the person who lost it might find it again."

"Ye passed by... " She trailed off, not sure whether to believe him. He'd seemed distracted when he said that, his gaze turning aside, but perhaps he was simply remembering noticing the cap. The proof was in Rory's hand. "Thank ye, Drummond Lathan."

Drummond sketched a brief bow. "Drummond will do. Again, milady, my apologies. I'll try not to bump into ye again."

She gave him a lift of her lips, not really a smile, and turned for home. He'd impressed her with his respectful treatment of her son. He hadn't ruffled his hair or touched him at all. For a moment, she let herself think it would be good to have a strong father figure for Rory.

Then she chided herself. They didn't need that. Rory saw the men in the village all the time. Her neighbor, old Kelso, took him riding whenever they visited. And this handsome stranger would be gone as soon as the raiders were vanquished.

THE NEXT MORNING, Drummond woke to the news that the raiders hit again during the night, evading his men and the MacComas men Angus's guard captain, Archie, had put on watch. The raiders took only a sheep. As annoying as that was, it could have been worse. But according to Angus, the steady pilfering was taking a toll. Winter was not that far off.

Angus didn't mince words. "I told yer da ye were too far away to do us any good, but even now ye are here, ye still canna put a stop to the raids."

Drummond gritted his teeth as Angus paced around his small solar, railing at the failure as though it belonged to the Lathan men. To Drummond alone. Though they'd been here only a day and his men had failed to find the raiders for months. How much did the man expect them to accomplish in one night?

"Why do I pay rent to the Lathan laird each year, when ye do naught for me or my people?" Angus had complained to Toran during the meeting at Lathan about its distance.

He had a point. The Aerie was too far away to be of use in an emergency, but by finding and destroying the raiders, Drummond meant to prove him wrong about their ability to help—if Angus didn't kick all of them out before he had a chance to do that.

Drummond hated to fail. "I'm determined to stop the raids at all costs," he assured Angus. If only he could find their hideout as easily as he found lost items for people in the Aerie —or wee Rory's cap. But that luck, or that tingle in his gut that sometimes seemed to tell him when he was close to a lost object, wasn't something he could depend on.

He found himself wishing he truly did have a talent like his siblings' to aid him in solving this problem. But nay, their abilities saved lives. His knack for finding lost odds and ends wasn't the same at all. And so far, he'd gotten along brilliantly without a talent like theirs. He'd continue to do so here. He was the Lathan heir, important enough on his own, without suffering as they sometimes did.

But where to start to put an end to these raids? "We'll

double the patrols. Keep them running all night, with a minimum of coverage during the day when everyone is up, active, and more likely to see trouble coming. If they're foolish enough to try a daylight raid, we'll be able to see them and follow to their hideout. At night, rather than riding patrols, we'll put a team in every pasture, every night."

Angus stopped pacing long enough to give Drummond a measured look. "Do we have enough men?"

"We do, unless ye have pastures yer men havena shown me."

Archie stood off to the side, smirking at seeing his chief berate the Lathans. Likely he was glad to have Angus's ire directed at someone else for a change. "My men willna like this," he said. "They've families, wives, they spend their nights with."

"They'll like even less starving this winter," Angus retorted.

The man grimaced and looked away.

"Very well," Angus said, his gaze direct and still angry on Drummond. "Do it. Archie, ye will cooperate. Our men will ride with the Lathans. All night, every night, until the raiders are dead or gone."

"The men who were on watch last night—"

"Can be on watch tonight," Angus said, cutting off Archie's objection.

"I suggest we start full up tomorrow night," Drummond interjected. "Ye said ye've never had raids two nights in a row. Let the men rest today and tonight, or they'll be asleep on watch tomorrow night."

Angus nodded. "Continue tonight. Dedicated patrols start tomorrow. Do it."

~

MORVEN SET down the basket she carried and knocked on Kelso's door. It opened quickly, and she smiled at her friend. "How are ye? I've brought ye what I promised. 'Tis a new leine and a length of oiled wool to keep the rain off of ye," she told him and glanced down at the basket by her feet.

"I'm well enough. Come in, lass, come in."

She bent to grasp the basket's handle, but Kelso shooed her away. "Let me get that for ye." He lifted it easily and waved her into his cottage.

Old Kelso lived beyond her croft, outside of the village. He didn't venture in all that often, preferring his solitude and his farm. But after Rodrick left her, he'd made sure she had meat for her table, fetched water for her from the village well, and occasionally kept wee Rory entertained while she worked. She thought of him as the grandfather Rory never knew after her parents died. She paid back his generosity with food and new clothes.

"How's my lad Rory?" He set the basket on the rough-hewn table near the hearth and gestured her to a seat.

"He's fine. In fact, he's outside, probably pulling up grass to feed to yer horse."

"Ach, that lad. Old Ebby wouldna ken what to do if Rory didna first stop by her pasture when ye come to visit."

"He's had much to entertain him the last day or two. Ye ken about the men Angus fetched?" She could guess he had not been into the village and seen them.

"Aye." He set a cup before her and filled it from a pitcher of mead. "Strange men, strange warriors, would indeed interest a lad that age. Any age. So what can ye tell me about them?" He gave her a mischievous wink and joined her at the table, filling his own cup.

She related her encounters with Drummond Lathan.

"Ye two bumped into each other twice? Well, now, in some

parts of Scotland, ye'd be considered married," he said, and grinned.

Morven shuddered, though she knew he jested. "Ach, nay. I've no intention of ever doing that again. The last attempt... well, ye ken fine how badly that ended."

"I do, lass, but ye are wasting yerself, and working too hard, raising that lad on yer own."

"I'm not alone. I have ye, and a few friends in the village. Somehow, I muddle through."

"I wish ye could do more than muddle. He's a smart lad. 'Tis just as well his da never learned of his existence."

"What makes ye say that? I sent letters—"

His brows drew together over hooded eyes. "I ken it." Then he looked up at her. "I just mean to say that the lad is well off with ye. Ye are a good mother to him, Morven."

"Thank ye, Kelso. Ye have been a good friend to us since Rodrick left."

"'Tis nay hardship when ye bring me warm clothes," he said, and gestured at her basket. "So have ye met any others of the warriors? How many are there?"

"I dinna ken. They're camped on the south side of the village, and they come and go so often on patrol that I havena tried to count them. At the village well, one of the lasses told me that she'd seen near to twenty strange men."

"Twenty! So many. Well, perhaps then they'll be able to put a stop to the raids." He took a sip.

"Have the raiders taken any of yer stock?"

"Nay, not yet, at least. They'll get around to this side of the village eventually, unless those men Angus brought can catch them. Now, enough talk of our troubles. What has my wee lad been doing while all this is going on?"

"Ach, digging holes looking for treasure that some supposed friends of his told him might be buried behind our cottage. When I found him, he was covered in dirt up to his knees."

Kelso laughed. "That's my lad. He'll be a trial to ye, but worth every bit of trouble."

"I pray ye are right."

"Am I not always?"

Morven laughed at that. "I willna argue with ye, auld man. I owe ye too much."

"Nonsense. I only did what the whole village shouldha done."

"Some have."

"Not enough, lass. Ye must think on something for me." He turned serious, his brow drew down and his eyes narrowed as he gazed at her. "Ye ken I've told ye again and again to find a reason to leave this village. I taught ye to read and write and do yer numbers so ye would be able to take care of yerself with yer weaving, or be of greater value to a future husband. Now that the Lathans are here, they may bring an opportunity for ye to do it."

"If ever I get the chance to move away from here and start a new life... " she parroted and trailed off. "Aye, I remember ye saying so a time or two."

"Ye'll take Rory with ye, of course."

"Of course. But why would I ever leave? Ye have taught Rory much, as well. I couldna ask for a better tutor for him."

He shook his head. "There are other tutors for the lad. The better question is why have ye stayed for so long?"

What was he talking about? Her life—her loom—was here. His continued insistence that her life would be better somewhere else confused and worried her. "Is there something I should ken? Something ye are not telling me?"

"Nay, lass." He reached across the table and squeezed her hand. "I just want ye to be happy. And here, I dinna think ye are. Comfortable, perhaps, aye. But not truly happy. Perhaps yer future—and Rory's—lie somewhere else."

"I... I dinna ken what to say."

"Just think on it. Perhaps that man ye have bumped into, or one of the others, will offer ye a better life than ye have here, on yer own."

Morven tossed off the remains in her cup and stood. "I should get Rory away from Ebby before he feeds her too much. Come with me. He's always pleased to see ye."

"'Tis because I let him ride her," he replied, and gestured her out the door.

"'Tis because ye care for him," Morven assured him, wondering again why, in that case, he was so eager for her to take Rory away.

4

Drummond woke to hear Angus calling his name, and there was no mistaking the anger in his voice. "They hit us again, damn it. What good are ye lyin' on yer pallet while my livestock gets stolen?

Drummond rolled out of his tent and stood shivering in his leine—and nothing else—in the early morning chill. "Again last night? Ye said they never raided two nights in a row."

"They didna. And now a man is dead. They never did that before, either."

Drummond's belly sank. "Who?" Not a Lathan, or that would have been the first news he received this morning. Instead, Angus had complained first about the missing sheep. Drummond glanced around the Lathan camp. Men were crawling out of tents, awakened, no doubt, by Angus's shouts.

"The dead man is... was a crofter," Angus said, more quietly. Regretfully, his gaze cast down. Then he met Drummond's frown with his own. "Likely he surprised them. They killed him and took every last one of his stock. They left naught behind save his broken-down old draft horse."

Drummond nodded to Eduard as he joined them. "This has

to stop. Tonight, it will." He knew his next words might not sit well with Angus—certainly Archie would object to them—but Angus needed to hear the truth. "Up to now, they've had free run of yer village's outskirts. They've taken what they want, with impunity. No more."

Angus got red in the face, but didn't react as Drummond thought he might. "Ye said that yesterday."

"Based on information ye gave us, Angus," Eduard interjected.

Drummond spoke up before Angus exploded. "They've done something different, changing their pattern, killing a man, whether on purpose or accidentally. The question is, will that death make them leave us alone for a few days, or embolden them? They've raised the stakes against themselves."

"They have to ken that," Eduard said, then added, "so it must have been an accident."

Drummond hoped Eduard was right. "Still, they've made us that much more determined to find and eliminate them," Drummond said. "They've left no room for compromise or mercy. They have a death on their hands. Theft is bad enough. Killing a farmer is unforgivable."

"Do ye think to reassure me with this?" Angus shook his head. "They could strike again, kill others. My people were worried before. Now they'll be afraid. We've lost one of our own." He ran a hand through his hair. "After we put him in the ground, I have to assure everyone in the village that the raiders will not—cannot—ride in and kill them in their beds."

"That is on all of us, together," Drummond said quietly. "Before the sun sets, we'll be ready. Archie and I set this up when we met yesterday. Lathans and yer men will be in position everywhere ye have villagers and animals. Others will ride out, searching for the raiders. We haven't stopped hunting them, and we willna. Ye have my word."

Angus snorted. "Yer word means nothing. Show me results. Bring me the heads of those raiders."

Drummond held up a hand. "I willna. Ye and yer men will bring them to yer people for justice. We'll help ye."

Angus crossed his arms and cast his gaze around the Lathan men standing outside their tents, watching in silence as the two leaders argued, made plans and promises. "Aye, that ye will. Or die trying."

Drummond frowned. Did Angus think a few cows and sheep were worth the lives of his men? "I have no intention of anyone else dying." Except that it was very likely going to be necessary to eliminate the reivers. "Not my men," he declared, "or yers, or your villagers. Whatever happens from here on out, the reivers brought on themselves."

RODRICK MONCREIFFE SQUARED off with his chief next to the makeshift pen where the livestock from last night's raid were contained. No one wanted them finding their way home. Or getting lost in the mountains. Not even the Moncreiffe raider chief, Diarmad, who, claiming to be older and wiser, had insisted on the slow and steady pilfering. He had been livid when Rodrick and his men returned, driving all these animals with them.

"Ye'll bring them down on us for sure," he roared. That was nothing to his reaction when he learned of the dead man. "Ye ken they've added men to help them hunt for us," he bellowed. "Why would ye do such a damned stupid thing?"

He went red in the face, and for a moment, Rodrick expected to be gutted where he stood. Diarmad Moncreiffe rarely gave in to his temper, but this time, he directed his fury full-on at Rodrick. Still, he was easily two decades older than Rodrick, and two decades slower. Rodrick could take him.

He'd killed the old man Kelso, his contact in the village, in a fit of rage after learning that he'd hidden news of his child from him. Rodrick had found him reading an old letter that Morven wrote to tell him she was carrying his child. She'd given it to Kelso to see it delivered to Moncreiffe. Instead, he kept it. When Rodrick confronted him about it last night, he claimed Morven lost the bairn soon after, so there'd been no sense in calling him back to formalize a marriage neither wanted on the technicality of a pregnancy unknown on the last day of the handfasting. Kelso claimed he didn't know if she carried a son or a daughter, but something in his eyes told Rodrick he lied. He'd had a son and lost him before he ever knew he existed. And he'd killed the man before he thought to ask him why.

Rodrick dared not admit how that news had dismayed and enraged him. Instead of confessing to losing control over a child he never knew, he lied. "He betrayed us. He wasna supposed to take other villagers' stock for his own and blame us. Each time we raided, he added to his herd. So I killed him before he could do us more harm and took all of his."

"Yer rash action may bring about the end of all of us. We've taken only what we need to survive—until now. Killing that man was stupid. And dangerous. Ye expect me to trust yer judgement after this?"

Rodrick clenched his fists. These men, these raiders, were outcasts, just like him. But Diarmad Moncreiffe had ambitions —ambitions that had gotten them banished. He wanted to establish another branch of the clan, to name an heir, stake a claim on land and resources, and build a permanent village. Rodrick looked around the ramshackle collection of cabins, tents, lean-tos, and wagons that made up their rough settlement, and frowned. They had a long way to go to achieve what the chief had in mind.

But Rodrick had the strength to do it. He was the one Diarmad should name his heir, not Rodrick's rival, Lorne. The

chief thought they were the two best fighters, the two best
reivers the group could claim, but Rodrick knew better. Lorne
could not compare to him. Rodrick bristled. "I'm the only one
smart enough and brave enough to do what it takes to protect
us."

Diarmad snorted. "Ye proved I canna make the decision
simply based on the better fighter or the better reiver. There's
more at stake." He glanced at the men around them. "My heir
must be a leader who can make rational decisions for the good
of all. With this killing, more men will be searching for us." He
lowered his voice and glared at Rodrick. "Ye may be brave, but
ye are also rash. Ye dinna think before ye act."

"I'm the one who shared what I learned in a year of living in
their midst," he objected. "Because of me, we have food in our
bellies, something to eat besides red deer and coneys. Who has
done better for our people? Tell me that!"

"I've told ye—I've told all of ye that we need stability, not to
be hunted down for stealing too much, too fast. Thanks to ye,
we'll be hunted with a vengeance." He straightened and continued. "My heir must help provide stability, not put us more at
risk." He looked over the people gathered around them. "Ye all
ken we lost many to cold and hunger after we were chased
from Moncreiffe. We lived well on the fringes of Moncreiffe
villages for a year after old William banished us. But he was
determined to be rid of us, and drove us off his land. In our
search for a place to settle, we turned to raiding other villages,
then tried to live here, but we canna grow food in these mountains. Last winter, we moved on, but lost more of our people, so
we had to come back to the one place where we had some help.
Now even that is gone, and the year is turning again. If we're
ever to be more than... this," he said, and waved a hand to
encompass their small settlement, "then we must have stable
leadership. For now, that's me. Someday, it may be one of ye.
I've decided to impose one more condition before I choose." He

narrowed his eyes at Rodrick, then did the same to Lorne, Rodrick's chief rival. "Ye must provide yer own heir. A son, to guarantee yer stake in the future of our clan. The first of the two of ye to produce yer son—with or without a wife—will take over when I am ready to hand over the job—or after I'm dead."

"Ye are daft!" Rodrick pushed forward, crowding Diarmad, a dangerous move, but a daring one the man would respect, even fear. "Ye canna mean to wait until one of us has a son. That could take years."

"Then it will take years," the chief growled. "Ye must ensure yer inheritance with a son—and prove ye can think beyond the tip of yer dirk about what's best for all of us."

Rodrick shook his head. The lass he married five years ago, before they left Moncreiffe, had given him only two daughters. And each pregnancy grew more difficult. He had little confidence she would live long enough to give him the son Diarmad required. Too bad he left Morven behind. She was strong. Perhaps he should seek her out and reclaim her as his wife. She would fight him, but he didn't care. He could handle her.

Or he could just kill the chief and Lorne and take over now. But nay, he needed time, and these men would give it to him. Their village needed much more than their few men could accomplish, especially when they spent many nights raiding the nearest village. Diarmad needed both him and Lorne if there was going to be enough of a village, and enough people in it, to create a viable clan of their own. Rodrick would need men when his turn came to lead, and killing those two, while it might satisfy his immediate urge, would weaken the clan and cause problems for him later on.

Something of his murderous inclination, before he turned his mind away from it, must have shown in his expression.

Diarmad backed up a step. His gaze sharpened. "The only way ye take over after me is to do as I say. Ye—or him," he added with a glance at Lorne, who watched them both carefully.

"I can do the job better than Lorne. Ye ken that. So why delay? Name me heir. Ye want me to have a son? Fine, I'll get a son if I must bed every lass for miles around. I'll enjoy it, too." He didn't like relying on chance. On random luck and timing. His rival could do the same thing.

"Ye enjoy too many things already. Like killing that crofter."

Rodrick fought not to react. He'd known old Kelso for years. In the moment, in his rage, he had enjoyed killing him. But now he'd cooled off, he regretted it. He would never find out why the old man wanted to keep news of the bairn from him. Had he wanted the handfasting to end? If so, why? Rodrick had never done anything to him. "It served him right. And it means we dinna need to risk another raid for a week or longer. They'll think we've gone, their patrols will get lazy, and then we'll hit them again."

He eyed the old man. He was right, and Diarmad knew it. The old chief's time was running out.

DRUMMOND ATTENDED the burial that afternoon. As the Lathan heir, it was his place to represent his clan, and to be seen to support Angus and the village, even in this tragedy. He went from person to person once the crofter was laid to rest, speaking quietly, offering his condolences and those of his men. Some turned away in anger, some merely nodded, accepting the sentiment with tears in their eyes. It was clear they'd known the dead man all their lives.

The grief he saw in Morven's eyes when he arrived made him want to comfort her, but she stayed near Angus's wife, offering her arm to support the woman, who seemed to have trouble walking. When Angus finished speaking and returned to his wife, Morven frowned at him, then left the gathering before he could say anything to her. At least she didn't, like many of the villagers, seem to blame him and his men for their loss. He accepted her rebuke and walked back to where his men camped, waiting for his return.

Later, after discussing tactics with his men, he walked to her cottage to offer his condolences. She sat in the garden outside, spinning yarn with a drop spindle he'd seen the lasses at the Aerie use. She still looked pale and morose, her gaze downcast on her work, but it wasn't just her gaze that told him how sad she was. She sat slumped, her shoulders rounded as though her belly pained her.

Nearby, Rory wandered the yard, collecting sticks. Kindling, Drummond supposed, until he lined them up and carefully broke them into different lengths. Drummond didn't know what he was up to, but he did know the lad's mother was here, and she couldn't turn away from him. Though she could get up, go inside, and close the door, this time she didn't leave.

"I'm sorry, Morven. I understand ye were friends..."

"Aye," she said, not raising her head to meet his gaze. She kept her attention on her work. He looked around and noticed fabric draped in the trees, flapping gently in the light breeze as it dried. "Yer work is beautiful," he told her, hoping to cheer her. "How do ye get such fine texture and softness?"

"'Tis all in the wool and the loom," she admitted, finally meeting his gaze. "And years of practice finishing the cloth."

"Tell me about the man who died. Why him, after all the raids that have plagued this village for months?"

She shook her head and set her spindle aside. "I dinna ken. Angus thinks Kelso surprised them. He wasna a sound sleeper, so likely he woke up. Maybe he heard something and decided to check on his stock."

"Ye were close?" He'd been her nearest neighbor on this

side of the village, but even so, how did she ken he didn't sleep well?

"Aye, he was like a second father to me. One of the few in the village who treated me well after..." she looked around and found Rory. She managed a small, secretive smile, then put it aside and shrugged. "The only reason I'm still here is that he befriended me, helped me when I needed it, and convinced some in the village to be kind."

"Why would they have been anything else, Morven?"

Tears came, then. She stood and turned away, toward the cottage, hiding her face.

Drummond intercepted her and took her in his arms, gently rubbing her back while she gave in to her grief.

"I only wish to comfort ye, lass," he murmured into her hair. "Let me help."

She shook her head and pulled away, as if embarrassed by her weakness and by the tear-stained spot on his leine that would remind him of it. "I'm sorry," she said. "Please, go." With that, she went inside and closed the door.

After forcing himself to turn away from her door, he made sure Rory was still nearby and safe, then reluctantly, Drummond did as she bade.

5

O nce Drummond left, Morven opened the door and considered going back outside to spin some more yarn, but her loom drew her. It was her comfort as well as her burden, and right now, she needed its comfort.

Drummond's questions raised old ghosts and reminded her of the pain she'd been through at the end of her handfasting, when her husband repudiated her before the entire village.

"Ye havena given me a son," he'd told her. "And ye are not breeding. I see nay future in this union. So I will go and leave ye to the next man foolish enough to hope for a son from ye."

The loom was the reason they spent the handfasting at her village. If the marriage took, he'd promised, then they would move everything to his. It didn't.

The irony still made her cringe, all these years later. He was gone, disappeared like the morning mist when the sun rose high enough to burn it away. She had not heard from him in almost seven years, and never expected to see him again. But the loom remained.

Likely he'd moved on, found another lass, another village

or keep, another life that suited him better. Perhaps even another son.

She was better off without him. Rory was hers and no one else's. So far, keeping her vow had been no hardship.

Then Drummond Lathan arrived. He was kind to her. And to Rory. And he'd held her in his arms while she cried. Oh, the feel of those massive arms around her, his chest warm against her face, his heart beating under her cheek, his scent. He was everything male and powerful she had forgotten how to crave. She'd forgotten what being safe in a man's arms felt like. But with him, she felt protected. He'd said he wanted to help. He had.

And yet, he'd done a painful sort of damage, too. She'd given up longing for a husband. A companion. She'd buried those longings under years of caring for herself and for her son. When Drummond Lathan ripped away the coverings and brought the urges back into her body, fresh and painful, like the spines of the thistle, beautiful and hurtful all at once, she'd pulled out of his arms and sent him away.

Her loom could not comfort her from this kind of pain.

She should go to Kelso's cottage and clean it. Angus would award it to someone in the village, but not right away. And while Kelso would want some of his things left for the new tenants, others he might want Rory to have. Ebby would be fine in her pasture, the lone animal left after the raiders took his milk cow and sheep.

She went back outside to tell Rory to come with her. She didn't see him, but she heard hoofbeats approaching, then saw three riders thundering up the glen, still far away. She couldn't see who they were, but their horses kept coming closer and closer. Surely not raiders, not in broad daylight, and not after killing a villager the night before. They had to know they were being hunted. Nay, they couldn't be raiders. So who were they? More of

Drummond's men? She didn't like the idea of more strangers.

"Rory! Come here," she called, trying not to let fear color her voice. "We need to go inside, now!"

As her son ran from behind the cottage to obey her, she recognized three MacComases riding hard, a great distance behind them, chasing the riders. So they *were* raiders, and they were headed right for her. She grabbed Rory and backed toward the doorway.

The nearest rider slowed his mount, hesitated and stared at her. Then he lashed his lathered horse and rode away.

The MacComas guards were too far back to catch the men before they disappeared into the trees. As soon as they got close enough to her to be heard, one of the guards shouted. "Which way?"

She pointed. "Where are the Lathans?"

He hung back as his companions took off in the direction she indicated. "Gone another way," the man answered. "Not with us." With that, he galloped after his companions.

So Drummond had missed these raiders—unless he managed to join the chase in the mountains. She hoped he did —and was successful. Even though he never knew her neighbor, he seemed to take Kelso's death personally. She wouldn't want to be one of the raiders if Drummond found them.

She hugged Rory to her, fretting. Who was the raider who paused and looked her over? Was she in danger from that man?

"Again?" Drummond let the disgust chilling his belly fill his voice. "Raiders rode right by the village, but none of the patrols were nearby?"

Eduard grimaced. "Three of Angus's men chased them, but lost them in the woods."

"They killed a man last night. What are they doing near the village in broad daylight today?" Drummond ran his fingers through his hair, then clenched his hands into fists. "That's the last thing we expected they would do. They're not behaving as Angus said they have the last few months. They've seen us and changed their tactics."

"Can we hope that means they're preparing to move on?" Eduard waved a hand. "To harass Moncreiffe or some other clan even farther away?"

Drummond shook his head. "Doubtful. They're taunting us. Letting us know they're not intimidated."

"So they willna give up?"

"I dinna ken, damn it." Drummond was at a loss for words, angry that they missed the chance to take on the raiders and disgusted that he hadn't been there to foil their show of disregard for the village defenses. "I want to capture at least one and question him. Too bad the MacComas men couldna catch them."

"They never even got close. The raiders rode fast horses, and Angus's men were too far back when they spotted them."

"I have to wonder why they came this way at all. Was it only a foolish risk, or were they after something?"

"What could they expect to find during the day that they couldna at night?"

"Good question. Exactly where did they ride?"

"I dinna ken where Angus's men first spotted them, but they followed them along the edge of the village," he said, paused and pointed, "then they cut back uphill into the mountains."

Drummond's belly clenched. Morven's cottage was on that side of the village, on its outskirts. Chances were, the raiders rode right by her home. Were she and Rory safe? He needed to know. Now. He took his leave from Eduard and hurried to Morven's cottage.

When he arrived, both she and Rory were inside. Through

her open door, Morven saw him coming, and she smiled as he walked closer. Drummond stood in the doorway for a moment, appraising the situation. Morven was laying out yarn samples, and had created several mixes, shading from light to dark. They both seemed calm and unhurt. He didn't like the open door, but she sat facing it, which Drummond approved. She would know who came toward her before they got too near. As long as she could close and bolt it before they reached her, he wouldn't complain. He understood her need for light to judge the color of her swatches, and air.

Rory sat off to the side, playing with twigs broken at different lengths. The ones Drummond had seen him breaking earlier?

"I heard ye almost had a visitor a few hours ago," Drummond said in lieu of a greeting.

She gestured him in. "We were not harmed, if that's what fashes ye. Three raiders rode by, chased by some of Angus's men, which ye probably already ken."

He stepped in and leaned his back on the wall by the door. "But something happened?"

Morven remained seated. A frown drew her brows together. "Aye, oddly enough. One of the men paused as he neared here." She glanced at Rory, then continued. "I had gone out when I heard the horses and was getting Rory inside. The man was being chased, but he paused and looked us over."

"Both of ye or just ye?"

"Me, I think. He didna say a word, didna gesture or smile. His expression didna change at all, as far as I could see. He just looked at me, then followed his companions up the hill."

"And ye didna recognize him?"

"Nay. He didna seem familiar."

Drummond pursed his lips. She didn't know anything to help identify or locate the raiders. But he didn't like that one of the raiders singled her out for special attention.

"Gotcha!"

Drummond turned to see what Rory had done to elicit that exclamation. "What are ye doing, lad?"

"'Tis my army. I'm setting up a defense against the raiders."

Drummond nearly smiled at the idea of a six-year-old making battle plans, but Morven watched him, so he moved closer to Rory.

"Do ye ken how to do that?" Drummond squatted by the lad and studied the arrangement of his twig soldiers. He seemed to have grasped the concept of a defensive perimeter.

"Of course," Rory replied. "The raiders canna get through this line," he said, and gestured at his outer perimeter. One tried, but they caught him."

"Indeed?"

"Aye. All of my men are close enough they can see each other, so no one can sneak between them. At night, they have to be closer together, of course. 'Tis dark out then."

"That's very good, lad. Who taught ye how to do this?"

"I made it up."

Drummond nodded, surprised. "What would ye do if ye didna have enough men to form yer line?"

Rory thought about that for long enough that Morven gestured Drummond to a chair. "Nay sense sitting on the floor when ye dinna have to," she told him. "He could take some time before answering ye."

Rory ignored her comment. He seemed focused on his pretend village, moving the sticks around, clustering them together in several clumps, then spreading them out again. Finally, he looked up at Drummond. "I dinna ken yet. I need to think about yer question some more. Can I call for help from other villages, or another laird, like our chief called for ye?"

"Aye, of course," Drummond said, impressed again. "Ye have seen it done."

Rory looked down at his diorama. "I need more sticks."

Morven clapped a hand over her mouth. The twinkle in her gaze told Drummond Rory's droll tone amused her.

"Go on then," Morven told him, "and find more sticks—ach, I mean men. But do not go far, aye? Just to the edge of the trees."

"I willna."

Rory ran outside, and Drummond shared an amazed glance with his mother. "Ye have a budding tactician on yer hands," he warned her. "He'll be of great value, whatever laird he serves in the future."

"So ye are already thinking of making a place for him at Lathan when ye are laird?"

"If ye come, too, aye."

His words appeared to stun her into silence. He recognized he had overstepped. "I'm not one to waste talent," he told her.

"Well, dinna depend on him overmuch. Lads change their minds many times before they're grown, but ye would ken that."

"Nay, not really. My future was determined at my birth."

"Ach, of course. The eldest. The heir. I'm sorry, that was unkind of me."

"Ye meant naught by it. *Dinna fash.*"

"Still, I'm sorry." She picked up some wool and her drop spinner. "What would ye do if ye were not the heir?"

"I'd still be a warrior. Beyond that, like Rory, I'll have to beg the favor of more time. There are many things I'd like to do, but I would need to think on it to pick a favorite."

"Granted," she said with a grin.

Drummond's pulse leapt. He'd never seen that expression from her. She looked younger, mischievous—and kissable. He took a breath to calm himself. "I hope Rory will be good at many things, not forever figuring out defenses against raiders." Drummond regretted his words as soon as he said them.

She sobered. "I willna argue with ye on that."

~

RODRICK COULDN'T BELIEVE what Lewis told him. "Ye are sure it was her?"

"Yer former wife? Aye. She was right where ye said she'd be. Ye described her often enough before ye wed again. If 'twas not her, she looked very much like ye describe. And she had a lad with her. He looked to be about six years old. She must have remarried right after ye threw her over."

"Did ye see a man with them?"

"Nay, but most are patrolling the area. We were chased on the way back from yer fool's errand. Damned daft to ride in broad daylight so close by the village we've been raiding."

"And would ye expect her to be outside in the middle of the night? How else would we ken?" As he shook his head, Rodrick grunted his disgust at Lewis's objection. But his mind whirled at this news and he quickly forgot his irritation. If the woman Lewis saw was Morven, then confirming she was still there satisfied his reason for sending the men, but discovering she had a wee lad the right age with her made his impulse a stroke of genius. He hadn't counted on there being a lad.

If old Kelso lied to him about Morven losing the bairn she wrote that she carried, then the lad Lewis saw could be his son. But even if he wasn't, he could be the answer to Rodrick's ambition. He could claim the lad, and his problem would be solved. Presenting old Diarmad with a six-year-old instead of a newborn would knock Lorne right out of the competition, unless he had bastards scattered around everywhere they'd been. That thought gave Rodrick pause. Did he? If he could find one older than the lad with Morven, Lorne could still win this. Rodrick needed to produce his son first. Once Diarmad named him his heir, Rodrick would move against him too quickly for Lorne to usurp him.

"We'll raid again the day after tomorrow, but we won't take cattle. I'm going to get my son."

"If he's yers. And as ye said about his mam, he'll be locked away in that cottage, asleep. Ye'll never get near him."

"I know. I'll observe during the first day or two and see when the lad is likely to be outside where I can take him. I'll grab him if I can, watch and wait if I canna. But I'll get him."

"How will ye avoid their patrols while ye do this?"

"Ye forget, I ken that area. Those people. We've avoided them for months. Most of those men couldn't find their dick if their wife pulled it out for them. I can remain unseen as long as I need to. But it willna take long. I'll have my son with me, one way or the other."

"What about his mother?"

"If I have the lad, I dinna need her."

"Yer wife isna likely to welcome yer son by another woman."

"She'll do what I say, or she'll be looking for someone else to take in her and her daughters. I dinna need them. I need the lad."

6

T he next few nights passed quietly. Morven was relieved that the patrols seem to be helping.

Yesterday, she put Kelso's cottage to rights and gathered up his belongings, including a box of accounts and papers she'd yet to go through, but she assumed they were tallies of crop yields and the animals he kept. She would give those to Angus, but wanted to go through them to remove anything Kelso would have wanted to be kept private.

His clothes might someday fit Rory, or she could give them to someone in the village now. She kept his dirk and longsword to give to Rory when he was old enough to need them. The biggest surprise was a cache of coins with a note that if anything ever happened to him, the coins were to be given to her to help her care for her bairn.

She sat at his table and wept, and again when she bundled up the new clothes she'd made him. He never had a chance to wear them. Before she left, she said a prayer for the repose of his soul. She hoped he knew the depth of her gratitude for all he had done for them. When she walked outside, she closed his door for the last time.

The village was calmer, the grief over Kelso's death fading fast. People were smiling again—even smiling at her—as the pressure of the raids eased. The raids had put everyone on edge, but hope returned after only a few quiet nights. Morven began to think things would be better from now on. She'd even seen Ilise outside the keep, walking slowly with her maid near at hand, speaking to everyone she passed. Morven spent a few minutes with her, then left her, so she could visit with the others who stood nearby, waiting their turn.

Adding to her good mood, Drummond even stopped by each morning after his nightly patrol to unwind and to spend some time with her and her son. She made sure to have food and drink on hand. "Being with ye grounds me," he told her. "Ye let me feel... normal... after spending the night on the hunt."

"Is it not much like hunting deer or a boar?"

"Nay, it isna. We're hunting men, always with the possibility of killing a man—or being killed. 'Tis necessary. And so far, 'tis working. The raids have stopped, at least for now. I'm glad of that. But that doesna mean I want to go straight to my rest, ride out again at the gloaming, and naught more. Spending time with ye, with Rory, gives me some peace."

"I'm glad to be of help," she told him. The heat of a blush warmed her face. She dropped her gaze. How much time did he spend with Angus? Surely the two leaders must consult with each other at some point during the day—or night. He had to spend time with his men, too. Surely he had more important things to do than sit with her.

But her son liked Drummond and basked in his attention, so she allowed his visits. Using Rory's twigs, Drummond began teaching him about tactics and strategy, making a game out of the lessons. Rory loved it. Drummond also made a small wooden sword and practiced with Rory, teaching him the fundamentals. Morven hated to watch that training. Rory was so young, and it meant he was growing up. She knew he would need those skills, but she'd never made a priority of having him taught. He was behind other lads his age, but Drummond's tutelage was helping him catch up and might someday save his life. That thought gave her some small measure of comfort whenever she watched her bairn and the much bigger man.

"Ye ken I will leave soon," he told her, breaking into her thoughts and making her heart sink.

"Nay, I didna realize..."

"I'm expected back at the Aerie in two days. If things stay quiet, we can assume the raiders have been chased away, and I can leave with a clear conscience."

"Can ye? Ye have made Rory a friend—one of few he has. He will miss ye." *And so will I,* she thought, but she couldn't say the words.

"I'm sorry for that. I'll miss him, too, but my responsibilities at home willna wait any longer. I'll find someone to continue working with him until he catches up with the other lads his age. He already has more skill with strategy than I've ever seen in one so young. Ye must find him a tutor, or it will go to waste."

"What if I dinna want my son fighting, or devising strategies so that others can fight?"

"Then send him to an abbey and make a priest of him. He willna be safe as he grows up if he canna defend himself, or if he has no skill he can sell to keep himself fed."

"He can be a farmer, or a blacksmith or..."

"Aye, he could, but all those can be called to fight for the laird. Ye ken these things, Morven. Ye think ye are protecting yer son, but ye are making it difficult—or impossible—for him to protect himself when he's old enough to need to fight."

She crossed her arms and hid her clenched fists at her sides. "'Tis easy for ye to say. Ye willna be here."

"Nay, I willna. So much for leaving with a clear conscience." He shook his head and stood to go. "I will think on this. The lad is young. He may choose among many paths in life. If I can help, I will."

THE NEXT DAY, Morven worked on the Martinmas celebration cloth the laird's wife wanted. Drummond's words kept her tossing and turning all night. Was she being unfair to Rory? Did every lad have to become a warrior, even if only at the laird's bidding? She knew better, of course. She'd lived in this village all her life and seen what other lads went through, how they trained, how they grew, and how some went to war and never returned.

But this was Rory. Her son. And that made all the difference.

Kelso had wanted her to leave, and to take Rory with her. Would that make her happy, as he'd suggested? Was there any place to go where her son would be safe? She remembered thinking there was more behind the old man's advice than he'd said, but she couldn't imagine what he wasn't telling her, what else there would have been. Kelso had not elaborated.

For a time, she lost herself in choosing the finest, softest yarns among those she had on hand to consider for the project. She knew Ilise's color preferences and had several to choose from, yet something was missing. A darker, thinner thread that would provide the shadow over which the color she chose would float like candlelight against a dark window. The finished fabric would appear almost as if made from golden threads, but she could not afford such finery. Nor could the chief's wife.

She thought about the underlying color she would need. Not black. It would be too harsh against Ilise's pale skin, and too difficult to get consistent color. Something softer, perhaps a midnight shade of blue or the deepest forest green would serve.

In the meantime, she would design the weave and set up the loom.

She was deep in thought when a low rumble intruded. At first, she thought it was thunder, but daylight streamed in her door. The wedge of sky she could see was cloudless and blue.

Horses! The raiders again?

Where was Rory?

She glanced around the inside of the cottage, expecting to see him, then recalled he was playing outside.

She jumped up and ran out the door. "Rory? Where are ye, lad?" Was he still digging for treasure behind the cottage? She rounded the last corner, expecting to see him, but nay, he wasn't there.

The sound of hoofbeats was louder now. "Rory! Answer me!"

"Here, Mam," she heard him call from the front of the cottage. She ran back the way she came as the thunder of hooves grew unbearably loud and the ground shook.

Three riders tore into the yard, trampling her flowers, headed straight for her son.

Rory watched them, frozen in fear, eyes wide and mouth open.

"Rory!"

He turned his head to look at her just as one horse veered to him. Its rider bent low, grabbed Rory's arm and pulled him, shrieking and calling out for her, on the rider's lap.

For a moment, she only saw Rory, held in a stranger's arms. The rider slowed and approached her. She lifted her gaze to his face. "Rodrick!" Her handfasted husband's name fell from her lips while Rory continued to cry and reach his arms out for her. "Put him down! Leave my son alone."

"Yer son? He's mine, and I've come to claim him."

"Nay!" She bit her lip. Why hadn't she told him Rory was someone else's child she was just watching for the day?

"I saw yer letter to me. Kelso kept it." Laughing at her, he kicked his mount into a gallop. Rory's screams echoed off the nearby foothills and combined with hers into a shrill chorus of anguish and fear.

What did he mean, Kelso kept it? She ran after them, but the horses disappeared into the trees, headed up the hill into the mountains, Rory with them. She cried out his name until she had no voice left, tears streaming down her face as she gasped for enough air to scream out her fury and pain again.

The rumble of horses galloping away and her screams brought villagers and some Lathans, including Drummond, running. She turned back to them, then collapsed to her knees. "Rory," she gasped. "Rodrick took him. It happened so fast..." She repeated the last two words over and over again, until her chest tightened too much to draw air. He'd said Kelso had her letter. Not letters. Which one—and why? And how did Rodrick know that?

She remained conscious enough to be aware of Drummond shouting orders to his men to give chase before he knelt by her.

"Morven, lass, breathe. We'll get Rory back. *Dinna fash*."

She shook her head. Nay, they wouldn't. She couldn't say the words, but her heart was screaming them. *His father took him.* The father who'd ignored him for six long years swooped in and stole him. Her son! Why, after all these years? And what had Kelso to do with any of it? Anger mounted, tightening her muscles until she thought her spine would crack. Rodrick couldn't be found when it mattered. When her son was born. When the village turned its back on her. Rory was *her* son. Not his. Where would Rodrick take him? Morven suddenly couldn't get enough air. The world went gray, then black.

～

DRUMMOND CARRIED Morven to her cottage while someone ran for the village healer. He stayed with her over the objections of one of the village's women. He was too concerned about her to leave her side. He would have taken her in his arms, held her on his lap and rocked her to quiet the groans and the tears that seemed to be all she could manage after screaming her lungs out, but the presence of the other woman stopped him. She positioned herself between him and Morven, and every time he attempted to get closer to her, to help her, the woman gave him a glare that could kill at twenty paces, much less in the same chamber.

When Morven glanced up, seeming to come out of the terrorized stupor she'd fallen into, she screamed, "Ye!" and fainted dead away.

"Out!" The other woman actually pushed him, throwing her body against him when at first he didn't budge, his gaze on Morven, everything in him calling him to go to her. The woman's fury finally penetrated his need.

"Nay," he told her.

"Aye," she said, and pushed again. "She fears ye right now." When he paled, she had the grace to tell him, "Likely she doesna ken ye in her present state. Ye are not helping her. Now go."

He went.

He paced outside the cottage until the healer arrived. Before he allowed her inside, he demanded she let him know Morven's condition. "Send me word," he demanded. "I must ken how she is."

"I will, lad. Ye need to see to yerself. Ye look afrighted over the lass."

"Take care of Morven," he growled and stalked away, furious at being so helpless to aid her. He hurried back to the Lathan camp, itching for a fight and knowing he dared not act on that urge. He needed to focus his energy on finding

Morven's son, and at the same time, ridding Lathan territory of raiders. Any and all of them. He stopped the first man he met. "Which way did the search go?"

Finn pointed. "Into the hills, that way."

"All of them?"

"Aye, to start."

Drummond knew they'd spread out once they got above the lower hillsides. "How many of us are still here?"

"Just me and Kevin. Sorley's up at the keep, breaking his fast. He's due to sleep."

"Get Kevin and saddle up. We'll join the search."

Angus showed up as Finn went after the other man. "The raiders?"

"Aye, who else?" They walked to Drummond's horse and he saddled his mount while they talked. "Morven said yer men chased three of them past the edge of the village a few days ago, but lost them. One slowed near her cottage. She thought he looked her over. Rory must've been what interested him, not her."

Angus frowned. "Why take the lad and not the lass? That is strange."

"When we catch them, we'll find out why," Drummond said. By the time he was ready, so were his men. Angus waved them off, and they headed into the hills, but at an angle from the primary search. They rode for several hours. Drummond stayed alert to any sound—or lack of it—in the forest, any movement, any tingling in his gut that might suggest they were close. That sensation came and went, seemingly without reason.

Eventually, they caught up with some men from the primary search. No one had seen anything. The raiders had disappeared. Frustrated, he and his two companions ranged around for another hour, but he never got a sense of where the raiders went. He tried to focus his thoughts on Rory, hoping that would spark some awareness, some tingle, but nothing seemed to work. If he had any talent at all, it was a useless one, good only for finding lost lockets and spindles for the lasses. Disgusted, he turned back toward the village, his thoughts still churning on the events of the day. The nightly patrols would be getting set up in a few hours. Drummond wanted to check on Morven first.

No longer content with stealing cattle and sheep from the outlying farms, the raiders had killed a man, then ridden right into the outskirts of the village and stolen a bairn. In broad daylight! Despite the MacComas patrols being augmented by the men he'd brought with him. They'd barely gotten the night-time sentry and patrol pattern set up, and the raiders adjusted, risking being chased while the sun shone, even though that made it harder for them to escape and evade Drummond's men.

And yet, they managed to disappear into the wilds above the MacComas village—with a screaming bairn. Had they knocked him out to silence him? Or worse? God's teeth, if they did the least harm to Morven's son, Drummond would see them hang, but not until he broke every bone in their bodies.

Before long, some of his men in the primary search returned, empty-handed. "Ye lost them, too?"

"Aye, up there," Eduard said and pointed toward the mountains. "We came back for fresh mounts and more help."

"'Twill soon be time for the nightly patrol. Ye willna find them in the dark. Our best bet is to capture one during a raid."

"Aye. They ken these woods even better than we feared," Eduard continued. "We were closing in. We heard them and thought we had them. They just... disappeared. Calum lost his mount over a cliff chasing the bastards. We almost lost him, too, but he managed to jump clear just in time, snag a sapling and hang on until we pulled him up. The horse didna make it."

"Damn," Drummond said, at a loss for more appropriate

words. Angus warned them about the terrain up there. Even wee Rory told him the same. By now, they should have been more aware of their surroundings, but likely the search had ranged farther than any had gone before.

"We kept going, but the tracks disappeared as soon as we hit rocky ground."

"They're not bloody ghosts!" Drummond clenched his fists. A real man took Rory, not some specter.

"Nay, they're not," Eduard answered. "But they may as well be, for all the good we did."

"Damn it! Unless the others are having better luck, we'll go out again at first light and track them." The urge to hit something grew. Drummond fought it down. He had railed at his men, but he knew they were as angry as he at losing the lad. He hadn't been allowed to help Morven. And he was mostly angry at himself for failing to find Rory. If the tingle in his belly was any sort of talent, then where they failed, he should have found the trail and located the lad. If his luck had held. But the sensation had come and gone, seemingly at random. If those sensations were tied to some talent, it was damned weak and unreliable. Useless. Good only for finding things lost in the Aerie—and Rory's blue cap. So far, it had been little help here.

"Could ye find where ye left off again?"

"Aye, of course."

"So we have a sense of where they went, where they might be headed."

Eduard shrugged. "They couldha gone in any direction from there, saving straight back at us."

"Fan out in every direction and find their tracks. Take some of Angus's men with ye and keep at it until the gloaming. By then ye'll be blind under those trees. Bring the men back for tonight's patrols. If we're lucky, after what they pulled off today, they'll stay away tonight. I'll check with Morven. By now she may have calmed enough to speak, and she may have some idea where they went. I'll tell Angus what has happened so far."

Eduard nodded and went to gather men to do Drummond's bidding. He retraced his steps to Morven's cottage. Her door was open when he arrived, and the healer stepped out. "She's calmer. Her voice is gone, but 'twill return eventually. She is still upset, so I gave her a sleeping draught. I dinna want ye in there. Anything ye do or say could make her condition worse."

Drummond pushed past her.

Morven sat at the small table by her hearth, a cup of something steaming in front of her. She paid it no attention, nor did she turn to Drummond when he came in. She stared off into space, appearing still lost in her fears, but perhaps the healer's draught was taking effect.

He knelt before her and put a hand on her knee to get her attention. "Morven," he called, softly. "'Tis Drummond. What can I do to help ye?"

"Find him," she croaked.

"I just got back. My men are still out searching. Can ye tell me where they might take Rory?"

Fresh tears leaked from her red and swollen eyes. "Ye didna find him?" She clenched her fists.

"Not yet, lass, but we will. What can ye tell me about the men who took him?"

"He has my son!"

Her focus on one man rather than the group of raiders was interesting. "What was the name ye said?" Could the lad's father be the one who took him? She'd never mentioned him and Drummond assumed he was dead. Villagers had told his men a few things about her past. Their opinion of her former husband was mixed.

"I saw him. He stole my son!" Her words came out as a painful cry, but fury danced in her eyes. She crossed her arms over her belly and rocked in her seat.

Drummond didn't understand how to help her, but it was clear she was in no condition to help him. Not now, but perhaps later, after she rested, and the healer's potion wore off. He'd come back in the morning, after the night's patrols.

"Ye ken I'll do my best," he told her. "I'm good at finding things."

Her head came up and fire flashed again in her gaze. "Rory's not a thing," she croaked. "He's my son."

So she wasn't just muttering, lost in her distress. She heard him, and was fighting the drug. "I ken it, Morven. We'll find him. Ye rest for a wee." When she didn't respond, Drummond left her. He'd only meant to give her hope, but feared he'd made her feel worse.

7

Morven woke during the night, exhausted, but restless. Moonlight filtering in around the window covering told her it was late.

Before she left for the night, the healer told her Drummond had ridden out until near dark, then took up the watch right outside her door. He insisted on guarding her in case the raiders came back.

She got up, wrapped a plaid around her, and opened the door. Drummond fell into the room at her feet. He'd been sitting with is back against the door. He must have dozed off. If it wasn't so noble of him, she would laugh.

"Come the rest of the way in and warm up," she told him. "Ye must be freezing."

"I've had warmer posts," he admitted as he rolled to his feet and entered. He paused, looking back outside as if checking whether anyone saw him fall in her doorway. "How are ye, lass?"

She closed the door. "Foggy. Bleary. I dinna ken. Go sit by the fire," she advised, then poured a cup of ale and handed that to him. Her fingers brushed his icy ones as he took the cup, making her wish she still had hot stew in the pot on the fire. After Rory was… taken… and during one of the intervals when the healer left her alone, she'd tossed it in the fire and scrubbed the pot clean, certain that until her son returned to her, she'd never be able to stomach food again. The smell nauseated her until it burned away. The healer had given her something to drink and expected her to sleep the night away, she supposed, because she hadn't left anything on the table for Morven to eat.

Drummond settled in the chair facing the hearth and set his cup on her small table. She became acutely aware of the humbleness of her home. The loom took up much of the space. Her bed against one wall, Rory's on another, a chest and storage cabinet on the third, and a small table in front of the hearth where she prepared their meals and where they sat to eat them, took up the rest of the small space. Certainly nothing like the home Drummond must be accustomed to. His clan must be powerful to lay claim to a small village so far removed. Why else why did Angus travel to fetch help from them? And powerful clans lived in castles with wealth Morven could only dream about.

She joined him at the table with her own cup. "Tell me about yer home," she invited, seeking distraction. "I dinna ken anything about where ye come from."

Drummond, his gaze on the smoldering peat in the hearth, took a sip of ale.

He still looked half asleep, or lost in thought. Perhaps he was still chilled, and his mind had slowed along with his body.

"The Lathan keep is called the Aerie. It sits on a high tor above a wide glen, with forests and mountains all around."

Ah, that was better. The pace of his speech told her he was warming up. Waking up. The ruddy color the cold had lent his skin was fading, and the tightness in his muscles seemed to have eased. She had no doubt, despite seeming half frozen when she opened her door, had a threat approached, he would have leapt up and fought without a thought for the cold. "How do ye get up to it?"

"There's a long trail that leads up the tor to the Aerie's gates. 'Tis the only approach, so 'tis easily defended."

"It sounds formidable."

"It survived a siege by a lowlander army after Flodden— before my siblings and I were born. 'Tis how my parents met."

"Yer mother was with the army?"

"Aye. She's a healer. She was kidnapped from her village months before. My da was visiting a clan near ours and got caught up in the fight when they were invaded. When he escaped, he kidnapped my mother and brought her home to the Aerie. That drew the army and they laid siege. Its leader wanted her back. To end it, Da killed him in single combat, and his army broke up and headed south, away."

She took a sip, distracted from her grief by his tale. "What an amazing time that must have been."

"Mother has said she had enough adventure then to last her the rest of her life. She settled at the Aerie, married my da, and has been our clan's healer ever since."

Her curiosity piqued, she asked, "How many siblings do ye have?"

"Two brothers and two sisters. Jamie, Lianna and I are triplets. Tavish and Eilidh are twins, two years younger."

"What is it like to have so many in yer family?" Morven was an only child, and so was her son. Her thoughts touched on Rory and skittered away. She could not break down, not now. Not until she was alone again.

"Do ye have any family besides yer son?" Drummond's gaze left the glow in the hearth. He straightened and looked at her.

For a moment, she found herself caught in his warm brown gaze. She forced herself to look away and shook her head. "Only Rory." Her throat tightened on his name, and she pressed a hand over her mouth, nostrils flaring as she fought back tears.

"I'm sorry, lass," Drummond said. "We *will* find him. We're going out again at first light to track them."

Suddenly his hand was covering hers, big, strong, and warm. The heat from the hearth had melted the ice in his blood. She inhaled and looked up into those deep brown eyes, so full of concern and determination. She let him take her hand from her mouth. As he did, before he enfolded it in his, his fingers brushed her lips, giving her a sense of warmth and calm that only lasted as long as his touch. Then her fears crashed in on her again.

"How can ye be so certain? The man who took him could be far away by now."

"He was one of the raiders, aye?"

She shrugged and left her response at that, reluctant to admit her connection to her son's kidnapper.

"Even if they moved, they will have left tracks. A trail to follow." He squeezed her hand, released it and sat back. "They canna hide forever."

Morven pressed her lips together and one hand to her roiling belly. Perhaps they couldn't hide forever, but they could hide for years. They could take her son so far away, he'd grow up and forget all about her.

Suddenly, her belly turned, and she bolted out of the cottage door, bent over, and lost the little ale she'd sipped. Once that was gone, she kept heaving, bringing up nothing but fear and fury and heartbreak.

Drummond's arms went around her, and she cried out, whether from surprise or shame, she wasn't sure, when they wrapped over her chest and grasped her shoulders. But his solid presence behind her, holding back her hair, calmed her and calmed her heaving insides. After a few moments, she was able to straighten, to lean back into his arms, to notice the cold on the front of her body and the raging furnace of his heat on her back.

"Come inside, Morven," he murmured. "'Tis too raw for ye to be out here."

Tears filled her eyes. "Rory is out here," she sobbed. "He's cold, and alone with strangers. Afraid. What am I to do?"

"Trust me."

Drummond's simple statement, spoken low and firmly against her ear, vibrated from his chest through her body. "I want to. What choice do I have?"

"Ye can, Morven. Men are going out in the morning when we can see their tracks. We'll get Rory back."

She turned then, in his arms, and leaned her head on his shoulder, her tears cold on her face.

Drummond held her until they ceased, then brought her back inside. They'd left the door open, so the cottage was cold, but Drummond got her seated, threw another brick of peat on the fire, and poured some more ale for her to drink. In moments, she warmed enough to look at him. His leine where his plaid didn't cover it, was transparent—wet from her tears.

She reached out and touched the wetness. "I'm sorry."

He put his hand over hers and held it against the fire of his chest. "I'm not."

He pulled her onto his lap and wrapped his arms around her.

She rested her head on his shoulder and watched the peat catch fire, low flames licking from one side to the other. When she was ready, she reached up and cupped Drummond's cheek. "Thank ye."

"For what?"

"For caring for me. And Rory."

"I do care for ye. More than ye ken."

She wanted to say *show me*, but she dared not. This man was too good a man, too devoted to his clan and his duty, to risk everything for. He would be gone soon, and she would be left with nothing but heartache and memories.

Then he kissed her. Gently, almost reverently, as if he knew how fragile she was and feared smashing her to pieces like a fine glass cup.

She let him kiss her while she absorbed his scent, his taste, the heat of his firm lips, the brush of his fingers through her hair. The comfort he offered. The memory she would cherish for the rest of her life. She clung to him, but dared not respond to his kisses, or she would go up in flames. And there would be nothing left of her but ashes.

DRUMMOND WANTED to ease Morven's grief. But he dared not, not in the way his desire for her would lead him to. She'd been years without affection, save for that from her young son. It appeared she hadn't had a man in her life since her handfasted husband left her. His men had related to him what other villagers had said about her, about her past. She'd had a hard time since the handfasting ended. And now? Drummond was not here to complicate her life, especially not to make it worse. Still...

He wanted her.

He was certain of that. But not at her expense. He must content himself with soothing her. Holding her. A few gentle kisses to comfort her. Right now, he could not say how much more he might want, or be willing to offer her. In the meantime, he meant to protect her—including from himself.

He glanced toward the one small window set high in the wall. A hide covered it but the soft, rosy quality of the light leaking in around the edges told him the sun would be up all too soon. It was time to go.

He lifted her hand and brought it to his lips. The backs of her fingers tasted of her tears, salty and bereft.

She looked up at him, wide-eyed, as his lips touched her skin. Color rose in her face.

"I must go, Morven. Ye dinna wish for me to be found here. Inside yer home, not so early in the day."

She nodded.

He couldn't read the expression on her face, in her eyes. Was she relieved? Or sad and about to object? She didn't say anything. Merely watched him, as a doe watches the hunter she knows is on her trail.

"Never fear," he murmured and helped her stand. She stepped away as he gained his feet beside her. "I will send a man to stand guard at yer door. I willna leave ye defenseless."

"The sun will be up soon," she said. "I will be fine."

Had she forgotten when Rory was taken? Nay, he saw her reaction as the thought crashed into her mind. She paled and dropped her gaze.

"Aye, ye will be fine, because I will put a man outside yer door. I need to ken ye are safe."

She pursed her lips and nodded before lifting her gaze. "Very well. Thank ye."

Her eyes again had that liquid look of unshed tears, but her lips were full and tempting. Drummond dropped his gaze to her hand, still cocooned in his, and brought it to his lips once more. He kissed her fingers gently, and released her hand.

"I'll check on ye later today. Get some more sleep, if ye can."

He left her without looking back. He wasn't sure he could keep walking away from her if he did. Instead, he returned to where his men camped, roused Eduard long enough to get the name of a man who'd had the chance to sleep last night and sent him to guard Morven's door. He wanted a man rested and alert, not one who dozed off leaning against her door as he had done last night.

Until she opened the door, he tumbled in, and everything changed between them.

"All was quiet," Eduard told him with a yawn that Drummond fought not to mimic. "No sign of the lad. The trackers ye ordered out just left. They'll send a man back to fetch ye if they think they're close."

Drummond glanced up at the sky. The sun was not over the surrounding mountains yet, but the sky had lightened enough that by the time the men reached the area where they'd lost the raiders yesterday, they should have enough light to search for the next set of tracks. He intended to go with them, but knew he'd be more help after a few hours' sleep. "If I'm not up when they return, wake me."

Eduard nodded and Drummond sought his own bed. Even if they didn't send a man back for him, he'd get a report from the trackers when they returned, and join the next patrol in a few hours. By then they'd have a better idea which way the raiders had gone, and perhaps that tingle in his belly would return and prove useful.

RODRICK GLARED AT HIS WIFE, Arabella, tired beyond tolerance of her anger and the lad's crying. He was tired of riding, tired of raiding, tired of living on the edge of survival. If only Diarmad had been successful in replacing the Moncreiffe chief—or had never tried at all. They'd still be living in luxury, relative to what they endured now. "Shut him up, or I will," he threatened.

"Ye brought him here. Ye quiet him. Or take him back to his mam. Have ye really sunk so low as to kidnap a child and claim he's yer own? Ye go too far with this scheme of yers."

He backhanded her, then turned to Rory, who watched their argument, wide-eyed, while he snuffled and whined for his mother. "*Haud yer wheesht!*" He was tempted to backhand the boy for good measure, but knew that would only prolong the crying fit.

Rory fell backward, wailed and curled into a ball on the floor.

"Ye frightened him!" Arabella grasped Rory's arm and helped him to stand, stepped away and rounded on her husband. "Would ye treat our daughters this way? How do ye expect to convince the chief this lad is yers if ye terrify him?"

"To achieve my aim, I'll treat him any way I must." He turned his glare on the lad. "Grow up. Be a man. Stop sniveling."

Arabella slapped him.

Rodrick's temper went white-hot. He swung at her, but she ducked out of the way and pulled the lad out of reach, too.

"He's only a wean—not a man, no matter what ye demand of him."

He'd had enough. More than enough of her. More than enough of her daughters. He had a son now. He would win the rest without her hanging on him like a weight on his back. "Get out," he raged. "Ye and yer daughters. Out! I divorce ye. Ye have been nay help. I have my son, and dinna need ye." Of course, tears. She would try to soften his ire with tears. Not this time. "I wager those lasses are not even mine. How many men have ye had?" She gasped and he laughed. "Go live with one of yer lovers. I'm done with ye." He knew he had no reason to suspect that of her. But he wanted her gone—now—and insulting her was the fastest way he could think of to get rid of her.

"Ye have lost yer mind. Who'll care for the lad?"

"That's my business. Gather yer brats and yer clothes and get out. And ye—" he said and pointed from Rory to the pallet in the corner, "Get over there and *haud yer wheesht* or I'll hit ye like I hit her."

Rory obeyed, silent for once, while Arabella moved around their cabin, gathering belongings and muttering under her breath. He caught a few words of her declaring she wouldn't have him around her daughters. God only knew what he might do to them. He almost hit her again for that comment. He wouldn't harm the lasses, but Arabella didn't need to know that. She'd earned his anger, and she'd suffered for it. The lasses had naught to do with what was or was not between the two of them.

He studied the lad and decided, aye, he looked like him, enough that the chief couldn't deny his claim. Morven could have lied at the end of their handfasting when she said she hadn't conceived. Perhaps, in truth, the lad was a year or two too young. But that's not what Rodrick would tell Diarmad. Though he was smaller than a lad his age should be, Rory could be his son, one he'd had for years, though he never knew it. As soon as Diarmad saw the lad, as soon as he saw the resemblance to Rodrick, he would have to name Rodrick his heir. Lorne would be furious, but that was too bad.

And then? The chief had better watch his back. Rodrick didn't intend to remain the heir for long.

In the meantime, what to do with the lad? He was whining for his mam again. "Crying again? Didna I tell ye to *haud yer wheesht*?"

Rory paled and tried to crawl back as far as he could against the cabin wall. Rodrick took a step toward him, but Arabella sniffed, distracting him.

There was only one solution. He should have seen it before he grabbed the lad. He must bring Morven back, too, even without her damned loom. Especially without it. If he had brought her home to Moncreiffe as he ought in the beginning, he would have known whether she was with child and been there to welcome his son. And raised him right. Not like this lad. He would have raised him as a man ought to be raised. He would not have been this weak-willed, crying excuse for a bairn.

8

D rummond woke to the sound of shouting, some high-spirited, some with a questioning lilt at the end. He rubbed his face, then rolled out of his tent and stood. The position of the sky told him it was mid-morning. The tracker patrol was riding in, escorting a bound stranger on a horse.

He waited until they stopped and got the man down. "Ye caught one of them!"

"Aye. Ran across this one and another as we headed back down the mountain. We wouldha had both, but the other one got away from us."

"Send a man to Angus. He'll want to question this man."

"Shall we take him to the keep?"

"In a minute." Drummond looked over their prisoner. Not a man, not yet. Thin, perhaps thinner than a recent growth spurt would account for. A hint of hair on his chin, not yet grown in. His clothing was worn and patched. Looking at this lad, Drummond could believe the raiders had only stolen to survive, and deserved some measure of sympathy. At least until someone they stole from died. He didn't appear old enough to be involved in raiding nearby crofts, much less killing a man. But he might know who did. And certainly, he would know where they were based. Still, he had a stubborn set to his jaw, and a glare in his eye that didn't bode well for getting information from him.

"What's yer name, lad?"

"Bugger off."

"Indeed? Do ye go by Bugger? Or Bug?"

From the twist of his mouth, the lad almost snorted a laugh. His face reddened with the effort not to react.

"Where do ye hail from, Bug?"

"Nowhere ye ken."

"I've never heard of that place. Is it nearby?" Drummond took a step closer.

The lad's bravado suddenly deflated. His gaze dropped to the ground.

"Ye look too young to be a raider. We're ye out hunting with yer da?" That brought his head back up, but he wisely kept his mouth shut.

"He had a dirk on him," one of Angus's men reported. "Not anymore."

That earned him a glare from their captive.

"Precious to ye, is it? Got it from yer grandda, did ye? And ye want it back?"

The lad shifted his weight, but kept his silence.

Drummond wanted to go easy on him, but he knew Angus wouldn't care about the lad's age or condition. "I'm not the one ye need to fear, lad. The MacComas chief will speak to ye next, and ye've a life to answer for."

"A life?" He swallowed hard. "I didna kill anybody."

"But one of yer men did. And I think ye ken who did it."

"I dinna."

"Tell me what I want to ken and I'll tell the MacComas to go easy on ye. Who leads the raiders?"

Silence.

"Where do ye live?"

More silence.

"I canna help ye if ye dinna help me."

The lad went back to studying the ground.

Drummond kept at him, but he ran out of time when Angus walked up with Archie and another man.

"Got one, did ye?"

"Aye. He claims not to ken anything. He's called Bug."

The lad's head shot up. "Am not."

"If ye dinna tell me yer name, then Bug ye will be." Drummond eyed him and waited while Bug considered.

"I'm..." He trailed off, apparently deciding Bug was preferable to giving up any information at all.

"Ye are in a lot of trouble, lad," Drummond reminded him. "This is the MacComas chief."

"And ye will now come with me," Angus told him. He tipped his head toward the keep, and the men who'd come with him took the lad's arms and led him away. "He's young," Angus said when they moved far enough away not to be overheard.

"And afraid. Stubborn. I tried going easy on him, but ye saw where that got me." Drummond paused and crossed his arms. "I'd say give him some time to think things over, but with Rory missing, time is not on our side. We havena found the men who took him yet, and the longer it takes, the farther they could go."

"Dinna tell Morven we have this lad," Angus advised. "No sense gettin' her hopes up."

"What are ye going to do?"

"Make him talk." Angus held up a hand. "I willna kill the lad, but I will have answers."

Drummond heartily wished the lad had opened up to him. "Have a care. When this is over, ye may wish to give him back— as a peace offering—but not if ye harm him too much."

"That's a good idea. Very well, keep searching. I'll do my part here."

Morven went about her day in a fog. She tried to eat, but nothing had any flavor, tried to work on her loom, but couldn't get it set up right. Her head felt wrapped in wool, layers and layers of it. She could barely see past the grief in her heart, the images and memories of Rory, from infancy until she watched him carried off by his father, screaming and reaching for her. Then the anger took over.

Drummond's man, a stranger outside her cottage, also disturbed her. He must have arrived while she was asleep, soon after Drummond left. He'd promised a man to replace him outside, and one was out there.

She could see him through the open door, hear him as he moved around, almost feel him. She couldn't live like this. Under guard. And worse, without her son.

She recalled a few things Rodrick had said about his clan. Moncreiffe. He'd always been vague about details, saying it was through the mountains a few days travel to the south and east. But he never said if that was on foot or on horseback. With wagons or without? And he'd never offered to take her there for a visit. He claimed his parents were dead, so there was no reason for them to make the trip until they were ready to move at the end of the handfasting. Did she know enough to be able to find it? Perhaps Drummond already knew. Surely as the Lathan heir, he would know a great deal about neighboring clans. And if not, well, surely a clan's settlement would be large enough that they would stumble across it.

Drummond would want to send men and leave her behind, but she must go with them. Her son needed her. The sooner she got to him, the better. She couldn't sit in her cottage and just wait for him to be delivered back to her. So many things could go wrong. She might never see him again.

Nay, Drummond could not leave her behind.

Determined, she went in search of him and saw him emerge from a tent where the Lathans had set up their camp.

He saw her and smiled. "Morven. Is everything all right?"

"What if the raiders are men from my—from Rory's father's clan? He could send them here because he kens the village and the crofts, the livestock and such. I think 'tis worth a trip to Moncreiffe to see if Rory has been taken there."

Drummond crossed his arms and listened while she talked, clearly considering her words. "I'm glad ye told me," he said, and nodded. "It makes sense. They seem to have a camp much closer than that, but 'tis a possibility. I'll send some men. If the Moncreiffe laird kens anything about a strange lad, we'll have Rory back as soon as the men can return."

"Nay!" She held out a hand to stop him. "'Tis not what I meant. I must go with yer men. They dinna ken Rory. If they brought back the wrong lad, I'd be heartbroken, and so might some other mother."

"Nay, Morven. Ye canna go. Whether the raiders are from of Moncreiffe or not, they are still out there. 'Tis too dangerous. One of yer village guards can go. They ken Rory."

"'Twas my idea. He'll need me. I must go."

"Nay. I willna allow it."

"Ye are not my chief, Drummond—"

"I dinna care, Morven. I willna change my mind. Ye must remain safe while we look for Rory. Ye willna leave the village. That is my final word."

Furious, Morven spun on her heel and stalked back to her cottage. She had to do something. She paced while she tried to recall everything Rodrick had ever said about where he came from. Rory's things mocked her, from the clothes he was outgrowing to his collection of broken stick soldiers, he was everywhere and yet... nowhere. She had to get him back. She would go alone if she must. Without Drummond's men, and without him.

She gathered provisions, blankets, cloaks for her and for Rory, and everything else she thought she might need. There was no time to walk to Moncreiffe. She'd take Ebby, Kelso's horse, and go. Her son needed her. He was her responsibility. This might be the daftest thing she'd done in her life, but all of Angus's and Drummond's men so far had failed. Finding him was up to her.

She waited until her guard went away from her cottage to relieve himself, and sneaked out.

COMING out of the keep after his midday meal, Drummond saw Brodie Lathan running toward him, shouting. Drummond couldn't understand him. But something was very wrong. And Brodie had been guarding Morven's cottage. "Raiders?"

"She's gone!"

When his words finally became clear, Drummond's belly dropped into his boots. "Gone? What do ye mean, *gone*?"

"She's gone," Brodie gasped as he reached Drummond, face red from exertion as he bent over, hands on knees, and tried to breathe and spit out words at the same time.

"Did ye hear horses? Was it the raiders again?"

He straightened, breathing more easily, and shrugged one shoulder. "Nay. Not a sound. Her door had been open all morning, but it was closed when I got back from taking a piss."

Drummond waved a dismissive hand. "When?"

"More than an hour ago. Mayhap longer. I knocked. She didna answer. I thought she might be resting, so I didna open the door." He held up a hand to forestall Drummond's reaction. "But I checked again a few minutes ago. This time I did open it. The cottage is empty. I looked nearby for her. She's disappeared." He looked away. "I'm sorry."

"I ken where she's gone," Drummond said as his muscles

tightened with remembered anger. "She thinks Rory may be at Moncreiffe, the clan his father hails from. I agreed to send some men, but she thinks she must go. We argued. She's gone alone." He clenched his fists. As much as he wanted to punch something, hitting Brodie wouldn't bring back Morven. "She sneaked by ye, most likely. 'Tis not yer fault. Tell Eduard when he returns from his search to keep the patrols going." He glanced skyward. The midday sun was high overhead, but night fell faster in the mountains. He'd have to find her before full dark, or she might get by him. Worse, the dark held dangers a woman alone was not prepared to deal with. This daft quest of hers could kill her. "I'll go after her. She canna have gone far on foot." And he wouldn't entrust Morven's safety to anyone else again. He was to blame for making her think she could do nothing to save her son. He wouldn't make that mistake again. She was his responsibility.

"What if the raiders find her and take her, too?"

Ice slid down Drummond's spine. "I'll find her before that happens."

In only a few hours' time, how could she go from taking comfort in his arms, wetting his leine with her tears, to charging off into the unknown on a desperate search? Foolish woman—the only thing she was likely to find was trouble. He didn't know whether to doubt her sanity or applaud her backbone.

"I'll get what ye need," Brodie told him and ran off to collect supplies.

While Drummond saddled his horse, Brodie came back with Ailbeart and enough blankets, food, and watered ale for a few days' travel, just in case.

"D'ye want me to come with ye?" Brodie's tone betrayed his guilt over Morven's disappearance. "Ailbeart can take the next patrol when Eduard gets back."

"Nay." Drummond swung up onto his horse. "I'll travel

faster and with less notice alone. Ye keep the men searching for the raiders and guarding the village with Angus's lot. One of the search parties might even find her."

"Ye'd be safer if one of us came with ye," Ailbeart objected.

"Bhaltair will kill us—slowly—if something happens to ye," Brodie muttered and shuddered.

"Yer da will do worse," Ailbeart added.

Drummond didn't bother to shake his head at their attempt to blackmail him into complying. "We're stretched too thin already. Keep the patrols going." Where was that tingle in his belly when he needed it? "I'll be back when I've found her," he said, turned his horse, and rode out of their camp into the hills.

9

By dusk, Morven had ridden deep into the mountains southeast of the village. Nothing looked familiar. She was long past the outlying crofts and pastures the raiders had hit. Long past any signs of people at all. She'd crossed a deer trail or two, forded a rushing burn, avoided a steep ravine, and spent knee-quaking minutes listening to crashing in the brush behind her. Her horse danced aside nervously, but just as she was about to kick it into a gallop, the noise moved away, rather than toward her. She could only guess what had startled her, but suspected a boar as being the only creature fierce enough not to care how much noise it made. She was lucky to have avoided it.

Second thoughts were beginning to plague her. She'd gotten away from the village and from Drummond's guard. She was proud of herself for how easily she had made her escape. But the reality of what she had done had set in. Around her, between here and Moncreiffe, were miles of emptiness, and she had few weapons and no tools, nothing save an eating knife and Kelso's dirk to defend herself. At least her da had taught her what to do with one of those. She wished she had the strength—and skill—to wield Kelso's longsword, but she'd left it behind, wrapped in a length of MacComas plaid, for Rory. While she was wishing, she might as well wish she was certain which way the raiders had gone, or where Rory was now.

Ahead she saw a rocky outcrop. There might be caves in it, or a sheltered area where she and Kelso's horse could safely pass the night. When she reached it, she found the rocks formed a natural amphitheater, shielded by boulders and screened by trees and underbrush. It would do. She tied the horse to a tree branch, gathered deadfall under the trees, then worked off some anxiety building and lighting a small fire in a natural depression in the rock. It warmed one side of her, leaving the other side in the cold.

Traveling like this was harder than she thought. She yearned to keep going, to travel all night, but she dared not risk moving about in a strange forest after dark. She could become hopelessly lost—if she wasn't already—or ride old Ebby over a cliff. Predators roamed the night as well, but she counted on her fire to keep them at bay.

She had never been this far from her village, but she imagined that she could feel her son, somewhere ahead of her, as desperate for her as she was desperate to find him. She wrapped herself in several layers of blankets, knowing she must rest, but determined to push on at first light. Night noises scared her and kept her fitfully awake for a time. Finally, exhausted by the lack of sleep the night before as she kept company with Drummond, and by the perilous events of the day, she slept.

DRUMMOND FOUND her by the glow of the embers of her small fire. She lay bundled up against the cold, asleep on the ground, her horse tied nearby, totally vulnerable to raiders, to wolves, and to the cold. As far as he could see, she had no weapons and few supplies. Nothing but determination and an old, broken-down farm horse. Fury boiled his blood in one moment and fear iced it in the next.

As much as he wanted to wring her neck for this foolish stunt, he sympathized with her determination to find her son.

He didn't know she could ride. They'd never discussed it. But because she could, she travelled farther from the village than he expected. Many times, he almost turned back, thinking he missed her, but his inner sense told him she was still out here somewhere. The tingle in his belly kept him going, that and the image in his mind of her lost and alone. He followed the sensation in his gut as it grew stronger, changed direction if it grew weaker. And here she was.

He dismounted and called her name, softly, to wake her without scaring her into running. Morning was still hours away, but he had to make sure she was alive.

She reacted to her name. Or to his voice, he didn't know which. And didn't care. As she sat up, relief eased some of the tension in his body.

She pulled an arm out of the blankets, rubbed her eyes and scowled at him. "What are ye doing here?"

"Looking for ye. What do ye think ye are doing out here alone?" He could feel his anger rising again. The cords of his neck stiffened and his fists clenched. "Do ye ken how much danger ye put yerself in?" He found her. Others could, too.

"Ye wouldna come with me," she said, as she fought to untangle herself from layers of wool.

She cut off the tirade that was beginning to boil up from his belly. He took a breath to calm himself. Then another. Showing his anger and fear for her would not make what he had to do any easier. In as reasonable a tone as he could manage, he told her, "It appears, now, that I am. Unless ye are willing to turn around and go home while I continue to search?" Not that he would let her go in any direction by herself. He was here now, and he meant to keep her safe. Besides, he'd bet a cask of fine French wine she had no idea in which direction the village lay. In truth, he was surprised—and relieved—not to have found her body at the bottom of a ravine.

"Nay. I willna return." She finally got herself untangled and threw off her covers.

He frowned at them, then noticed the dirk she unearthed from the tangle, and turned a fierce stare on her. "Did ye think to defend yerself while wrapped up like that?"

"I had to stay warm," she said, her wrinkled brow making it clear he was a fool not to understand that. She pursed her lips. "How did ye find me?"

"Just lucky, I guess." He squatted next to her, eyed her meager pile of kindling, added a few sticks, and told her, "Sleep until sunrise. Then we'll go."

"Ye need sleep, too."

"Fine," he said, settling on his haunches with his back to a rock. "I'll sleep. Ye guard us. Wake me if ye hear anything." A screech sounded nearby.

"Like that?"

"That owl? Nay. Like horses. Or wolves howling."

She shivered. "Mayhap ye are better able to deal with those."

He snagged one of the blankets and pulled it to him, then wrapped it around her shoulders. "Since I have weapons, and ye dinna seem to be prepared to use what ye have, I suppose so." He ran a hand through his hair, frustrated by her naïveté. "Why are ye here, Morven? Why did ye not talk to me again?"

She narrowed her eyes. "Ye said *nay* when I asked to go with ye and yer men. I didna see any sense in wasting my breath."

"So ye'd rather waste yer life?" He held out his hands, palms up, questioning. "What would Rory do without ye, if ye came to mischief on this quest?"

She gathered the blanket more tightly around her. "He's without me now. I'm trying to find him and bring him home."

"So am I." He studied her until she looked away.

"Aye, well, what did ye intend to do? Pluck a random lad out of the woods and bring him back with ye?"

"I ken Rory."

"Ye have seen him with me, in the village."

"I have."

"But do ye really think ye'd ken him if ye encountered him in a strange place? With anyone else? Strangers? He'd look like any other lad to ye, away from familiar surroundings."

He shook his head, sure he'd never met a more stubborn woman. "Why are ye so certain I wouldna?"

"Why are ye so certain ye would?"

"Because I am more observant than most." He proceeded to describe her son to her, including the color of his eyes, the marks on his skin, the cowlick in his hair, what he'd been wearing when they last met, what they'd talked about, and how Rory's voice sounded. "I would ken Rory anywhere, with anyone, Morven. I care about the lad. Ye needna fear I'll over-look him."

She shivered again and adjusted the blanket around her.

In the firelight, he could see the shine of tears in her eyes. "Ach, Morven, come here." He pulled her into his arms and covered them both with her other blankets.

"We shouldna do this," she protested, then sighed. "But ye are so warm," she murmured.

"And yer hands are like ice," he told her, clasping one in his. "Ye've been cold too long. Sleep, lass. We'll rest and go when the sun comes up."

When she didn't answer, he held himself still. In a moment, her soft breathing told him she'd already fallen asleep.

She had to be exhausted and sick with worry. He let her

sleep snugged closely against him, her arm draped over his chest and her head on his shoulder. This wasn't how he'd imagined holding her, or how lying with her the first time would be, but he'd enjoy it while he could. He wouldn't fall asleep with her in his arms. The feel of her, the scent of her fueled his desire for her. He was too stimulated, alert to any sound or movement around them, longing for the woman in his arms. The brave, foolish, fierce, loving woman who had captured his heart.

THEY LEFT Morven's campsite at first light and headed a little south of east. "Ye were generally in the right direction," Drummond told her, "but ye would have missed the Moncreiffe keep behind a range of hills and kept going until ye reached Dundee, or the sea beyond it."

Morven flinched, thinking that her fears had been well-founded. She'd had the barest amount of information to start with, a mother's instinct to drive her, and fear for her son keeping her going, but she'd been a fool. "I'm sorry I put ye through this," she finally said. "Ye didn't deserve to spend a cold night on the ground."

The look he gave her melted any last vestiges of ice in her fingers and toes. It was full of heat and desire. "I was right where I wished to be. With ye in my arms."

She swallowed and nodded. "I was, too. Ye make me feel warm and safe. How can ye be so kind to me—someone ye barely ken?"

"How can ye ask that? I care about ye, Morven—ye and Rory. Ye are coming to mean more to me than ye ken."

She smiled gently as she held his words to her heart, right next to the memory of being held in his arms. And his kisses the night he put himself at her door until she opened it and brought him inside, out of the cold. Could she admit she felt the same?

They rode in silence for a few more miles. Drummond seemed preternaturally alert. What did he sense? Or was he simply, as he'd said, unusually observant, and that was what she noted in his posture and the sweep of his gaze around them.

She did her best to be as observant as he, studying the trees, listening for birdsong or the grunt of a red deer buck, the scurry of long-eared coneys in the undergrowth, and the chitter of red squirrels in the trees. It all seemed normal, as though they passed by as easily as mist, invisible to the animals, or unconcerning.

By midday, Morven was certain they had to be close to their destination. She was heartily sick of riding. Her rump and legs were numb and her back ached. They reached a cliff and turned aside to travel along it, searching for a way down and onward. She was about to ask Drummond to stop and let her walk the stiffness out of her body when he held up a hand.

His gaze darted about them, seeming to inspect each tree, each rock. The frown drawing down his brow frightened her. But the voice coming out of the trees ahead of them nearly made her faint with terror—and hope.

"Stop right there," Rodrick said. "I have men all around ye." When Drummond rested a hand on his sword's hilt, Rodrick added, "If ye want to live, dinna do it. Pulling that blade will be the last thing ye do in this life."

"Who are ye?"

"The man ye seek. Aye, Morven," Rodrick said, smirking as he appeared before them, his mount stepping silently out of the trees, "I have Rory. I mean to keep him."

"Nay! He's my son. Ye must give him back to me."

Beside her, Drummond shifted in his saddle. "Why did ye take him?"

She'd been so focused on Rodrick that Drummond's voice at her side startled her.

"'Tis none of yer concern," Rodrick admonished. "But I've come for the lad's mother. Ye saved me a day's ride. How thoughtful of ye to meet me here."

"*Meet* ye?" Morven didn't have to feign the outrage in her voice. "I'd sooner skewer ye. Where is Rory?"

"Safe. Ye'll see for yerself soon enough."

Relief filled her. Rory was safe—for the moment. But she and Drummond were not.

Rodrick tapped his horse's sides and approached her, reached out and jerked the reins from her hands. "Come along now. I'll take ye to him." He tipped his head toward Drummond and gave a look full of meaning to the men who'd appeared as silently from the woods as he had.

Drummond! She looked around at the sound of steel sliding from leather. At the other men's appearance, he'd pulled his sword.

"Leave her be," he warned.

Rodrick laughed. "I'm merely granting the lady's wish, and taking her to her son. Surely ye canna object to that."

A slight noise behind her was all the warning she or Drummond got as Rodrick's men attacked. Morven screamed, "Nay!" as Rodrick pulled her mount out of range of the fight.

Drummond couldn't win against five other men! "Dinna do this!" She cut a glare at Rodrick, but he paid her no attention. His gaze was on the defense Drummond put up against his men, the grin on his face growing as they edged closer to the cliff.

Then one of the men got behind Drummond and hit him across the back with the flat of his sword.

Morven screamed his name, helpless to do more as Drummond fell from his horse and disappeared from view, over the cliff edge and down. Only then did she realize how close they'd come to the steep drop. Thuds and the sound of something heavy crashing a long way down through the brush filled her belly with ice. How could this be happening?

Rodrick called back the man who went to peer over the edge, looking for Drummond's body. "'Tis not worth risking our necks to make sure he's dead. With that fall, he must be."

Morven choked and clapped her hands over her mouth to stifle the scream that wanted to tear itself from her throat. Rodrick had her now. Drummond was gone. Badly hurt at the very least, but likely dead.

Sharp pain pierced her chest. Nay, he couldn't be. Dear God, what if he was down there, too injured to save himself? Someone as alive as Drummond Lathan, as determined and fierce, could not die this way. Someone she cared about could not disappear forever right before her eyes. Her vision went gray, and she fell forward over Ebby's neck. "Drummond," she moaned, regretting that she hadn't told him how she felt about him when she had the chance.

Rodrick jerked her upright.

She rounded on him, fury giving her the strength to set aside her grief and challenge him. "Why are ye doing this?"

"That brat ye raised won't stop crying for ye. A weakling like that canna be my son, but ye were my wife, so we're going to pretend he is. Just long enough for me to take care of some business."

Morven's heart leapt into throat. He still didn't know Rory was his bairn. What would he do if he found out? And what would he do with them once his business was concluded?

10

R odrick laughed at the dismay on Morven's ashen face. For a moment, he had thought she was going to leap from her horse and follow her companion over the cliff. Was that man Rory's father? Nay, she called the lad *my* son, not *ours*.

He didn't care. He had her. She'd calm the lad. She'd confirm for Diarmad the notion that the lad was his. His plan would work. And if she thought she could frustrate him and not cooperate, he'd make her. He'd threaten the boy—even beat him if he had to—until she did everything he told her to do, exactly as he told her to do it. "Let's go," he barked, kicked his mount into motion, and jerked on her reins, forcing Morven's horse to follow along. Her sharp cry told him he'd surprised her. She grabbed her horse's mane and sent him a glare.

"Ye didna have to kill him." The censure in her tone made his jaw clench.

"What did ye think I would do? Bring him with us and set ye up with him in a cozy cottage? Ye are more a fool now than ye were when ye handfasted with a stranger if ye think I would leave him alive to follow us."

She looked back as they rode away from the cliffside, silent, probably fuming. Or grieving. He didn't see any sheen of tears in her eyes. Maybe she'd developed a backbone these last seven years.

"How is my son?" She glared at him, then asked again, "Have ye hurt him?"

He didn't bother to answer. Why would he take the lad if he only meant to harm him? If she didn't realize that, she'd find out soon enough.

"I..." She let go of her mount's mane with one hand and reached toward him. "I shouldna have asked ye that. I ken ye wouldna harm a bairn on purpose."

He gave her outstretched hand a long look, but made no move to take it, or to come close enough for her to touch him.

Finally, she drew it back, her lips pursed and her eyes wide. "Ye must tell me! What have ye done with him?"

She kept after him, her voice rising in pitch and volume with each question, irritating him. "*Wheesht*, or ye'll not like what I do to ye."

"Ye never acted this way before. Why are ye doing this now? What happened to ye?"

"Naught happened to me. We lived in yer village while we were handfasted. I had to be good to ye. I dinna have to do that anymore."

"Why did ye disappear? I tried to contact ye. I had news..." Her face flushed and she ducked her head.

"What news?" He pulled her horse closer to his, reached over and grabbed her arm. "Am I his father?" Was her lad the bairn she claimed to be carrying in the letter Kelso had been reading before Rodrick killed him? "I was told ye lost a bairn."

Her head lifted. "Who told ye that?" She didn't wait for him to answer. "I sent word. Both when I was sure I was carrying and after Rory was born," she railed. "I tried to send word to ye. Ye didna answer. Where were ye?"

"I went where I said I would go. Back to Moncreiffe." And

remarried. She didn't need to know that yet. And a few years later, got caught up in a revolt. Banished along with the others involved. She didn't need to know that either.

"Is that where we're going?"

"Ye'll find out soon enough." He let her arm go and kicked his horse into a trot. Perforce, hers followed. Damn it, there must be another letter in Kelso's cottage. He should have known the old man lied to him. She hadn't lost the bairn she carried. Rory was his son. Rodrick was glad he'd killed Kelso. He'd deserved to die for keeping his bairn a secret. But why had the old man done it? Why hadn't he found out first what he had done to Kelso to make him want to keep his wife and son from him?

"Ye are not who ye said, are ye? Why are ye doing this?"

He pulled on his reins to slow their mounts, then reached across and hit her arm with the back of his hand. "If ye want to see yer son again, ye'll *wheesht*." He was fighting a losing battle to control the rage rising in him. He should have searched the old man's belongings instead of taking his word that she'd lost his bairn. He would have known, damn it! If the old man hadn't kept her letters from him, he wouldn't be here today. His body felt stiff all over, hot, his heart pounding as if trying to burst from his chest. She had no idea the peril she was in. "If ye say another word, I'll throw ye over that cliff back there and ye can join yer lover at the bottom."

Nay. He couldn't kill her. He needed her. He had plans for her. But she didn't need to know that, either.

DRUMMOND WOKE UP. He thought he'd hit the bottom of a steep hill because he lay on his side on level ground. Unless he'd landed on a ledge. When he opened his eyes, the only thing he could see was a head-sized rock next to his face. He shifted his position carefully, first clenching each fist, twisting his feet, and bending his knees. Nothing seemed broken, but every part of him hurt. Even before he moved, everything hurt. How far had he fallen?

He turned his head slowly, so as not to overbalance and fall farther if he was on a ledge. Nay, he wasn't. He could see trees and scrubby undergrowth. He lifted his head, fighting the aches and the spinning sensation in his belly, and looked around. He was facing away from the cliff and couldn't see how far he'd fallen, but he could see level ground stretching away from him. It was safe to move.

He pressed up to sitting, a groan escaping when he put his weight on his left arm. Not his sword arm, thank the saints, and not broken. But wrenched, or so bruised in the fall that the pain made him dizzy. If the infernal swirling in his head would stop, he'd feel better.

He hadn't felt like this since he and his brother, Jamie, got into a keg of French brandy when they were fourteen. Their father had been furious, and their mother, once she was certain they would take no lasting harm, refused to heal them. She'd let the headaches and sick stomachs teach them a lesson they'd never forgotten.

He checked his other arm and legs. Nothing broken, but he'd be sore for days. He eyed the rock he'd woken up to find blocking his view. Had he hit his head on it?

Then he remembered how he'd gotten here. Where was Morven? Och, nay, the fight. The raiders had her. On horseback. They were probably long gone. He needed to get moving. How long had he been out? He rolled to his hands and knees, grasped a nearby tree trunk and pushed to his feet. He clung to the tree, waiting for his belly to stop threatening to climb up his throat. His head still spun, but if he moved slowly, he could tolerate it. The worst damage was to his pride that he'd let someone hit him from behind—that and the pounding headache. He could be dead right now. They probably thought he was.

He studied the steep hillside. Broken branches and crushed undergrowth marked the path he'd taken tumbling down. No wonder he felt the way he did. But even if his head wouldn't settle down, he could climb it. He hoped the raiders hadn't taken his horse. After a careful walk to the steep hillside, he reached up for a handhold and a place to put a foot, then climbed. He had to pause often to rest and breathe, so his spinning head wouldn't throw off his balance. He clung to thin tree trunks, exposed roots, rocky outcrops, anything that he could use to lever himself upward. He didn't want to fall again, and the higher he climbed, the more fervently he felt that. Another fall might kill him. He was lucky this was more of a steep hillside than a sheer drop, or he would not have survived. As it was, he probably fell a few feet, then rolled down the rest of the way. That would account for some of the pain he could feel on his torso, legs, and arms.

When he finally reached the top, he pulled himself over the verge and lay panting, letting the world and his pulse settle down. His head pounded in time with his heartbeat. Slower was easier to bear, so he stayed on the ground and breathed until his heartbeat slacked off. After a few minutes, he sat up, then forced himself to his feet and looked around.

Where was his horse? Gone, of course. They'd taken it. He'd have to walk. The men who took Morven would get far ahead of him, but he could track them. One small blessing—he found his sword caught in some undergrowth at the edge of the cliff. The raiders must have overlooked it, peering over the edge and searching for his body down below. He could use it as a walking stick until he needed to use it to kill the man who took Rory and then Morven.

He suddenly realized he would find Morven even if he couldn't read tracks. She was like a beacon ahead of him.

He paused, staring in the direction she had gone. How did he see that so clearly? Was this what his mother and siblings had, each in their own way? Nay, they saved lives with theirs. He'd never really believed his facility at finding things could be a version of their talents. But it felt like the fall somehow changed an ability he'd spent years comparing to his siblings and dismissing. Or had he somehow tapped into it fully, now that his ability was a matter of life and death for Morven and for Rory?

They weren't lost *things*. They were people he cared about. A woman he loved and her son. Did his love and their danger make this difference?

He set out, then stopped at the first burn he found to drink and wash. He splashed cold water on his pounding head, but it didn't help. Then he searched along both banks until he found tracks. Lots of them, all going in the same direction.

The kidnapper might think he was dead, but he was clearly smart enough to try to confuse the trail in case he wasn't. Too bad for the kidnapper that Drummond could now follow Morven to the ends of the earth, if need be.

THE VILLAGE where Rodrick brought Morven was a rude camp made of tents and lean-tos, a few rough cabins, and one mud-daubed stone structure. As they rode in with the other five men and Drummond's horse behind them, Rodrick leaned closed to her ear. "Go along with whatever I say or yer lad will suffer."

Morven stiffened but nodded agreement. What choice did she have? She saw a few dispirited women and dirty children, who turned to stare at her in surprise, eyes wide and gaze flicking between her and the man who held her captive. The women looked thin, tired, and all were engaged in some task, from mending clothes to gathering firewood, to caring for the bairns.

Soon, she would be one of them.

As Rodrick dismounted, leaving Morven on horseback above him, an older man appeared in the doorway of the stone structure. Rodrick pulled her reins down with him and held them in one clenched fist, crushing any thought she might have entertained of galloping away. The men who'd ridden with them were still behind her, so they would have caught her in moments if she ran, but she wouldn't. She couldn't. She was here for her son. Still, the thought persisted. If only she had Rory on horseback with her, she would at least try to escape.

"What have ye brought us?" The man stepped out and walked toward them, his gaze fixed on Morven in a way that made her want to dismount and put the horse between them.

"My wife, mother of my son," Rodrick declared, then raised his voice and turned to regard all the people watching them as he repeated his claim.

Another man stepped out of the crowd, frown directed up at Morven as he stomped toward Rodrick. "Is that true?"

Rodrick tensed, but didn't look at her. Nonetheless, she knew what he expected her to say.

"Aye, 'tis. We have a son together. Rory."

"Ye are the one he handfasted with all those years ago?" The old man's gaze sharpened.

"I am."

"That makes me the heir," Rodrick pronounced. "Not only do I have a son, he is not a bairn in arms. I have had a son all these years, and only just discovered him."

"Why did she not send word to ye?"

"I did," Morven answered before Rodrick could speak. "To the clan he claimed was his. Moncreiffe. He lied."

Laughter broke out at that assertion. Out of the corner of her eye, Morven could see Rodrick giving her a cold stare.

"He didna," the older man said. "We were once part of Clan Moncreiffe. With time, we will be a clan of our own. A clan to be reckoned with."

"What she believes doesna matter," Rodrick insisted beside her. "I have found her and my son. Ye must name me heir."

"Nay!" The other man who'd questioned her stepped toward the older man. "He lies. He's kidnapped a lad and a woman, a ready-made family to convince ye."

"Bring the lad," the older man commanded, gesturing to one of the nearby women.

In moments, Rory appeared. With a cry, Morven slid from her horse and ran to him. No one moved to stop her. He stood frozen, staring at her as if she wasn't real. She knelt and wrapped him in her arms, tears wetting both their faces.

"Mam! Ye are here," he choked out. "I called for ye, and ye came."

"Of course I came, love. I searched for ye and I found ye. All will be well, Rory. *Dinna fash.*"

She looked up to the older man. "What will ye do with us?"

"That is up to Rodrick. The resemblance is clear. The lad is his son."

A woman standing with two young girls cried out from behind a closed fist. She eyed Rodrick with hatred, then turned her gaze to Morven and the hatred in her eyes dissolved into pity. She shook her head and turned away.

Rodrick widened his stance and grinned, fists on hips as the man who'd questioned her grimaced, then spat at Rodrick's feet.

Rodrick ignored the slight, took her arm and pulled her up from where she knelt with Rory. "Let's go," he ordered and led her to one of the rough cabins. He gestured for her to go inside, then tied their horses to the branch of a nearby tree. Rory led the way inside the cabin. Clearly this is where he'd been kept since Rodrick took him.

Morven looked around at the sparse furnishings. A cot, a pallet that Rory headed to without being told, a chair and small table, and a chest that must contain clothes and weapons. That was it. She'd always thought her home in the village was spare, save for her loom. But compared to this, she and Rory had lived in a palace.

Where would she sleep? Surely not in the cot with Rodrick.

He came in as she took in her new living arrangement.

"Sit," he said and pointed at the chair.

She complied, having nothing else to do, and not wanting him to take out any perceived disobedience on her son.

"Ye will act as my wife, whether ye consider yerself to be or nay. We must keep up appearances until the old man is gone and I take over." He crossed his arms and smirked. "I'll make sure that happens soon. Then ye can go wherever ye want."

"Rory, too."

"Aye, ye and the lad. I willna need ye any longer."

She didn't believe him. Before long, she would know more about him and his band of reivers, so she expected that rather than let them go, he'd kill her and keep Rory. Unless he got her with child and she gave him another son. The old man said they were building a clan. A clan that Rodrick would now inherit. He would want more than one heir. And he would want sons he was certain were his. She'd admitted in front of his chief and all the people gathered around them that Rory was his. Did he believe her? If he did, he'd never give him up. And given the way he was strutting and planning to succeed the chief, she was sure if he kept Rory, he would beat him to make a man out of him. If she found she needed to convince him Rory wasn't his, would he kill Rory, or just disown him?

She had to believe they would be rescued, and until then, she would do her best to protect her son. She'd go along with Rodrick until Drummond came for her. He had to be alive! Or until the Lathans captured a raider and forced him to lead them back here. Or she found a way to get them both away from here. She couldn't let her son be subjected to this kind of life.

Resolved, she stood. "Where can I go—"

"I'll show ye," Rodrick said, taking her hesitation for what she meant. He gestured her out of the cabin and down toward a burn. "Down there. I'll wait here."

She paused, startled at the sight of Drummond's horse tied out with Rodrick's and old Ebby. Was there no end to what Rodrick considered his? What he would take? She continued down the hill, surprised to be allowed on her own. Rodrick must be certain she wouldn't run as long as he held Rory. He was right.

Coming up the hill was the woman who'd cried out when the chief acknowledged Rory as Rodrick's son. As they passed, the woman whispered to her, "If ye want to live, run when ye can. Soon. With or without the lad."

Morven nearly stumbled but kept going. So even that woman thought Rodrick would kill her when he achieved his aim of taking over, but he would keep Rory. That confirmed her worst fear. Rodrick would strike soon. She couldn't wait for the Lathans to rescue her. She had to find a way to get Rory—and herself—out of here.

11

Drummond reached the raiders' encampment just before dark. The pearly glow of the gloaming was fading from the sky, giving him enough cover in deep shadow to circle the camp and find a vantage point hidden in the bracken where he could see without being seen.

The scents from the camp's central cooking fire tortured his belly as much as his injuries made moving a test of his will. His last meal had been the little he and Morven shared before they broke camp and set out just after sunrise. He'd searched without success for berries or anything else edible as he followed the raiders' tracks. He didn't want to take the time to hunt and cook a meal, so he'd kept going, fearing what would happen to Morven once the raiders reached their base. Now he smelled the meat roasting on a spit over the fire, and something else. Perhaps a stew made of meat scraps and the vegetables they'd stolen from Morven's village. His belly rumbled loudly enough for him to fear anyone nearby would hear it.

There! Morven and her son walked from a rough cabin toward the camp's central cooking fire with the man who'd taken her from him. The man Drummond suspected was in

charge of the raiders. Morven had a determined frown on her
face and an arm around Rory's shoulders, urging him forward.
His gaze kept darting between his mother's face and the blade
in the hand of the man at their side.

The fear in Rory's eyes broke Drummond's heart. He didn't
know how he was going to get them away from that man and
out of an armed camp, but he would. He'd sworn to protect
them. So far, he'd failed, and that failure ate at him. He gripped
the hilt of his dirk. That would change. He would do whatever
it took to free them.

Morven probably thought he'd died in that fall and her
future would be tied to this rough camp for as long as her
captor kept her alive. It was up to Drummond to help her, but
what could one man—one injured man—do?

He had his sword, but he was battered by the fall he'd
taken, and his head still pounded with every heartbeat. He
could use the help of his mother or youngest sister, Eilidh, to
heal the damage the fall down the cliff had done, but they were
days away on horseback, a sennight or more on foot. Saving
Morven and Rory was up to him, no matter what it cost him.

He settled in to observe the camp routine, to see who went
where and when. All he needed was a moment when Morven
and Rory were together and unguarded. Their horses were tied
behind the cabin he'd seen them leave. That gave him an idea.
Once it got dark, he'd take the supplies he hoped were still on
his horse and hers. He couldn't steal their mounts, not yet. If
they disappeared, the raider chief would know he lived and had
followed them. But he knew how much food should be left, and
there were blankets on both. If he could take enough of those
supplies to cache away from here, when he got Morven and
Rory out, they all might stand a better chance of surviving.
He'd leave at least a blanket on each horse, so it would appear
they were undisturbed.

The people of the camp lined up to collect their food.

Drummond counted a dozen men he hadn't seen before, the five he'd fought, and the man with Morven. Were there more? He hadn't seen any guards as he circled the settlement, but perhaps a few had gone to raid the village's outlying crofts again. And where was the man who'd been with the lad he called Bug? Did they know the lad had been taken, or were they used to their men being away for days at a time? If he wasn't already here, how soon would his companion return? When they heard about the lad, surely they'd get concerned about MacComas coming for them. But for now, the camp was quiet.

Another man carved roasted meat and gave each person a share. Next to him, a woman, one of a handful Drummond could see, ladled something from an iron kettle just off the fire. Once each person had their share, they walked away and settled on logs that ringed the cooking area.

As Morven and Rory moved up to collect their food, the man with them turned back with his full plate to watch. Rory bumped into him and spilled some of his meal.

With an oath, the man backhanded the boy, knocking him to the ground.

"Nay!" Morven cried out, and dropped to her son's side.

Two lasses sitting nearby turned their heads and looked away. Had the man mistreated them, too?

Morven's captor hauled her to her feet, swearing at her as Rory whimpered. "Leave him. I'll nay have a *greetin'* bairn for a son," he said, bending over Rory. "If ye want to eat, *wheesht* ye and get up."

Drummond half rose from his crouch in the brush, then settled back down as Rory obeyed the man, ceased crying, wiped his nose, and got to his feet. Morven gave him a plate, and in a few moments, they had collected their food and moved aside to find a seat.

Drummond watched them eat, his own hunger forgotten. He couldn't help them now, not when they were in the midst of the raiders' camp. His need to protect them spurred him to action, but he had sense enough to know he had to bide his time. And collect their supplies from their horses.

He swore that as soon as he could, he'd kill the man who'd hurt them.

THE NEXT MORNING, Drummond saw Morven make her way down toward the burn that ran fast and cold near the raiders' camp. She was alone. No doubt, the man holding her and Rory knew she wouldn't run as long as he had the boy, so she was given the freedom of the camp.

Drummond stayed in the cover of thick undergrowth and paralleled her path. She glanced around when she reached the undergrowth along the burn, then stepped into the bushes on the opposite side of the path. A few minutes later, she stepped out again and went to a clear area at the edge of the burn to wash her face and hands. She dried them on her skirt, then stood, hands on hips, staring across the burn toward home.

So far, they were alone, and he would know if anyone started down the path toward the water. Drummond saw his chance. "Morven." He called her name softly enough that only she would hear him, yet loudly enough that she would recognize his voice.

She started, jerked upright and whirled about, looking for him. "Here." He moved quietly toward her, then, after making sure they weren't observed, stood and beckoned her to him. She glanced around, as if checking for observers, then stepped into the brush and came into his arms. "I feared ye died. Drummond, I'm so glad ye are alive!"

In answer, he kissed her. He meant it to be a kiss of greeting, of relief that they were both alive and well. But when she didn't pull back from him, it turned into more. He couldn't stop.

When she grasped the back of his head to pull him closer, he ran his tongue along the seam of her lips. She opened for him, and he devoured her until the sound of a voice up in the village brought him back to his senses. He fought his reaction to the feel of her in his arms, the taste of her on his tongue, glanced around to make certain they hadn't been discovered, then told her, "We need to get out of here. Now."

"But Rory—"

"Now that I ken where this is, we can come back with enough men to free Rory and rid the area of the raiders."

"Nay, I'll not leave without him." She pulled back out of Drummond's arms. "Rodrick threatened to harm him, even kill him, if I didna obey. What do ye think he'll do if I disappear?"

"Who is this Rodrick to ye? Is he the one who took ye both?"

Morven took a breath, frowning and looking aside as if coming to a decision. "He's Rory's father," she finally said.

Drummond's breath froze. "Yer handfasted husband?"

"Aye, the one who left before I kenned I was carrying."

Drummond reeled at that news. Rodrick had a legitimate claim on his son—even on Morven, given that she became pregnant during the year-and-a-day of the handfasting. "Ach, Morven. Then ye *are* married to him. And Rory belongs to him. With him."

"Nay!" She stepped farther away and held up a hand. "Nay and nay," she hissed. Fury snapped in her gaze at Drummond's words. "He repudiated me, and I him. We are *not* married. And I willna allow Rory to be raised as Rodrick means to do. I willna. If I canna get Rory away from here by any other means, I'll kill Rodrick, even if it means my death, so long as Rory is free of him."

She pulled away from Drummond and started on the path up the hill. Perforce, Drummond followed, but stayed in cover. "Morven, nay." He reached out to her, but she avoided looking at him and continued to ascend the hill. They were getting too close to the top. If he was going to do either of them any good, he could not expose himself. He ducked farther into the bracken, fuming, as he watched her stride away from him.

At the top of the hill, Rodrick appeared, holding Rory's arm in one big fist, and calling for her. "Wife, ye've been gone too long." His lips twitched in smug satisfaction when he spotted her. He twisted the lad's arm up behind his back, making Rory cry out. "Come, Morven. I see ye there, and ye ken what I'll do if ye dinna obey me."

Drummond wanted to rush after her, to keep her away from Rodrick, but she was out of his reach, in full view of Rodrick and others from the village who'd gathered to watch.

She squared her shoulders and marched bravely into Rodrick's clutches.

He let go of Rory and backhanded her, knocking her to the ground.

Rory cried out and dropped down to her as Rodrick warned, "Dinna disappear like that again." Then he stalked off.

Drummond clenched his fists and growled in frustration. That man would die—and soon.

Morven was in hell, waiting for Rodrick to kill her, and mourning her inability to protect her son. But Drummond was near. She held on to the hope that he would come back for her —for both of them. He could not think that Rory should stay with a father who lived this way, who treated him this way. And if she was wrong, and he did think so, if he left them here, then someday, somehow, she would free them.

For now, she had to wait. Even if Drummond decided to help her, he couldn't do much by himself. She knew that. But now that he'd found her, now that he'd seen the raiders' camp and knew how many people were here, if he returned to his men and brought them back here, she and Rory might stand a chance of getting free. It needed to happen soon, before Rodrick killed the chief and took over. She'd be next and Rory would be trapped.

At the midday meal, she noticed a few unfamiliar faces. Rodrick stayed at her side, making his claim known to any villagers who hadn't seen them arrive or been at the evening meal yesterday, by touching her, ordering her to bring him more food, and glaring at any man who ventured too close.

If Rory strayed too far away, he called him back and cuffed him for leaving his mother's side. Morven hated that. She didn't want Rory to associate her with punishment. But that was exactly what Rodrick wanted, she was certain. He wanted to make her son hate her, make him his father's son, then raise him to be violent and cruel—a side of Rodrick she'd never seen all those years ago. What had happened to make him this way?

When he wasn't ordering her or Rory around, he did the same to others in the camp. Especially the woman who'd warned her to run, and her daughters. Morven didn't have a chance to speak to her again, but she vowed she would find out who they were, and why the woman cared enough to warn her away.

Noise from a disturbance on the outside edge of camp made Rodrick stand and head in that direction, leaving Morven and Rory in peace for the first time since they'd begun their meal. Her sense of peace evaporated quickly as she realized Drummond might be the cause of the commotion. She stood, peering in that direction, but could see nothing there, then looked around, her gaze tracking the perimeter of the camp. Nothing. She saw no sign of him. As much as she wanted to see him, she was glad she didn't. She and Rory were surrounded. Drummond could not risk appearing, not in broad daylight. He'd never get away. And Rodrick would kill him. She had no doubt of that. He'd left Drummond for dead easily enough at the cliffside.

Drunken shouts and the unmistakable sound of fists hitting flesh soon drew most of the villagers toward the disturbance. As long as Drummond wasn't involved, Morven didn't care who was fighting, but fear twisted her belly that he might be the one being beaten. She told Rory to stay where he was and followed the others.

"A MacComas patrol? Ye left him with them?" The older man, the chief, was toe-to-toe with a younger man, and clearly furious.

"I had nay choice. If I'd tried to get him back, they'd have me, too. The lad willna tell them anything."

Rodrick stepped up and yanked the younger man around to face him. "Did they follow ye?"

"Nay! I'm sure of that. I went out of my way. 'Tis why I'm so late returning."

Rodrick turned to the older man. "We've begun to settle here. 'Tis a chance worth taking."

"Diarmad," another man stepped in and said, "the safety of the clan comes first. We need to move."

Rodrick bristled. "Lorne, I am the heir, not ye. Step back."

Lorne didn't move. "Ye have set the MacComas village against us. If they make the lad talk, if they choose to attack, we're finished." He appealed to Diarmad. "We've got to move."

Rodrick shoved Lorne aside. "I said step back."

"Rodrick," Diarmad interrupted. "I will hear him." Then he raised his voice and addressed the gathered crowd, "And anyone else who has an opinion or an idea to share."

"Nonsense," Rodrick spat. "If ye canna make a decision, I'll make it for ye."

The crowd gathered closer, clearly anticipating trouble.

Lorne glared at the chief. "This is the man ye want to follow ye?" His disgust was clear in his tone and in the curl of his lip.

"The decision is made," Rodrick reminded him.

"He will learn, given time," Diarmad said.

The crease between his brows told Morven he lacked confidence in his choice. Was he doubting his decision already? Morven clenched a fist, wanting to run, but hemmed in by the avid watchers.

What would Rodrick do if Diarmad stripped him of the title and named Lorne his heir? And what would he do with her and Rory? A woman near her muttered, "'Tisna good, this." Morven had to agree.

Rodrick's hand had gone to the hilt of the dirk he kept at his belt.

In response, Lorne pulled his. "Dinna do something foolish," he warned.

"Both of ye stand down," Diarmad ordered. "Or I'll be forced to look elsewhere for a man with more sense to replace me."

Lorne took a step back, but Rodrick held his ground. He hadn't yet pulled out his blade, but his jaw was tense enough to make a muscle jump.

Then Rodrick let his hand drop to his side. For a moment, Morven thought the tension would ease and that Rodrick would do as Diarmad said.

Lorne spoke up again. "If ye hadna killed that old crofter ye were working with, we wouldna be in this mess."

Morven froze. Rodrick killed Kelso? "Why?" She didn't realize she'd cried out her anguish until Rodrick turned to her.

"Because he kept yer letters from me. He kept me from my son all these years. He ruined my life. Yers, too. He deserved to die."

"He wasna using our raids to cover his own thefts from the villagers?" Lorne didn't hide his disgust at Rodrick's lie.

"Nay. He was too stupid to try something like that."

"He was a friend to me and to yer son," Morven shouted. "And ye killed him."

"Ye deserve to hang for murder," Lorne swore and charged at Rodrick.

Rodrick leapt out of the way before pulling his own blade. "I'll kill ye before that happens," he threatened, and waved his blade. Men crowded closer—to pull them apart or egg them on?

"Not if I kill ye first," Lorne taunted, then stumbled over someone's foot.

Rodrick moved in to finish him off.

"Stop this!" Diarmad shouted, his voice ringing with anger. "Stop at once!" But his words had no effect, so he pushed forward and grabbed each of the combatants by their shoulders.

Morven flinched, certain Rodrick would take advantage of the older man's mistake.

He did. He twisted around and pushed the chief onto Lorne's blade. Then, as though aiming for his rival, defending his chief but missing, Rodrick's blade pierced the older man's back.

Lorne stepped back, aghast. Rodrick merely stood by and watched the old man fall dead at his feet. Then he looked up at the gathered onlookers. "I'm chief now. Ye will obey me, or wind up like him." He toed the old man's shoulder with his boot, then gestured to Lorne. "Ye killed him. Get rid of him."

For a moment, no one moved. Faces around the circle registered shock, then a few of the men nodded. Rodrick's supporters, Morven guessed. The woman who'd warned her away started to cry, tears that soon spread to other women. Most turned away and went back to their tasks, she supposed, but two stayed to help with the old chief's body.

Lorne looked ready to continue the fight, but after a glance at the people surrounding them, he gestured for some of the other men to help him, bent and grabbed one of the old chief's arms. The other men took his other arm and legs. They carried the body off into the woods.

Morven was sure Rodrick had killed the chief, not Lorne, and that he wouldn't bother to give him a decent burial. She hoped the others would.

12

After the fight in the camp and the murder of the old chief, Drummond knew things were about to get worse for the people there. He had to get Morven and Rory out of there soon. He hoped to steal them away from the cabin without anyone seeing or hearing them go. Once they got far enough away that the horses wouldn't be heard, he'd put Morven and her son on one, and with luck, they'd be able to ride back to the village before anyone missed them and raised an alarm. But when he moved back near the cabin they shared, he groaned. The horses were gone. Damn it! They must have been moved earlier in the day, while he was away, scouting the area.

Without the horses, they faced a long walk, especially for a six-year-old. During the afternoon, whenever it was safe, he circled the camp again, looking for where the raiders kept their horses. Every time Drummond moved, hoping to get close enough to feel something, he risked discovery. He knew they couldn't be too far away. He counted on his new sense to tell him when he was getting close, but he never felt a hint of a tingle in his belly.

Finally he found them, on the downhill side of the camp. He dared not take Morven and Rory to them—their village lay in that direction, so it was the first place Rodrick and his men would look for them. Disgusted, he made his way back to where he could see their cabin and the central cooking-fire area, and settled in to wait.

That evening, he watched Morven and Rory go into their cabin. Rodrick remained by the central fire with the men, drinking and celebrating his victory.

Drummond figured this was his best chance. He crept toward the cabin, paused beside it and leaned around the corner. No one had moved from the central fire. He crouched down and made his way to the front door, opened it carefully, and slipped inside.

"Drummond! What are ye doing in here?" Morven kept her voice pitched low, but her fear was unmistakable, eyes wide under lowered brows.

He closed the cabin door behind him and stepped farther into the room. She'd been settling Rory on the pallet on the floor. He sat up and the sound of Drummond's voice. "Gather what ye need for travel," Drummond told her quietly. "Cloaks, blankets. We need to go, now. Rory, lad, ye, too."

"If Rodrick comes back and ye are here..."

"He's drinking by the fire. We'll be long gone before he does. Have ye any food in here?"

"Nay," she answered without looking at him.

The door rattled and Drummond ducked behind it.

Morven tensed, waved a hand at Rory to lie back down, knelt, and continued pulling the covers over him.

The door opened and Rodrick leaned in. "Good," he said. "I'll be back soon. Dinna think to go anywhere," he added, laughed, and slammed the door shut.

Drummond stepped out from behind it while Morven stood, pale and shaking from the close call. He took a deep breath, trying to slow his heartbeat, leaned into the door for a moment and listened. He could hear Rodrick moving away, shouting at someone as he went.

Drummond turned back to Morven. "Get moving. He sounded drunk. No telling when he'll take it into his head to come back."

Morven made sure to dress Rory warmly first, then put on as many layers as she could, taking some of Rodrick's clothes for Rory and herself as well as the blankets from the bed and pallet.

"'Tis all there is," she said when she finished.

"Let's go. Without a sound."

Rory's eyes were wide, but he nodded.

Drummond opened the door a crack, peered out, and closed it again. "Someone passing by," he reported, let out a breath, then looked again. "Clear. Let's go."

He led them around the cabin and into the woods up a slope.

"Where are we going?" Morven whispered.

He pointed up the hill. "We canna head back toward yer village, not yet," he answered in a low voice. "They'll search that way first. We must go higher into the mountains."

"We're on foot!"

"I noticed. Lass, I hoped to steal back our horses, but they've been moved somewhere 'tis daft to try to get them. These mountains are full of hollows and caves. I'll leave ye and Rory in a safe place and come back for horses. 'Tis the best I can do for ye and the lad, to keep ye out of that bastard's hands."

When they reached the cache of food and supplies Drummond had hidden, he gave half of it to Morven to carry, hefted his sword and led them onward. He'd explored up here in the time he'd observed the raiders' camp, and had found a likely place for Morven and Rory to wait. Not the nearest cave. Likely the raiders knew of it, too. But another, farther up and much harder to find, had probably escaped their notice. They reached it before midnight. Drummond had been forced to carry Rory, who'd become too exhausted to walk after several hours of the uphill trek.

"Sleep," he told them after they took shelter.

"Ye are exhausted and hurt. Ye must rest, too," Morven reminded him. "Or ye'll be nay good to us."

"I plan to. I'll sleep a few hours, then sneak back for horses."

But it was broad daylight by the time he awoke. It was much too late to steal anything from the camp and be able to get away safely. Morven and Rory were still asleep. He moved silently out of the cave and surveyed the area. He could see down the mountain where the camp should be, but trees, or the shoulder of a hill, hid its location from view. Smoke from the central cooking fire should mark its location, but the sky remained clear. Perhaps the camp was farther around the mountain than he believed. That didn't reassure him. But he didn't see any sign that they'd been followed.

He left them that afternoon to walk back to the raiders' camp. It was a faster trip down the hill than it had been coming up, but as he neared the camp, he slowed and stayed hidden, waiting and watching for any sign of patrols or sentries, moving and pausing again. That way, it was in the gloaming by the time he reached the camp.

It was gone. The raiders left nothing behind but the stone structure, the cabins, lean-tos and scraps.

Drummond stayed out of sight, watching for any inhabitants.

The camp remained quiet and still. No one stirred. Even the birds seemed subdued as if respecting the silence the missing people left behind.

The gloaming was fading to full dark when he noticed a

faint glow from the central firepit. So they'd left today. He gathered some deadfall and stirred the ashes enough to spark a stronger glow that caught on the dry wood. Some dry grass wrapped around a bundle of twigs soon caught and smoldered enough to make a weakly flickering torch. It lasted long enough for him to get a look inside the remaining structures for anything left behind.

There was nothing. No food, no clothing, no weapons. They'd taken all the horses and the livestock they'd gathered. There was nothing left at all.

His stomach sank. He didn't want Morven and Rory to have to walk back to their village, but now they had no choice. If he dared take the shortest route back, he could make it easier on them. But if they were still being hunted, and he had to expect that Rodrick and his men were out looking for them, going straight for the MacComas village would be the surest way to be caught. So he'd stick to his plan, take them a roundabout way that gave them a chance to succeed. They'd survive.

A lot went through his mind as he made his way back to the cave. He could hunt. The days were shorter and the nights longer and getting colder. Water would be their first concern. And being hunted, by raiders or wild animals. But he would make sure they got home.

MORVEN HAD NEVER BEEN SO glad to see the light of early morning begin to paint the eastern sky with pinks and purples. She'd been awake all night, too worried to sleep. Instead, she sat with her back against the cold stone wall, watching the entrance to their shelter for Drummond to return. She kept imagining seeing him walk into the entrance, his body a dark outline silhouetted by starlight behind him.

When he finally did arrive, morning light behind him kept

his face in shadow. But she knew his shape. His walk. It was him, not any of their pursuers. "Drummond!" She stood and went into his arms. "Are ye well? What did ye learn? Where are the horses?" She realized he was leaning on her, so she tugged him farther into their cave. "Here, come sit by the fire and warm up."

He nodded.

She threw the rest of the fuel Rory had gathered on the glowing coals and blew on them to coax the fire to life. Settling next to him, she took his cold hands in hers. "What can I get ye? Water? We've little to eat, but ye are welcome to what's left."

He shook his head and cleared his throat. "They're gone. The camp is empty."

She gasped at Drummond's news. "They're gone? All of them?" The horses, too? They would have to continue walking. How long could Rory continue like this?

"Aye. Naught left but the structures. They took everything they could carry or herd along with them. Do ye have any idea where they would go? Did they talk about moving while ye were there?"

She had no idea. "The whole camp is gone?" She shook her head. "Lorne wanted to move them, but Rodrick refused. He never said if he had a destination in mind. Does that mean they're not searching for us?"

Drummond shrugged. "Some may be. Since they dinna ken where we are, or whether we might luck into a patrol from yer village or my men, I suspect the rest moved for safekeeping."

"Safekeeping? They raided my village because Rodrick kenned it and the area around it. And if he wasn't lying, because Kelso helped him. Where can they go and have the same?"

She handed him a water skin and he took a long drink before answering.

"I think they raided to survive. Ye saw how thin and tired

they all looked. Angus said they only took one or two animals at a time. Added to anything they managed to hunt, it would be enough to last a day or two for a group that size, nay more. They took a huge risk, raiding that way instead of cleaning out all the livestock from a crofthold, but perhaps they couldn't manage them, so they had to chance being caught again and again to survive. I'm not making an excuse for them, for what they did, especially when they killed a man, whether on purpose or by accident, but it didna look like they were going to survive the winter."

Morven couldn't believe he would have any sympathy for them. "It sounds to me as though ye are making excuses." She bit her lip, sorry for taking out her shock and dismay on him. He'd walked the whole way there and back. He deserved her sympathy and thanks for his effort, not her censure. But she couldn't stand the thought of Drummond making allowances for anything the raiders had done.

"Nay, I am not."

"Ye said whether they killed a man on purpose or by accident. My friend died. 'Twasna an accident."

Drummond shook his head. "A war or a raid or even a battle between two opponents can get out of control. If yer friend went out to see what was causing a disturbance and tried to prevent the theft of his livestock, in the dark, not kenning who or how many men he was up against, aye, anything could have happened, none of it good."

"Rodrick killed Kelso." She put a hand between her breasts and pushed back the stab of grief that pierced her chest. "He admitted it in front of the entire village."

"Why?"

"Because Kelso hid Rory's existence from him. I dinna ken why he did that. But the raiders did the rest."

"I'm sorry. I didna ken. Except when they raised their voices, it was difficult to hear what they said, and then the fight started. Rodrick took advantage of that opportunity so easily, it makes sense to me that he's killed before. And I want to say something else—"

"What more could there be?"

"Rodrick is cruel and controlling. There was nay life for ye there. I was wrong, too," he added with a glance at Rory, who still slept on the ground near their low fire, "about Rory belonging with his da. There is nay life for yer son with him, either."

"Is that an apology?"

"'Tis the truth."

"At least we can agree on that."

DRUMMOND KNEW they'd have to rest soon, but he wanted to put another hill behind them before they stopped to eat a midday meal. Morven had been quiet, following him without complaint. Surprisingly, Rory had remained quiet as well, trudging along with his mother much better than Drummond had imagined he'd be able to. For a wee lad, he seemed attuned to the mood of the adults with him. Drummond had given him and Morven a talk before they set out about traveling safely—and silently—and they both appeared to have taken it to heart.

Even when Rory stopped, unable to take another step, he hadn't cried out. Simply looked to his mother, who in turn clutched Drummond's sleeve to get his attention. He'd picked up the lad and carried him for the last hour. Rory had gone immediately to sleep in his arms.

The feeling of receiving such trust, and of having such care for a young life was something Drummond never thought to experience. Certainly, he'd looked out for his siblings, often more than they wanted, but never had they been in the position of relying so totally on him. It was humbling.

And exhausting. Drummond still ached from his fall down the cliff at the hands of Rodrick's men. Along with Rory's weight, he bore his claymore slung on his back, and too few supplies to sustain them on their trek. His headache teased him, fading, but still with him, pounding harder when he exerted himself—which was most of the time on this trek. He hoped after another sleep, he'd wake refreshed and pain-free.

Ahead, he spotted a shaft of sunlight in the trees. A clearing. A small one, but perhaps it would serve to give them all a few minutes in the sun to warm their bones, rest their tired feet, and eat. Even better, he heard the unmistakable rush of water nearby. They could drink and wash a bit before moving on.

He turned to look behind him to let Morven know they were close to a stopping point. He didn't see her. Fear filled him with ice and he fought not to drop Rory and run back, searching for her. Where was she? He clutched Rory more tightly to his chest as he retraced his steps past several large trees. There! He took a breath, the first, he realized as his starved chest expanded, since he noticed her missing.

He waited until he reached her to speak. "Morven?" She sat on the ground and leaned against an ancient oak trunk, eyes closed.

"I couldna take another step," she admitted softly. "I'm sorry we're such a burden to ye."

He knelt and put Rory, still asleep, next to her so she could put an arm around him.

She gathered her son to her and leaned down to kiss the top of his head, then tilted hers to look up at Drummond, giving him a tired smile in thanks.

"Ye are not a burden," he reassured her, keeping his voice low to match hers. "Ye have both done very well. We've come farther than I hoped we would by now," he added. It was a lie, but if it served to encourage her, he could be forgiven for it. "I was about to tell ye we could stop in a few minutes. I spotted a sunny clearing just ahead. But if ye need to rest now—and aye, I see ye do—then here will do as well."

"Where are we?"

"I dinna ken, exactly, but we are headed around that mountain," he said and pointed at a peak partially visible through a gap in the trees beside them. "Our path will soon bend toward yer village. I ken this is hard on ye, but 'tis safest to take an indirect route back. If they are still searching for us, they'll expect us to make our way as fast as we can, directly there."

"This is hard on ye, too. Ye are still injured."

"'Tis not so bad. I can still keep ye safe."

She gave a soft sigh and gifted him with another smile. "I ken ye will."

He pulled out the last of the bread and cheese he had on him that he'd taken from their horses before they left the camp, and a skin of watered ale. That was nearly gone, too, but he could refill the skin in the burn. "How much food do ye still carry?"

Morven looked at what he held. "About that much. Not enough to get us home, is it?"

"Nay, but I'll hunt. We willna starve."

"The closer we get to the village, the more likely we are to be found by Rodrick's men."

"Or mine. Or yers. By now, I'm overdue returning home, so the laird will have sent more men to find out what happened. If we meet them, we can ride rather than walk. *Dinna fash*, lass. I will get ye home. Now eat. I'll save some for when Rory wakes."

"Nay, ye need yer strength to carry him. Ye eat what ye have there. I'll share mine with him."

Drummond knew she was right, but he hated to finish what he had in front of her.

"Bide ye here for a wee. I'll go refill a skin at the burn."

She nodded.

He surveyed their surroundings carefully. All seemed

normal. The trees stood sentry, late summer leaves and undergrowth providing cover, and birdsong and squirrel chatter
added a comforting note. Reassured, he followed the sound of
the burn to its bank and refilled his water skin. He ate half of
the bread and cheese he had left, drank his fill of water, refilled
the skin again, and took care of his other needs. Refreshed if
not full of belly, he returned to Morven and Rory. The lad was
awake, and Morven was handing him bits of cheese and bread.
Good, they were eating. Even the small amount of food they
had left would lend them the energy to go on.

"Take this skin and give me yers. I'll go fill it."

"Nay, I think we're ready to find the burn with ye." She
encouraged Rory to his feet, and with a hand up from Drummond, gained hers.

He kept hold of her hand as he led them to the water,
needing the comfort her touch afforded him, if only for a few
minutes. At the burn, he filled their water skins twice over after
they drank their fill, then stood sentry, his back turned to them,
as they did what was needful. Watching the cold, clear water
race by, he suddenly longed to strip naked and let the chill ease
the aches and the bruises purpling his skin. But they needed to
keep moving. Taking care of his injuries would have to wait.

They walked on. Luck was with them. Before sunset, they
came across a small cave just as the evening mist rolled in.
Drummond used his dirk to hollow out a shallow bowl in the
dirt of the cave floor and built a fire using sticks Rory gathered
nearby. "This will keep ye warm and keep wild animals away,"
he said. "And the mist will hide any smoke that rises. I'm going
to see if I can catch us some dinner. I'll be back as soon as I do."

"Are ye sure ye should go?" Morven gave him a worried
look.

"Ye'll be fine here. I willna go far, I promise ye."

Lips compressed, she nodded. She might be reluctant for
him to leave them, but she knew they needed food.

His luck held long enough to kill a coney with his dirk, making him glad of every session spent practicing with his brothers throwing dirks at a small target. He skinned and gutted it, then collected some sturdy, thin deadfall to use as skewers and allow them to roast it over their small fire. Berries the deer had missed filled his pouch and would make a sweet finish to their simple meal. Hot food would do more than fill their bellies. It would warm them and improve their morale.

13

M orven bit into the haunch of hot meat, juice dribbling down her chin. She caught the juice with her hand and sucked it into her mouth. She'd worry about table manners when she was at an actual table. This was the best meal she'd ever eaten. She knew hunger and exhaustion colored her opinion, but she didn't care about that, either. Drummond had provided for them, just as he'd said he would. And she was grateful. She insisted he eat fully half of the meat he provided. She split the rest with Rory.

When they finished their meager meal, Drummond emptied a pouch of berries and shared those. The sweet-tart flavor nearly brought her to tears.

"We should find more of these from here on out," he said with a grin. "As we drop down out of the mountains, there will be more bushes the deer haven't found."

"I like these," Rory announced with a grin. "Are there more we could eat now?"

"Sorry, lad, those are all I found before it got too dark to see. We'll keep an eye out for more as we go tomorrow."

Mollified, if not satisfied, Rory nodded. "Then can I go to bed?"

"Aye, ye can," Morven told him.

He lay down, and she covered him with one of the plaids. In moments, he was asleep.

"He's bearing up better than I would expect a young lad to do," Drummond told her as she came to sit by his side.

His praise warmed her, as did the fond look he gave her son. "This has been hard on him."

"And on ye, too, lass." He put an arm around her. "But he's a good lad when he's not being kidnapped." He grinned. "Ye have raised him well."

"Thank ye." She rested her head on his shoulder, suddenly spent. He felt so good. The man was as warm as the small fire where they'd cooked their supper. When his hand started making soothing circles on her back, she took a deep breath and let all her worry go. For a moment, at least, she could pretend this was normal. Being held by a caring man, a big, strong man who also cared for Rory. She snuggled closer and wrapped her arm across his broad chest. It took moments before she realized she was mirroring the movements of his hand on her back, caressing his chest. She straightened, lifting her head from his shoulder, but he pulled her to him. His lips descended on hers, warm, firm, tasting faintly of their supper, but mostly of Drummond.

She lifted a hand to his throat, his scruff prickling her fingertips as she traced the cords in his neck and then speared her fingers into his hair.

His tongue teased her lower lip, and she opened to him, welcoming his gentle assault with a low moan that seemed to ignite something in him.

With a groan, he pulled her onto his lap, and she couldn't mistake the hardness against her hip as he tugged her closer.

He ran a hand from her waist up her ribs to cup her breast, all the while teasing her lips and throat with kisses.

Her blood flamed through her veins, scorching her with longing to fill the emptiness at the crest of her thighs. Her hips rocked against his hardness while her blood pounded in her ears and swelled her breasts. She moaned his name.

"Lass, ye ken I want ye," he murmured in her ear, his fingers finding the hem of her dress and sliding beneath it. His hand drifted higher, cold air a sharp contrast to the heated trail his fingers left on her calf. He paused at her knee. "Will ye have me?"

She put a hand over the cloth covering his hand. "I want to. I want ye. But Rory…"

"Is sleeping the sleep of the innocent and willna wake."

"I canna do this," she told him, regret suffusing every cell in her body. "I canna risk it."

"Then let me please ye," he coaxed and his hand drifted higher while his tongue traced the shell of her ear.

Despite her misgivings, Morven's legs fell open at the gentle urging of his fingers, and Drummond took immediate advantage, stroking higher, making her pant with wanting his touch. Finally, he was there. She could have cried out with relief, but his touch drove her higher. She trembled in his arms, writhing at the sensations he gave her, until suddenly, it became too much. Bright shocks of pleasure radiated from her center, making her gasp. Drummond covered her mouth with his to muffle her cries until she subsided and went limp in his arms.

She'd never felt so warm, so replete. She wanted more, but she'd already refused him. Still she could please him, too. After a few moments of floating, the aftermath of the release he'd given her, she laid a hand on his hardness and caressed it, then tried to grip him through his trews.

"Nay, lass," he said, picked up her hand and kissed it. "Ye are exhausted." He smoothed her skirts back down over her legs and pulled a plaid over them. "Sleep now. I'll keep watch."

DRUMMOND LAY AWAKE, aware of every movement and sound near them. Trees swayed and whispered in the growing breeze while owls and other night hunters searched for prey. He'd let their fire burn down to glowing coals, and fed it only rarely. Rory snored softly, and Morven shifted now and again, but didn't seem to wake. Outside their refuge, the night breeze blew away the mist, and stars blazed in the arc of sky he could see from the mouth of their wee cave. He had a weird sense that the raiders were nowhere near, and headed away from where he was. That was strange. He expected Rodrick to be closing in on their path. Did that mean Lorne was leading them now? Why could he sense, even weakly, a group, but not get a feel for the single man, alone or not, that Drummond must guard against to keep Morven and Rory safe?

Drummond knew he and Rodrick had more in common than he'd ever want to admit. Ambition, control, even overprotectiveness. But comparing himself to that man did not paint a pretty picture. He saw his worst tendencies exaggerated and rubbed in his face. There were lessons to learn there, not that he'd admit that to Morven or anyone else. But he would think about what they meant for his own future.

His thoughts turned to Morven and her son. She didn't hover over the lad, yet she kept a sharp eye on him. Drummond approved. Respect for her grew every day. She had fought for her child—and was still fighting for him with every step they took on this long, arduous journey.

As the sky brightened, Drummond realized he was coming to care for Morven—and Rory—in a way he'd never experienced before. He could imagine her by his side, not at the village, but back at the Aerie, part of a family that was his alone. That thought kept him occupied, imagining better days —and nights—ahead, until the day brightened enough to wake her.

Rory woke slowly, groggy and still tired. Morven soothed him with promises of the treats to be had once they got home. "Only a little farther," she told him.

Drummond smothered their fire and got them on their way.

As they left their latest campsite behind, Drummond hoped she was right. They were all tired of being hungry and footsore. Rory, most of all, since his short legs demanded at least two steps for every one the adults took. If they were lucky, today they might encounter a Lathan patrol and make the rest of the trip on horseback, with an escort to keep them safer than Drummond alone and injured could do. But if not, he wouldn't let himself give in to exhaustion, or to the pain that plagued him since his tumble down the hill. He would lead them home, carry Rory, hunt for food, whatever it took to keep them alive.

"How are ye feeling?"

Her question surprised him. She seemed to have read his mind. "Well enough," he answered.

"Ye took harm in that fall down the cliff."

"Yet here I am."

Morven walked at his side, Rory trailing a few steps behind. She kept glancing behind to make sure he kept up with them.

"He's fine, too," Drummond assured her.

"I ken it. But I canna help checking on him."

"Ye are a good mother."

"Am I?"

Her tone told Drummond she wasn't convinced.

"Ye ken ye are. Rory is smart and strong, wise for his years. Ye have taken good care of him."

She looked around her, and Drummond knew she was taking in the deer track they followed around this mountain, the trees near them, and the glimpses of blue sky and beautiful vistas visible when the trees thinned. "If that is true, why are we here? Would I have let Rodrick steal Rory from me?"

"That is not yer fault," Drummond told her with the conviction he drew from every fiber of his being. "Ye didna make Rodrick do what he did."

Her shoulders slumped. "Did I not? I let him end our handfasting, though I was carrying his son."

"Ye didna ken that."

She sighed. "Nay, I didna."

"Ye ken why we're here, and ye ken fine who is at fault. His father. Perhaps Kelso, too. Dinna take that burden on yerself."

She continued on in silence after that. Drummond knew she worried, and he could do nothing about that save keep leading them home. His new sense remained quiet, or absent. Perhaps it had been a figment of his imagination. Or perhaps he didn't need it because Morven was right beside him.

A few hours later, he began to wonder if he was wrong, and the ability he feared was real. Had it become the anxiety that occasionally tingled in his chest and made his headache worsen? Those feelings came on again, yet nothing around them seemed out of the ordinary.

Before they'd gone another mile down the trail, Drummond bent nearly double at the stabbing tingle that hit his gut and radiated out from there, stealing his breath. He straightened as he turned, searching for the source.

Rodrick darted out of the trees. He grabbed Rory.

At Drummond's side, Morven gasped at Rory's cry. Rory had lagged a few paces behind them, giving Rodrick time to put a blade to his throat before either of them could react.

"Ye thought to evade me?" Rodrick jeered. "I went over these mountains a thousand times while I lived with ye—and since. I ken every trail, every path ye might choose to make the journey easier for a bairn. Ye were doomed to failure even before ye set out."

"Let go of him," Drummond warned, menace in his gaze and his posture, but dismay and anger in his heart. He'd put Morven and Rory through miles of a roundabout route, trying to avoid this man, and failed. He didn't need Rodrick to tell him that.

"I thought I killed ye." Rodrick pressed the blade more firmly against Rory's neck, but kept it flat rather than using the edge.

"Yet here I am. Care to try again?"

"Nay. Ye'll behave yerself and stand there while I take my son. He belongs with me at home in our camp."

Drummond frowned. "There's no one there. Two nights ago, I went back. They were all gone."

"Ye lie."

"I dinna. They took everything they could carry. The animals, too."

"That bastard Lorne!" Rodrick slumped, as if the news dismayed more than angered him, but when he did, his blade pressed against Rory's neck.

Rory jerked against Rodrick's hold. The blade's edge cut a shallow line and blood began to trickle down his throat.

"Rory!" Morven's cry echoed from the surrounding hills. "Ye're bleeding."

Rodrick's surprised reaction, pulling the blade away from Rory's neck, gave Drummond the chance he needed. He shoved Rory aside and went for Rodrick, determined the lad would not shed any more blood.

Morven grabbed her son before he fell and pulled him clear of the men. While they circled each other, she pressed her skirt to his neck to stop the bleeding.

"Give it up, Rodrick," Drummond said as the two men brandished their dirks. Drummond wanted to pull his claymore from the sheath on his back, but doing so would leave him vulnerable to Rodrick's charge. He would have to win this fight with his dirk. "Those people have left ye. Ye dinna need Morven or Rory. Go on yer way and leave them be."

"I'll find my people, and when I do, my wife and son will be by my side."

"Ye could be searching a long time," Drummond warned.

"Aye. Perhaps ye have a point." Rodrick grinned. "I'd be faster on my own. I can always start another family."

Rodrick's words chilled Drummond. If he made the wrong move and lost this fight, he feared Morven would see Rory's father kill her son. Or Rory would see him kill his mother. Drummond would die before he let either of those things happen.

He and Rodrick continued circling each other, slashing and thrusting with their dirks. Drummond dove aside as Rodrick swung at him. He felt the punch and a sharp pain, but he glanced down and saw no blood. Instead of a blade, Rodrick's fist had connected with Drummond's side. He rolled, and came to his feet at the ready. Rodrick danced back and circled toward where Morven stood with Rory. Drummond got in his way. "Ye'll not touch either of them again," Drummond warned him. He feinted a punch, then sliced Rodrick's arm with his dirk. The wound wasn't mortal, but it would pain him, and the blood lost from it would slow him.

"They are mine to do with as I please," Rodrick insisted, clutching his bleeding arm.

"We are not!" Morven shouted from the side.

Her exclamation distracted Rodrick into looking at her.

Drummond took advantage and rushed him, stabbing him in the shoulder.

Rodrick fell to the ground with an oath, face pale and eyes wide on Drummond as he struggled to get up—and failed.

When Drummond moved in to finish him, Morven cried out. "Dinna kill him in front of his son!"

Drummond glanced at her in surprise, then at Rory. The lad's wide-eyed stare froze him.

Morven moved in front of Rory and hid Drummond's next move from him.

Frustrated, Drummond nonetheless understood her concern. He closed in on Rodrick and when he raised up on an elbow to defend himself, Drummond hit him on the point of his chin, snapping his head back and knocking him out. He didn't want to spare him. But the only thing he could do to keep from traumatizing Rory and further was to let him lie there and bleed. If he died after they left him, Drummond would be satisfied.

"Come with me," Drummond ordered when he was certain Rodrick wouldn't wake any time soon. He moved down the path, away from him.

Morven, her back to him, turned her head and nodded over her shoulder, then put Rory on her side away from the man on the ground and walked to where Drummond waited. He led them away, into the brush, one hand on his side.

"Is he dead?"

"Nay. I did as ye asked." Angered, he hoped they wouldn't regret it. "I should take him back to Angus. 'Tis his place to deliver justice for Kelso, but I canna carry Rory and Rodrick, too."

"Ye are hurt."

"I'll manage. Rodrick has a horse, or he would not have gotten ahead of us." He whistled, but there was no answering neigh. "It must be hidden nearby. Let's get away from here. We might find it on the way, else I'll circle around and look for it."

"Dinna go!" Rory's voice sounded small and weak.

Drummond knelt to be at eye level with him. "If we dinna find it first, I willna go far, and I will return," he promised. He waited while Rory thought it over, then nodded, before he stood and led them farther down the track. He kept glancing behind them, but felt sure that it would be hours before Rodrick woke up—if he ever did.

Finally, he moved them off the path and into cover, then circled around. Finding Rodrick's mount would save them time and exhaustion. The horse must be well hidden, and trained not to make a sound. Drummond's quick search came up empty. There was no time to keep looking for it. They had to keep moving in case Rodrick woke up or had men nearby who would come looking for him. Drummond returned to Morven and Rory and hurried them away, quietly, hoping to escape any more confrontations. With luck, Rodrick would be the last impediment in their way.

Rory did his best, but before long, Drummond had to pick up the exhausted boy.

"Thank ye," Morven told him. "Are ye sure ye can manage him?"

"Aye. He's a good lad, aren't ye, Rory?"

Instead of answering, he buried his face in Drummond's shoulder, hurt but stoic.

"Ye'll be home before ye ken it," Drummond assured him and gave Morven a reassuring lift of his lips. He hoped that was true. He was thankful the cut on the lad's neck was not deep. The village healer would see that it did not fester. And if it did, he'd take the lad to the Aerie on the fastest horse available.

Drummond suspected one of Rodrick's blows might have cracked one of his ribs, but he couldn't do anything about it except keep them moving. If the man didn't die where they left him, he'd come after them again. Drummond kept watch as they went, hurrying Morven.

"We'll go directly to the village now," he told her. "We've been found once. I dinna want that to happen again."

DRUMMOND SET a punishing pace for a six-year-old, but Rory endured it well. They'd been walking for hours before he complained, "I'm tired," collapsed to the ground and sprawled, looking boneless.

Morven knelt by him, but Drummond stood over him and said, "Up ye go, lad." He'd carry Rory the rest of the way to the village if need be, just to keep them moving.

"We need to rest," she informed him. "We canna keep going like this."

"We must." He heaved a sigh, and Morven pounced on it.

"Ye must rest as well. Yer injuries still vex ye—aye, they do," she said, holding up a hand and interrupting him when he started to object. "Ye canna carry this lad all the way home. Let's find a place to hide for an hour, then go again until dark, aye?"

She was right. As much as Drummond wanted to travel fast, caution was still warranted. Rodrick might still be alive. Any men he had with him were probably still in the area, and when they found him or his body, they'd have a good idea whom to blame. They'd come after Drummond with even more fervor than Rodrick had used to claim Rory and then Morven.

Drummond regretted not taking time to find Rodrick's horse. But it was too late for second thoughts, and best to stay hidden as much as possible. The closer they got to Morven's village, the more likely they were to run into trouble. If Rodrick was still alive, he'd show up soon.

But Morven was also right that an hour's rest might make the difference in how far they could go this day. He looked around at the undergrowth. Some areas were thicker than others. Perhaps one of those would serve. "Stay here."

He moved off to inspect prospective lairs. Thorny brambles covered a large area, but none of them needed the scratches those would inflict. The bleeding they caused would weaken them. However, the fruit they bore would help feed them. Drummond picked a few berries to take back to Rory, then moved on. A dense cluster of bracken at the edge of a small clearing caught his eye. He carefully probed the mass, trying not to visually disturb it, and found an open area between two of the trees it fronted. The gap was small, but large enough for Morven and Rory to shelter in.

"I found a bramble with these," he told Morven when he returned to them and handed her the berries.

She studied them, sniffed, and touched one to her tongue to taste it. "Blackberries. And sweet. But not a place to hide."

"Nay, but there's a mass of bracken nearby that will serve as a resting place for a wee while."

She nodded, coaxed Rory up with a berry, then looked to Drummond. "Show me."

He bit down on a groan as he picked up Rory, then led her to their hiding place. "Go in through there," he said and pointed out the natural gap he'd found low to the ground. It wasn't a tunnel used by an animal. There were no broken stems as far as he could see into the mass.

"Will we all fit?"

"I dinna think so. Ye and Rory go in. I'll investigate the blackberry bramble and collect more fruit while I'm at it. I can hunker down there if I need to."

"Be careful," she said, her gaze intent on his.

He set Rory down by his mother. "I'll give ye an hour and come to fetch ye."

"Rory, come with me. I'll go first, and we'll have a wee sleep."

Drummond watched as she dropped to her knees, then crawled into the bracken. As soon as she was fully inside, Rory looked up to Drummond. "Go on, lad."

"Ye willna leave us, will ye?"

Drummond softened at the fear and pleading in his eyes. "Nay, Rory. I'll be nearby, keeping watch. Get some rest."

Rory followed his mother.

Once Drummond was certain they couldn't be seen, he moved away, his mind on Morven. She had worked with him without complaint to keep them safe, to help keep Rory quiet. She was strong, caring, sympathetic, concerned about him as much as her son—or nearly so—and even after days of rough travel, beautiful. As Drummond walked to the blackberry bramble, a certainty flooded his body that he wanted her with him. Forever. As his lover and his wife. If the lad wasn't with them now, he might do what his body called him to do and seduce her, but this was not the time or place—or the way to win her heart.

He found a way to hack into the bramble with minimal damage to it or himself, and settled in to wait. His side hurt enough to keep him awake, and he relied on the forest sounds to alert him to any changes as he rested, but nothing did. After what he judged to be an hour, he carefully made his way out of his lair. He stayed low, listening and looking for any hint of strangers in the area. Then he stood, picked as many berries as his pouch could hold, and made his way back to the mass of bracken.

Again he watched and waited, making certain no one observed them before calling Morven and Rory forth. He rewarded their silence with the berries he'd picked, then they continued on their way.

14

A t first, Rodrick didn't know where he was or why he felt
so weak. Then the pain hit like a blow to his shoulder,
arm and back, and he recalled the fight. That bastard with
Morven stabbed him, but other injuries, whether from bruises
or broken bones, soon pained him as much as where a blade
had pierced his shoulder. Yet he lived. He rolled slowly to his
knees, each degree of movement like a new blow or blade
piercing his flesh. He grasped a sapling in reach of his good
arm and forced himself to his feet.

His head whirled for a moment and everything went gray.
He held on, leaned against the tree, and breathed through the
pain until his vision cleared. Once it did, he staggered from tree
to tree toward his horse, holding on to stay upright as he went,
pausing when he had to, his forehead against the stout wood,
while he breathed and his head swam.

He'd hidden the horse in a thicket a good distance from
where he confronted Morven and her protector. As punishing
as it had been to reach it now, he was glad. Any closer, and it
wouldn't be here, waiting for him. They would have taken it
and been long gone, back to that damned village. They

wouldn't trust he died here today. They would expect him to try again. His son would be harder to take away.

He looked around for the men he brought with him. Where were they? He needed some help. Getting on his horse with one good arm and other painful injuries presented more of a challenge than he wanted to deal with. He grasped the saddle with his good hand, trying to find some strength. Trying not to scream. They'd abandoned him! Had they seen the fight and left him to bleed out and die? Or were they doing as he'd bidden, still looking for his son? If they knew what was good for them, they'd be tracking his bitch wife and son.

Then he remembered he'd left two men in a clearing some distance away to wait until he called for them. He shouted until he had no breath left. If he tried to call out again, he'd pass out and never get up. They couldn't hear him. He'd have to find them.

He gathered himself again, tossed the reins up across the horse's neck, lifted a foot into a stirrup with his good arm, grasped the pommel and somehow hauled himself up to sprawl across the saddle. Though it hurt like hell, he swung his leg across and twisted into the seat, his upper body still supported by the horse's neck and shoulder.

When the rush of agony subsided, he pushed himself upright and waited, breathing hard, until everything stopped spinning. Once he could see the blood he'd left dripping down the horse's mane, he grasped the reins and pulled them to him, kicked his mount and turned to follow his quarry, his men forgotten. Then stopped. Where would they go? Farther into the mountains to hide as they had been doing? Or now that he found them again, had they decided to abandon pretense and head straight home? He groaned. It was too dark to track them. He'd have to chase them in the morning.

He rode to where he left his men and stopped at the edge of

the clearing, dumbfounded, then energized as fury roared a blaze of heat from his belly to his extremities. "Lewis!" His men didn't move. Instead, it appeared that the whole time he'd fought the man with Morven, and while he lay wounded and unconscious, they'd waited here, drinking and falling asleep. No wonder they hadn't heard him calling for them until he could call out no longer, until in agony, he had to pull himself on his horse.

His fury was so hot, he knew he would have the strength to mount again. So he slid off his horse and walked up to them, making no attempt to be quiet. They didn't awaken. Aye, they were drunk and passed out. These were the sort of followers he was left with after Lorne stole away his entire clan? Everything he'd planned for, what he learned while living among the people in Morven's village, all the knowledge he'd shared, everything he hoped to build, had come down to these two. He couldn't bear it. Disgusted, he stabbed Lewis and slashed the other's throat before they could rouse sufficiently to defend themselves. He left them to bleed out, mounted again before the power bestowed by his outrage deserted him, and headed into the darkness.

HOURS LATER, Drummond found a sheltered spot and built a small, protected fire, and roasted another coney he caught. Morven realized they were lucky to have the comfort they did, things Drummond had ensured they brought with them, and food and fire he provided along the way. Still, she longed for the safety of her village, though she knew that sense of safety was a lie. Rory had been taken from there. Kelso had been killed, and the village livestock had been raided again and again.

But at least there, she would find the coziness of her own

bed. Hot food from her own larder. Her loom. And a few friends. And Rory would be home.

If the raiders were really gone, life could return to normal. But if the raiders moved away, Drummond would go, too. He and his men would return to the Aerie, leaving the village as it was before they came. Safer, perhaps, for a time, since they'd driven off the raiders, but she'd be even more lonely than she'd been these last few years.

Drummond had shown her caring and compassion. He'd risked his life to save her son and her. If she was to fall in love with another man, Drummond would be the one.

But she could not. After this trauma, her son would need her even more than before, and she needed him. He needed time to heal. They both did. She stared at the glow of the small fire Drummond had built, and couldn't imagine leaving the only home Rory had ever known, not for a very long time.

Then Drummond, as if reading her mind, interrupted her thoughts.

"What will yer life be like in the village once ye return?"

She looked at him. He was a few feet away across their low fire, leaning against the trunk of a large pine, one of several that made up their protected hollow. He appeared relaxed, one knee raised, the other leg out in front of him, as if taking his ease after a full meal and hearty drink, not exhausted and hurting. His longsword lay on the ground near at hand. "Much the same as before. Why would it not? I'll weave as I have done for years to keep us fed and clothed."

Drummond opened his mouth as if to speak, but closed it again and stared off into the surrounding forest before saying what was on his mind. "The lad is nearly old enough to foster, ye ken."

Morven went cold, from her belly to her fingertips. She could not think of sending Rory away for years of fostering, not when she'd just gotten him back. How could Drummond even suggest such a thing?

"I would bring him to the Aerie. He'd be safe there. If Rodrick still lives, he couldn't reach him there." Drummond paused again and met her gaze.

Surely he could see the dismay written on her face. She felt lightheaded, as if she'd gone pale. She wrapped her arms around herself to keep from shaking and turned her head to watch Rory sleeping at her side, wrapped in one of Rodrick's cloaks and covered with several plaids.

"Ye could come, too." He said it quietly, as if it meant something to him. Something more than just accompanying her son to safety.

"Ye'd both be safe," he added.

But he didn't say *and with me.* Disappointment that he hadn't added those words swamped her, and that surprised her. Did she really want him to take her away with him? What he proposed was a big change for Rory, but for her, too, whether she stayed home without him, or went with him and Drummond. "What would I do there?"

"What ye do now, if ye wish. I'll move yer loom and anything else ye need. A keep the size of the Aerie always needs more skilled craftsmen and women. Ye would be welcome, and yer work valued."

It sounded too good to be true. Could it happen exactly as he said? If she made a home where people didn't look down on her for her past, but valued her skill and helped her take care of her son, he could grow up to be the kind of man she wanted him to be. More like Drummond and not at all like his father.

But it was too fast. "After this, Rory needs his home—his familiar place with people he kens. I canna imagine taking him away from that. He needs stability and healing, not another trek to a strange place."

Drummond leaned an arm on his raised knee. "Even if it

means that he is safe? He would adapt quickly. Ye would, too. Life at the Aerie would be good for both of ye."

"I'll think about it," she promised. And she would, but not any time soon.

THEY REACHED the village outskirts by the middle of the next day. Morven couldn't believe how wonderful it looked, how normal. The people rushing toward them with open arms, shouting surprised greetings, lifted her spirits. Rory clung to her skirts, but she took his hand and smiled. "We're home, lad. They want to welcome us." Drummond stepped forward, as though he still needed to keep them safe. But these were faces she knew, some of them friends. She put her free hand on his arm and held him back.

Glenna got to them first and wrapped Morven in a hug. "Ye are here! Where have ye been? Ye have been gone for days!"

"'Tis a long story. Perhaps easier told to everyone at once, aye?" Morven looked up from her to see the MacComas Lady approaching on her husband's arm. "Ilise! How good to see ye out of doors!"

Ilise laughed and took her hand. "'Tis naught next to having ye returned to us. Thank ye, Drummond Lathan."

Drummond bowed over her offered hand. "'Twas a difficult journey I'm glad to see end, but I'd do it again if it meant bringing these two home to ye."

Ilise smiled, glanced aside at her husband and nodded.

Angus took that as his cue and offered his hand to Drummond. "Ye did well, lad. 'Tis a great and good surprise to see ye walk into the village like this. I'm sure the tale will be long in the telling."

"It will," Morven said, inserting herself into the men's

conversation. "But I beg leave to tell it later. We are tired, hungry and dirty. I'd like to take care of my son."

"And so ye shall," Angus promised.

"Glenna, ye ken what to do," Ilise said. "Will ye take charge of these two?"

Angus added, "I must insist on taking a few minutes of Drummond's time before he sees his men."

Only then did Morven notice Eduard and the other Lathans she knew on the edge of the crowd, but with them was another bigger man and a few more strange faces. "Drummond," she said, "it appears ye have more men here."

He nodded as though he'd already seen them. "Laird Lathan is as good as his word. I knew he'd send men to find out why I was late."

"Their arrival is well timed," Angus said. "Just an hour or two ago, in fact."

Drummond looked down at Rory. "Are ye ready to go home, lad?"

Morven worried when he didn't answer right away. He looked uncertain, but perhaps it was just the press of the crowd making him uneasy. "Let's go, Rory, aye?"

He looked from Drummond to her and back again. "Ye willna leave us, will ye?"

Drummond met her gaze for a quick moment, then knelt to meet Rory's worried gaze. "I'll be here after ye have had time to eat and get a bath," he said, and made a face, which made Rory laugh, "and mayhap a wee sleep, as well?"

Rory nodded. "Soon, then. I'll see ye soon." Then he took Morven's hand and led her toward their cottage, Glenna on his other side, followed by a parade of lads bringing firewood and others hauling buckets of water for their bath.

Before they took more than a handful of steps, she heard Angus order Drummond to go with him. It wasn't fair. Drummond was just as tired and hungry and dirty as she and Rory, even more so. Hurt, too. She turned and caught Ilise's eye. "Dinna let him keep Drummond for long," she pleaded. "He's injured, as well as hungry and tired."

"I'll see he's well taken care of," she promised.

Morven nodded acceptance and turned away again, oddly disturbed by that promise. She wanted to be the one to take care of him. But she wouldn't get the chance. Not today. Maybe not ever.

15

After taking the seat Angus pointed him to, Drummond told him about the conditions he observed at the raider encampment, their numbers, the murder of the old chief—and the raiders' disappearance. "I expected Rodrick's men would still be patrolling near here, given that Rodrick had to know this was our eventual destination, so I chose to take a longer way back. With that in mind, we'll stay a few more days to make sure the raiders don't regroup and begin again. But they may have moved on, especially if Rodrick is dead."

"I hope they are far from here," Angus said. "Why do ye doubt that he is dead?"

"For good reason. Morven prevented me from killing him in front of Rory, but he was gravely wounded. He may have survived—or he may have bled out in the forest."

Angus clenched a fist on his desktop. "I hope ye are right about that last. He sounds not at all like he was when he lived here. He treated Morven well enough, then he left. And ye ken the rest."

"His ambition led to all of this," Drummond said. "They raided here because Rodrick knew the area and had help from

Kelso. Rodrick killed Kelso because the old man had Morven's letters about Rory's birth in his possession. Long ago, he must have suspected Rodrick was trouble and sought to protect her and her son. When Rodrick found out he needed his own heir in order to be named Diarmad's heir, he set up Rory's kidnapping."

"I dinna like his persistence, especially if he is alive. Still, he achieved what ye said he wanted—the chieftainship. Why would he still need her or his son?"

"Only he can answer that." Drummond stood to go.

"I hope he never does." Angus waved a hand, dismissing him. "Ye heard my wife promise ye would be taken care of. If I understood her, ye need the healer as well as food and rest."

"It can wait. I must talk with my men. Ye met the ones who arrived this morning?"

"Aye, Eduard brought Bhaltair to me. They were organizing more sorties to search for ye when ye simply walked into the village."

"Too bad they didn't get here a few days ago. We would have preferred to ride back to the village."

Angus chuckled and waved him out with a caution. "Dinna let my wife find ye leaving or ye'll have to deal with her before ye see yer men."

When he emerged from the keep after his meeting with Angus, he glanced around, but knew better than to expect to see Morven. Villagers had pulled her away from him, offering food and help, and care that he suspected she'd been without since her handfasting ended. She'd had to earn every bite of food and every bit of goodwill she'd ever received. From her high color, he knew their sudden attention overwhelmed her, but she gratefully accepted it all. Drummond was happy for her, yet if it meant she would decide to stay in the village, he would regret it. But he would support her decision. In familiar surroundings, with people she knew, her loom, her life and her son, she would be most comfortable, at least for now.

He made his way to the Lathan encampment. Bhaltair greeted him with a rough hug.

Drummond groaned at the pressure on his ribs, and grimaced as the pain from his fall flared up. He pushed back, and waved the big man off. "Sorry. I'm battered. Da let ye come?"

"Ye're lucky he isna here himself," Bhaltair told him. "I had to argue with him to prevent it. 'Tis good I won that fight. Ye look like hell."

Drummond winced and scrubbed hard at the stubble on his face. "Well, we're back, safe and mostly sound. The trouble-maker is most likely dead and the raiders cleared out their camp. I dinna ken where they went, but the threat might be over—or it might not."

Drummond heartily wished he hadn't let Morven talk him out of finishing off Rodrick. He'd sleep better if he knew the man could no longer threaten her or Rory.

"We continued patrols while ye were gone," Eduard told him. "Our best trackers are still out looking for ye."

"I took the long way around," Drummond told him. He hoped the trackers were able to find the raiders, but if they did, that news would have to wait until they got back. "Send someone back to the Aerie to tell the laird we've returned and what has happened."

"I'll go," Bhaltair said. "But." He huffed out a breath and tilted his head away from the group. "Come with me." When they'd moved out of earshot, he continued, "Yer da expects ye to come back with me."

"I am not finished here. 'Twill take a few more days to be sure the raiders are gone."

Bhaltair crossed his arms over his massive chest. "Are ye

sure ye want me to deliver that message? Ye fought not to come at all. Yer da expects ye to leave the rest to our men."

"I ken what ye are saying," Drummond told him. "And I ken that the treaty lairds will arrive in less than a month. But I have my reasons to stay, at least for a few more days."

"They wouldna have anything to do with that lass ye brought back and her son?"

Heat crawled up Drummond's chest and neck to his face. He fought it down and pursed his lips. "It has to do with finishing the job I came here to do."

"And the lass," Bhaltair insisted. He clapped him on the back and laughed. "Very well, I'll tell yer da ye'll be along soon. Nay more than a sennight, aye?"

Drummond elbowed him. He might as well ram his elbow into a stone wall. "Go on with ye. And be careful. We dinna ken where the raiders went."

"I will. Ye take care of yerself and the lass. I'll tell yer mother—"

"Ye'll tell her naught, damn ye." He lifted his chin toward Bhaltair's horse. "Go on with ye."

Bhaltair laughed again, shook his head and left him.

THE NEXT MORNING, Ilise surprised Morven at her cottage. She looked up from cleaning their few dishes to see her standing in the doorway. "Milady!"

"May I come in?"

"Of course!" Morven nearly dropped the earthenware bowl she'd just dried, set it aside, and pulled out a chair at their wee table. "Please, sit down. How are ye feeling?"

"Better today, enough to come to ye instead of sending someone to fetch ye. 'Tis a lovely morning, and I've spent too many of them indoors."

"I'm glad ye are better."

"I, too. I will rest with ye a few minutes before I hazard the walk back to the keep. 'Tis farther than I recalled. Or perhaps 'tis just because I'm slower than I used to be."

"Ye will regain yer strength and speed soon," Morven said, hoping it was true.

"Well, as to that, I suppose only God can decide. But enough about me." She paused and fastened her gaze on Morven's face. "I came to share something with ye that I didna want ye to hear from anyone else."

Morven sank into the seat opposite her. "Aye?"

Ilise hesitated long enough for Morven to begin to worry.

"Tell me about the Lathan who brought ye back. Drummond, is it?"

Why did she ask? Ilise knew his name perfectly well. "What do ye wish to ken, milady?"

"Dinna *milady* me, Morven. Answer the question."

Morven frowned. "He brought us home. He carried Rory when he was too tired to walk, even though Rodrick's men knocked him over a cliff in a fight. A fight I thought killed him. He was hurt, yet he hunted to keep us fed and searched out safe places for us to sleep. He took care of us." She dared not mention how he'd cared for her one night while Rory slept.

"So ye have fallen in love with him." Ilise's words were not a question.

Morven dropped her gaze. "I... I'm grateful. We have been through so much together."

Ilise reached out and took her hand. "Then ye will not welcome what I have to say, but ye must hear it."

Morven looked up, suddenly afraid. What could be so terrible?

"While ye were gone, while everyone worried for yer safety, for yer very lives, one of his men who remained behind let it slip that he is betrothed. He is to meet the lass for the first time at the clan gathering the Lathan is holding soon."

Morven fought to remain calm. She wanted to cover her mouth with her hand and choke back a cry of *nay*. Drummond had never given any indication—but that's what men did, wasn't it? Lie? Leave? "Does he ken?"

"The man didna say anything about that. Only that he expected a betrothal would be celebrated soon. I'm sorry to be the one to bring this to ye, but ye needed to ken."

Dear God. "Thank ye for telling me. But ye needna *fash*. We have nay understanding between us." The lie came easily, but the heartache behind it hit hard. Her chest felt as though it would crack open. But she could not let Ilise see how she'd upset her. Ilise would be hurt by her pain, and Ilise had more than enough of her own.

Morven stood and went to the loom, both to give her time to get control of her roiling emotions, and to gather up the yarn samples she'd studied as possibilities for the Martinmas dress Ilise wanted. It would give them something else to talk about until Ilise was ready to venture back to the keep. Morven would help her, of course.

"Do any of these combinations please ye, Ilise? Milady?" She amended her question to put some distance between them, distance she felt they needed at the moment.

Ilise met her gaze steadily, as though she understood what Morven was doing, but she studied the samples before her. "Not that one," she said, picking one up and holding it in a shaft of daylight entering the doorway. "This I like," she said, fingering another. "And this one. Ach, I canna decide. Will ye bring them to me tomorrow? I'll think on them, and make a decision once I see them in my chamber."

"Of course."

"Well, let me be on my way." She pushed herself to her feet. Morven cringed at the effort it took and the pain etched in her features. Fortunately, Ilise's head remained down as she pushed up from the table. Morven had time to soften her expression before she looked up. "Would ye like me to escort ye back? Ye could study the samples ye like and tell me what ye prefer tomorrow."

"That's a good idea. But ye dinna need to escort me. The walk will do me good. I'll take them with me. Ye stay here with yer son."

Morven saw her to the door and watched as she went, step by painful step, back through the village. The pain Morven suffered didn't show like hers did, but the effect seemed just as devastating. How could Drummond treat her the way he had and say the things he said if he had a betrothal waiting for him? She had once believed that nothing could hurt her more than when Rodrick repudiated her and left. This pain was worse.

DRUMMOND CONTINUED the Lathan patrols paired with Angus's men, and sent some ranging farther away to look for the raiders or any stragglers who might still be in the area. They found no one.

After another five days of constant patrols and guards stationed at outlying crofts to protect their livestock reporting no activity, both Drummond and Angus believed the raiders had left the area. Drummond had to go, and it was probably safe for the rest of the Lathans to leave, as well. He had always known this day was coming. In truth, he looked forward to returning to the Aerie and taking his place at his father's side during the clan chiefs' gathering. His future was there, set and sealed on the day of his birth.

But unless his future included the woman and child he met and fell for at MacComas, there would always be something lacking. If only Morven would hear him and understand what he offered. But she kept her distance. Something had changed in her once they returned to the village. At first he thought it had to do with her and Rory's sudden acceptance there, but the longer it went on, the more he suspected something else was keeping them apart.

Was it something he'd done? He racked his brain, trying to recall, or imagine, what might have offended her. He could think of nothing. She'd been happy and grateful when they first arrived. But before long, she became distant. Even cold. Over the last few days, Drummond saw her often, but only in company of others in the village. If he didn't know better, he would think she deliberately avoided him.

It appeared that after hearing the story of what Rodrick had put her and Rory through, the villagers completely changed their opinion of her and now treated her as one of their own who'd had a lucky escape. As they should have all along. He was happy for her.

But not for himself. He had entertained the notion of Morven at the Aerie with him, as his bride. Yet he could not take her from here if, finally, she had been allowed to fit in. She would have to agree to go with him, or agree to let Rory foster at the Aerie. If she visited often, Drummond might still have hope of gaining her hand. He would try to convince her, but he was running out of time.

He stopped by her cottage that afternoon, hoping to speak to her without an audience of her new friends. He found her at her table, humming a lovely tune as she worked preparing their evening meal. Drummond leaned against the shadowed side of the open doorway, content to wait for her to notice him. Until she did, he could listen, and look at her. She'd recovered quickly from their ordeal. She seemed happy as she worked. Drummond envied her that. She'd once asked him what he'd do if he wasn't the heir, and he'd begged time to consider his answer. He still didn't have one, except that heir or not, he wanted to be with her. To love her and have her love him in return.

Would she? Or was he dreaming?

Finally, she glanced toward the doorway and saw him. She stopped what she was doing and sat back. "Drummond. What brings ye today?"

Just the sound of his name on her lips made his blood heat. "The fabric on yer loom looks soft and rich. My mother would love that color," he told her. "Perhaps one day, ye could make another for me to give her."

She pushed away from the table and regarded him before she cocked her head toward the pallet Rory used. Quietly, she said, "He was up very late. Bad dreams." She stood and came to Drummond.

He took her in his arms, enjoying the sensations she elicited and knowing this might be the last time he would hold her.

She leaned back, frowning. "Let's go outside," she suggested, then closed the door behind them. "Rory should be up soon, but I dinna want to wake him."

"The kidnapping?" Drummond walked beside her, letting her set the pace.

"His dreams? Aye. The healer says they'll fade over time. I hope they will soon."

"For his sake, I do, too."

"Ye asked about the cloth. Once ye leave here, 'tis likely we will never see each other again."

"Why would we not?"

She hesitated, making Drummond study her more closely than he usually enjoyed doing. Something was amiss. Perhaps she *had* been avoiding him. But why?

"What is it like to have a mother ye care so much for? And to worry her as ye must do?"

Her questions disarmed him. Drummond chuckled. "Is that not what mothers do? Worry?"

Morven nodded and shifted her gaze aside to where Rory's kidnappers had trampled her garden. "That has been my experience."

"What of your mother?"

She brought her gaze back to him. "My parents died of a fever before Rory arrived. 'Tis one reason he is so dear to me. As if they gave part of themselves to him when they passed."

"They did, through ye," he said.

"And yer family?"

"I always knew I was the heir," he told her, "taking on airs, but also responsibility. Looking out for the siblings I told ye about. They think me overly protective."

"I canna imagine why," she said wryly. "Ye have such a large family. I used to dream I would, too, someday, but I gave up on that wish when Rodrick left me."

"'Tisna too late," Drummond told her, but he didn't know if she believed him. He paused, then took her arm and stopped her. "Morven, I need to talk to ye. I came to tell ye that we are leaving in the morning."

16

M orven's hand covered her mouth. Behind it, she said, "So soon?"

"Ye ken why I must return. If ye are willing, I will take Rory with me to foster. Ye said ye needed to think on it. Have ye decided that is what ye wish to do? If ye will come, too, I will escort ye and all yer belongings—including the loom. Ye will be welcome..."

He trailed off, aware of the pallor of her complexion and her silence.

"I dinna think so." She looked away.

Losing her son terrified her, but something more than losing Rory, even more than coming to the Aerie with him, was on her mind.

"Ye willna lose him, lass. Ye can be with him, in a safer place..."

"I want to wait a while longer—maybe another year, she finally said. "He is smart and wise for his years, but in other ways, he's young for his age. After what we just went through, I canna uproot him. Not yet. He needs familiar surroundings."

Drummond feared she'd never agree. He took her hands

and turned her to face him, trying to hide the dismay roiling his belly. "Ye ken I want ye with me. Come to the Aerie. Make a life there, with me or nay. Rory will adjust. In fact, I think he will thrive there. And so will ye."

After their recent experience, her reluctance was understandable, but he couldn't help feeling rejected. He thought they had something together, but her son always came first. She had told him that, and he believed her at the time, but he thought he could change her mind. Despite everything they had been through together, she hadn't budged. She was locked in her past.

Drummond realized he'd done all he could. She had to make the decision for herself and her son. He would not force her into something she wasn't ready for.

"I will accept yer decision," he told her as they turned back to the cottage door, "for now. But I want ye to keep thinking about my offer. Send word if ye are ready to take me up on it. I will come for ye myself, with wagons for yer belongings and yer loom. I willna abandon ye, Morven. This is only a temporary separation, unless, that is, ye dinna want to see me again." He waited, heart pounding, for her answer.

She narrowed her eyes. "Will yer betrothed, or perhaps in a year, yer wife, welcome me? Will she think Rory is yer son?"

She asked as they reached her door. Drummond froze. "My...? What are ye talking about?"

"I was told ye are betrothed, or ye will be at the clan gathering ye are so eager to return to." Her words came at him fast and clipped, like the impact of a handful of pebbles. "So what kind of future do ye plan for me and my son at yer Aerie? Do ye anticipate that I will be yer leman? Because I tell ye now, that will never happen."

"Who told ye such a tale?" Drummond snarled the question, but he couldn't help himself. "I am not betrothed. I have no plans to be—none that dinna involve ye. I would never—"

He threw up his hands and grasped her shoulders. "I would never suggest such an arrangement. I couldna do that to ye, Morven. I would never insult ye... hurt ye... God's bones. Who told ye this lie?"

She shook her head, uncertainty replacing the anger in her eyes. "While we were missing, Ilise heard it from one of yer men. I dinna ken who, but she thought it important enough to make her way here, to my cottage, every step pure agony for her to take, to tell me herself. I had nay choice but to believe her."

"So that is why ye have been so distant with me lately. If she had nay reason to lie to ye, or to want to hurt ye with such accusations, she must have misunderstood something she overheard. Perhaps one of my men was talking about me and ye, if, nay, *when* we made it back. After I spent so much time alone with ye—aye, and Rory—he might have assumed that ye would be compromised, and that we would have to wed, whether we wished to or nay. Ilise might have overheard such a conversation, and didna ken what he meant."

Morven crossed her arms and stepped back, eyes wide and brows arched.

Drummond reached for her, but she evaded his hand.

"Ye have plans that involve me?"

"Ye ken I do. Only I wish to give ye the time ye need to be confident ye and Rory are well recovered and ready for a new life. At the Aerie. With me."

She studied his face, her gaze roving over him as if trying to read his mind.

How could he convince her he was telling the truth?

She stepped forward and cupped his cheek. Her lips twisted as she shook her head. "But not so soon." Tears shone in her eyes, giving him hope that she would remember him, and yearn for him.

He'd never felt this way before. His heart was fluttering in his chest like a caged bird. Yet he was certain only moments ago, it had dropped into his belly. His head felt woozy, like this was the end of a night of drinking. Morven had tossed his emotions about like a heavy surf tossed a coracle. But he'd landed onshore full of hope and longing. "I'll be waiting, and when I can, I will come to check on ye and Rory. And to ask ye again." He dipped his head and kissed her, pulling her into his arms while he fought to memorize everything about her. The way she fit against him, her taste, her scent, her caress. "I will ask ye as many times as I must, until ye say *aye*." He kissed her again, to seal his words as a promise.

She broke the kiss and stepped out of his arms. "Wait here," she said, then slipped into her cottage. He thought she would wake Rory, so he could say goodbye to the lad, but she came back a moment later with the fabric he'd admired. "I finished it. This is for yer mother," she said. "A token of my gratitude for the way she raised ye, the man I fell in love with. The only man I've truly loved."

Drummond's emotions overcame his ability to speak for several long moments. His heart swelled with love, and with awe that she would do something so heartfelt. So generous. And so meaningful to him and to his family. Finally, he found his voice. "I fell in love with ye, too. I dinna wish to leave ye."

"But ye must. I ken it."

"What will ye give the clan's Lady?"

"I'll make something else for her. Once ye said yer mother would love this, I decided to finish it for her. I put my heart in it for her. For ye."

Drummond took her hand. "Morven, come with me."

"Ye ken I canna. I still owe Lady MacComas her fabric. And Rory needs a home he kens."

How could he argue with her? She was as diligent, as driven, as controlling as he. Independent. And still fighting for her son. Though she tried to make him believe she feared giving up her only source of livelihood, Drummond knew her son was the reason. Though she loved him, Rory had to come first, at least for now.

"Tell Rory goodbye for me, and that I will see him again soon." He wanted to see him now, but understood Morven's instinct to protect her son from watching him leave. It was likely they would be gone before he woke up tomorrow morning. "And thank ye for the gift. I hope someday soon, ye will see her wearing it."

He consoled himself that he'd finally succeeded in doing the job he'd been sent to do, had no excuse to stay longer, and had every reason to return home for the clan chiefs' gathering. He was the heir, and he'd best remember that, rather than letting Morven distract him. Though she was the most attractive woman he'd ever met, his role at the Aerie was his responsibility alone. No woman—no matter what he felt about her, no matter that leaving her behind was going to break his heart—could change that.

He left her standing in her doorway, her son sleeping inside.

MORVEN WATCHED the Lathans ride away early the next morning, her gaze locked on Drummond. She regretted every word she had uttered to turn him away from her. She had missed her chance to tell him the truth. Waiting until he left was too late by far.

If only she could call him back and admit she wanted to go with him, but she was afraid. She feared how another change in Rory's life would affect him, certainly, but she also feared for herself, that she wouldn't fit in. Drummond was to be the laird of his clan someday. She was no one. He might come to regret bringing home a woman with a son, not the sweet, virginal bride she was sure his family expected him to wed. And most of all, she was afraid to risk her heart again.

She'd sworn to love only her son. With Drummond's help, she had gotten him back and regained the chance to do so. She would live her life as she planned it, and be strong for him. Despite everything his father had done, everything his father had been, she would ensure Rory grew up to be a good man. Still, she wondered how much of Rodrick would live on in Rory. His wanderlust made sense after Rodrick talked about how he'd wandered the mountains until he knew every trail. What other traits would they share?

Suddenly, her stomach sank. She'd been wrong. Rory needed more than her influence. He needed a strong father figure—a good man like Drummond—to guide him. And she'd just let the chance ride away.

Once the Lathans were out of sight, she went back to what was familiar while she dealt with the grief of letting Drummond go. Her loom. Her work. Only to her, it wasn't just work. The fabrics she created were her art. Something she'd always loved. But suddenly, the act of creation that had sustained her for all these years did not satisfy her as it once had. She knew what was missing. Drummond. She blamed herself for the emptiness she now felt. She should have been honest with him and told him how deep her feelings for him had become. Feelings that were worth exploring, to see if they could lead to a future that would make both of them happy.

Desperate for distraction, she turned to Kelso's box of accounts. As she expected, most of what it contained would be of interest only to Angus. But near the bottom, she found her second letter to Rodrick, telling him of his son. Her heart sank as she read it. She'd been so happy then, thinking the news would bring Rodrick back to her. She turned the letter over. Kelso had written something on the outside of it. It took a moment to decipher what he wrote. Two words. *Rodrick* and *trouble.* What had Kelso known that led him keep her letters and to take such a drastic step? Had he seen something of what Rodrick would become? Lately, she'd suffered a taste of the misery that old man had saved her from. If only he knew. She crumpled the letter, threw it on the fire, and pulled out the next. She found nothing more of interest until she reached the very bottom of the box.

There, she found a folded missive with her name written on it in Kelso's broad strokes. She held it up to the sunlight streaming in her open door, looking for another name, another person he wanted her to give it to. Finding none, she turned it over. He'd sealed it with melted wax. What could be so important? She broke the seal, curious, yet something made the pit of her stomach hollow out with dread.

She took a breath and unfolded the letter, hardly daring to hope Kelso had left her the answers to her questions.

Lass, he wrote, *if ye are reading this, I'm dead and gone and naught can hurt me, so 'tis long past time I atone for what I've done and tell ye the truth. Ye'll be wondering why I kept yer letters to Rodrick Moncreiffe rather than sending them on to his clan, why I took a special interest in ye and wee Rory, and why, as ye probably ken by now, I helped the raiders.*

My sins against ye began while ye were still handfasted to that wretch. Aye, he treated ye well enough for the year he was with ye, but men are different when there are nay lasses nearby. I'll nay go into it all, but he wasna the man for ye. Ye thought ye loved him and didna see the fury in his eyes. If ye ever crossed him, ye wouldna survive the beating he'd give ye when his temper overtook his sense. Blacksmithing made him dangerously strong. Yer life and yer lad's wouldha been forfeit. The cruel way he ended yer time together was only a wee portion of what might have come.

When ye asked me how to get yer first letter to Moncreiffe, I saw my chance to free ye from him forever. So I took it and hid the letter away. Because I deprived ye of a husband, as long as ye remained without a good man at yer side, ye became my responsibility. I meant only to do right by ye. I thought I'd saved ye. But I was wrong.

More than a year ago, Rodrick entered my cottage, demanding to ken what had changed in the village, who kept livestock, and more. Despite his threats, I refused to help him. 'Twould be no great loss if he killed me. But then he threatened to find ye and drag ye away with him. I couldna let that happen to ye or to Rory. I ken now he planned for his men to raid us. At the time, I thought only to protect ye and yer wee lad.

I'm sorry for every hardship ye have endured because of me, yet I hope by the time ye read this, ye will ken that I did the best I could for ye.

He signed it, *Ever yer friend, Kelso MacComas*

Morven laid the letter aside. She could no longer see it. Her eyes filled with tears and her throat closed with grief and longing. Why hadn't he told her? Or told Angus? If he'd told someone—anyone—he might still be alive today. And Rodrick would not have been able to send men close enough to the village and to her cottage to discover Rory. Her son wouldn't have been taken. Nor would she. Rodrick had hit both of them, just as Kelso predicted. He tried to protect them, but in keeping the secret of Rodrick's involvement with the raiders, Kelso made everything else inevitable.

Including Drummond.

God, why had she let him go? She'd made the same mistake as Kelso. She hadn't told Drummond how she felt. And now he was gone. Perhaps forever.

Her friend, Glenna, arrived before she could spiral herself into tears and sobbing that would frighten Rory.

"Well, they've gone," Glenna announced, as if Morven wasn't aware of the lack down to her bones.

"Aye, they have," Morven agreed, fighting to keep her voice

from betraying her grief. "We can go back to life as it was before the raids began." Only without Kelso's help.

"Nay strangers in the village, camped at its edge," Glenna said with a glance out the door, as if looking for the Lathans. "And nay raiders stealing our livestock, so we'll starve this winter," she added.

Rory came in the cottage in time to hear her comment, and Morven cringed when his eyes widened.

"Are we going to starve?"

"Nay, laddie," Morven said, determined to reassure him. "We never were. And now the raiders are gone, we never will. Ye have naught to *fash* over."

"I do!" He stuck out his lower lip and frowned.

Morven saw the signs of a belligerent mood Rory rarely suffered. "What do ye have to *fash* over, lad?"

"Drummond is gone. Ye are sad. And so am I."

"He had to go home, Rory. Just like he helped ye to come home, he has one to return to, as well."

"He should live here."

"Nay, laddie. He's his da's heir. He couldna stay with us."

"I wish he was my da. Not that mean man who stole me from ye. Then he could."

Morven swallowed tears. Rory missed Drummond, too. When he said he wished Drummond was his father, she wished that, too, with all her heart. He'd treated Rory so well, she knew he'd be a wonderful father to his own children someday. She glanced aside at Glenna, looking for some help to distract Rory. But even her eyes glimmered with revealing wetness. It seemed they weren't the only ones who would miss the big, handsome Highlander.

"Glenna." Morven said her name to break the spell of sadness that had overtaken them all.

"Ach, aye, I came for a reason. Angus asked to speak to ye. When ye can," she added. "'Tisna urgent."

She nodded. "Can ye stay with Rory for a wee? I'd best go see what the chief wants." The distraction would do her good.

"Of course. Go on with ye."

ANGUS GESTURED Morven to a seat when she arrived at his solar door. "Come in lass."

"What can I do for ye?" She settled onto the chair he'd indicated and waited. Had his wife asked for something? If so, why had she not sent for her, rather than Angus? Did he want a special gift? A surprise for his wife? Or did he have news for her? Perhaps there was news from Moncreiffe about Rodrick. She felt her heartbeat pick up speed and took a breath to calm herself.

"'Tis more what I can do for *ye*," he said, surprising her. She tipped her head to the side, waiting.

"First, I must apologize for how the clan has treated ye since the end of yer handfasting."

His words drove her to her feet, nerves jangling. This was not a conversation she wanted to have with anyone, least of all, with him. But he waved her down, so she sank back onto the seat.

"I should have put a stop to it," he continued.

"How could ye? Ye canna make people befriend me. They must be willing to on their own." Her gaze dropped to her hands. She was embarrassed so few had bothered, and that Angus was well aware of it.

"Well, I should have done something to make yer life better. Perhaps now I can."

She brought her gaze up and met his under a questioning frown. "What do ye mean?"

"Ye've been through a trauma, what with the raiders carrying off wee Rory, then what happened to ye and the Lathan." He paused a moment as if gauging her reaction to the reminder, then smiled. "Ye need a man of yer own to protect ye, lass. If ye wish, I will find ye a husband."

Morven froze. She did not want Angus to find her a husband. She'd turned Drummond away, a man as kind and honorable as any she'd ever met. Why would she accept a stranger?

"I see from yer expression ye need to think over my offer. Very well. Take all the time ye need, but think on it, lass. There are several men here who would make ye a good mate, or I can reach out to neighboring clans, though we'd hate to lose ye."

They'd hate to lose her loom, and her skill with it. Morven crossed her arms, certain Angus would try to push her to one of the men of the clan, and she could not think of one of them she would be willing to accept.

"There's another thing I can do to help ye," he continued when she didn't react. "I can arrange to foster yer son away, someplace where he'll be safe, well cared for, and trained up as a lad ought to be."

Morven knew she must have gone pale. She felt suddenly weak and dizzy, and the pace at which Angus continued speaking told her he knew he had upset her, and he was trying to justify the suggestion.

"Then ye wouldna have the burden of caring for him, or the worry that he'd get into trouble if the raiders come back. Lathan might be a good place for him. I understand he and Drummond Lathan got on well."

The mention of Drummond's name was like a dagger to her heart. Why had she let him go without telling him how she felt? She was a fool. "Nay... Angus, nay," she choked out, her voice growing stronger on each syllable. "Rory was returned to me so recently. We both need time..."

Angus waved a hand, as if turning her world upside down was of no import.

"Think on it. On my offer to find ye a husband, too. Ye'd be better off. Safer. Someone to share yer burdens with would make yer life easier, lass."

She wanted to argue her life was fine, just as it was. But she knew that wasn't true. The hole in her heart where Drummond used to be was proof enough that her life lacked much—love, companionship, someone who cared for and protected her. And just as she had feared would happen, Rory, who wished Drummond was his father, felt the lack, too.

She took her leave of Angus on shaky legs. His offers rattled her nearly as much as discovering Rory had been taken. They cracked the idealized image of her life she'd quickly constructed since her return and sudden acceptance by the clan. The offers, made so casually, yet with the power of the laird's will behind them, forced her to acknowledge that things wouldn't remain the same, no matter how much she might want them to.

17

F rom his hiding place just outside the village, screened by
gorse bushes no one bothered to trim, Rodrick watched
Morven walk to her cottage. Morven used to like the yellow
flowers when they were in bloom. Apparently she still did. Or
perhaps she derived some dye from them for her cloth. Either
way, they provided him a perfect shelter while he observed the
activity around her cottage. Their cottage. It had once been his,
too, before he walked away from it—and her.

What a fool he'd been. His life could have been so different.
Instead of being on the run, injured and sick, he could have
lived here, or taken Morven back to Moncreiffe. To keep her
home and keep her child safe, she would have kept him from
renouncing the current Moncreiffe laird three years ago.
Instead, he'd forced the wife he'd married a year after he left
Morven to join Diarmad's splinter clan with him. He shifted
and groaned at the pain in his shoulder and the soreness in his
slashed arm. Perhaps with Morven, he wouldn't have been
outlawed along with those who followed Diarmad. He wouldn't
be sitting here, half out of his head with fever. He wouldn't have
lived the last three years on the edge of starvation, chased away

after a year of raiding Moncreiffe. He wouldn't have brought their small clan to the mountains to raid MacComas, or depended on Kelso to tell him who had new lambs or what defenses Angus was mounting against them. Aye, it was all Morven's fault. But nay, she'd tried to tell him, he suddenly remembered. His head was hot, then cold, then full of wool. Kelso had kept her letter. Nay, letters. He hadn't delivered it. Them! All of Rodrick's troubles were his fault. Rodrick was glad he'd killed the man. Kelso had ruined his life. It was time for paybacks. And someone in this village would have to pay. But who?

Morven looked pale and shaky, stopping often to steady herself by putting a hand on a tree or the side of a building. But she straightened her spine as she reached her own cottage, forced a smile to her lips and disappeared inside.

What news had she gotten that she needed false bravado to keep it from her son?

It didn't matter. Whatever was going on in the village didn't matter. She would be gone from here soon. She and his son. As soon as he was able, he would take them away. She would help him.

He shifted and grimaced at the pain in his shoulder and the heat that seemed to crawl along his bones. First, Morven must heal him. She was his wife, especially since his other wife disappeared with the rest of his clan. It was Morven's duty, and she would do it. He'd see to that.

He had plans. So many plans. He needed to be healthy and strong, so he could take his revenge on the man he thought he'd killed. The man who'd taken his family from him and led them back here, through the mountains. His mountains.

A blonde lass left the cottage. She didn't close the door! He could walk in. Nay, someone else approached. A man. What was a man doing with Morven? She'd just lost her protector. Had she taken another so soon? Was he her lover, too? She'd pay for it if he was. And if her protector had been, she'd pay for him, too.

He shifted again and groaned at the pain the movement caused. He had to be certain any bairn she birthed was his. As the laird of his own clan, he must ken that his bairns were legitimate, so they could inherit and keep his line going. Forever. He was strong. His new clan would be, too, as soon as he could gather back the people in the raiders' camp. Diarmad had named him heir. He was their chief. Not Lorne.

He stayed hidden and watched for Morven and Rory, shivering all the while, his head pounding in time with his shoulder. But the man came out first. As he left, a woman approached. There were a lot more people around them than there used to be. Foolish sympathizers. If only they knew the great things he planned for his wife and son.

But with all these new friends of hers, how would she keep him undiscovered in her cottage until he was healthy enough to take her and Rory away, to fulfill his plans? His destiny? He intended to build up a clan strong enough to take his revenge on her protector, the man who injured him, who tried to kill him—until Morven stopped him. Aye, he was alive thanks to her. Soon, she would restore him to health and strength, too.

He'd figure something out. But first, he needed to get in there, to keep his little family together. He couldn't have the lad running to the others in the village and telling them his father was back.

DRUMMOND KNEW LEAVING Morven behind was the wrong move —at least for him. He thought it was the wrong choice for her to make, as well. But she wanted to stay, and he had to return home. His responsibilities there would not wait any longer. Still, something kept pulling him back. To her. The tingle in his belly had increased to the point it now pained him. Why? He knew exactly where she was.

He couldn't deny something happened during his fall down the cliff. Something caused the headache that lasted for days. Something also awakened or increased the sense he'd always thought of as the combination of luck and observation, giving him this weird sense of knowing where to find Morven and the lad. He couldn't decide if the other faint, inconstant impressions he felt came from people he knew were in the village, or if they were just his imagination at work.

Even now he could sense Morven and her son, miles behind him. How long would this last? And from how far? Would he still sense her when he reached the Aerie? He hoped not. That knowledge would torment him. Yet he also hoped that the connection to her would survive. He would take comfort from knowing she was where she thought she belonged.

Wouldn't his family be surprised? No longer would he be the only one without a talent. He'd finally become like his mother and siblings. Thinking of them, Drummond pictured Morven there, at his side, at the Aerie. If only she had agreed to come with him. His family would love her, and especially Rory.

He clenched his teeth. He'd asked, and she'd refused him. Twice.

Eduard pulled up beside him and gave him a head shake. "Ye look fit to bring up a thunderstorm, and I'm not eager to ride through a heavy rain. Are ye still *fashed* over the lass?"

Eduard must have seen the direction of his thought on his face. Drummond nodded. "This feels wrong."

"Leaving her? Then turn yerself around and go back to her. Ye canna leave her like this. Ye must declare yerself and see if she feels the same."

"'Tis easy for ye to say." He held up a hand. "I thought we did, but she chose to remain behind."

"Yet here ye are, trying to guess her feelings. Yer own, too, I'll wager. Talking yerself out of what ye already ken. We havena gone so far that ye canna be back with her today. If ye're this *fashed* about leaving her, ye need to turn around. And on the way, decide what she means to ye. What ye mean to each other."

"I'm needed at home." Drummond shook his head. That excuse sounded weak, even to his own ears.

"And once ye arrive, yer da will wrap ye up so fast in everything he needs ye to do, ye'll never find the time to clear up things with the lass. Ye ken better than to let that happen."

Eduard was right. He hadn't said anything Drummond hadn't already told himself.

"I'd be wasting my time."

"Ye dinna really believe that."

"At this point, I canna tell the difference between what I believe and what I only hope is true."

"Ach, lasses. They can twist a man in knots, they can."

"And there ye have it."

"Yet ye have never let a lass do this to ye before. Why now?"

Why now, indeed? Because Morven was different. Kind, smart, determined, fierce, loving, all those things and more. And she called to him. Worse, or better, she called to this new sense of his. What if she continued to refuse him? Would he ever be able to be with another woman without feeling that Morven and Rory were bound to him?

Perhaps the answer was to continue on to the Aerie and see if that connection persisted over the time and distance that would separate them. His mother would be able to tell what had happened to him, and if need be, heal it. Stop it. Make it go away.

Did he want that? He shook his head. Nay. He'd miss her too much.

Eduard apparently took his gesture as an answer. "As I

thought. Ye dinna ken. And ye never will until ye two are honest with each other."

Drummond grimaced. "'Twill have to wait. Da expects me at the clan chief's gathering. I canna spend any more time at the village. Not until afterward. Perhaps by then, I will ken whether what I feel is real—and permanent—or not."

"Aye. And perhaps by then, trouble will find her and the lad again, and ye willna be at hand to put a stop to it."

Drummond tightened his grip on the reins in his hand. "I tried to convince her to come with us. To foster Rory with us. I canna be at the Aerie and the village, both, at the same time. She will be fine. And if the raids start up again, Angus will send word. 'Tis the best we can do for now."

Decision made, Drummond felt the weight of it lift off his shoulders and sat up straighter in his saddle. He needed time. Perhaps they both did. After the gathering of lairds, he could return to speak to her again. To see if what they had was real or if they'd simply reacted to the danger they were in and looked to each other for comfort. Perhaps even bring both of them to the Aerie for a visit, so she could see what their life could be like, if only she would do what he asked.

Eduard snorted, but after that expression of disgust, he rode beside Drummond in silence.

His thoughts returned to Morven. He could still so easily picture her at her loom, or speaking to Rory with a mother's compassion, helping to keep them safe as they made their way through the hills back to the village. Confronting Rodrick.

Suddenly, ice slid down Drummond's spine and the painful tingles in his belly spread to his chest, his arms, his fingers. He could barely hold the reins.

Rodrick wasn't dead. And he wasn't far from Morven.

"I've got to go back," he told Eduard. "*Now.*"

"Then someone must go with ye."

"Send Ailbeart after me. Ye rest go on ahead to the Aerie.

I'll follow soon, with her, I hope." Without giving Eduard a chance to object or question his decision, he turned his mount and galloped back the way they'd come, praying he'd arrive in time.

MORVEN WAS at her loom when she heard a noise outside. A thud. A muffled cry. Had Rory fallen? Something didn't sound right. "Rory?" She looked toward the door, then surged to her feet, aghast.

Rodrick! She went cold, her mouth flooded, and her belly twisted.

He dragged Rory into the cottage, his arm across Rory's neck and shoulder, Rory's head lolling to the side.

Certain she was going to be sick, she clamped her jaw shut, swallowed, and fought the sensation. She took a step toward her son, but Rodrick's glare stopped her. "What have ye done to him? Put him down!"

Rodrick slammed the door and dropped the bolt. "He'll sleep for a wee. Ye are going to take care of me."

Only then did she realize he looked like hell. The stab wound in his shoulder must have festered. He was flushed and sweaty, likely fevered. He brandished a dirk in his other hand.

"Ye must heal me, make sure I live. Keep everyone out. No one is to know I'm here."

She planted her hands on her hips. "And how am I to do that?"

"That is up to ye. One slip, and we'll both be without a son." He dropped Rory.

He landed in a heap of loose limbs.

"Rory!" Morven reached for him.

Rodrick took her arm and forced her back. "But we can make another. And we will. Several in fact, to help establish my branch of Moncreiffe. Ye'll be the Lady of my new clan. I ken ye want that."

She pulled her arm free from his grip. "Nay! I dinna."

His eyes narrowed. "Do ye want to keep Rory alive?"

"Of course." Dear God, how was she going to keep him from harming their son?

"Then ye'll do as I say. Now help me with this damned shoulder."

If she could get away from him, she could summon help. But Rory would be in danger as long as Rodrick controlled him. "I need to fetch more water from the village well."

"Ye will use what ye have here."

"I dinna have everything I need for a poultice." Desperation gave her an answer, or so she hoped. "I grow some of the plants on the south side of the cottage."

"I'll get them."

She shook her head. "Ye dinna ken what to pick—or how."

"I'll bring them all."

"Nay! Ye'll destroy plants I will need later." She kept her gaze on him, hoping to convince him with her calm bearing. "I'll get them. Ye have Rory. Ye can trust I will not go anywhere but to pick what I need for your shoulder."

He studied her, then growled. "Go on."

She unbolted the door and opened it.

18

As he rode near, Drummond could see the closed door to Morven's cottage. He didn't see Rory outside, and that worried him. He tried to convince himself they were both inside, preparing their supper, but he didn't believe it. He was close enough to sense they were near, but his strange sense told him so was Rodrick.

Caution led him to dismount at a distance and cover the ground to the cottage on foot. He didn't want the sound of approaching hoofbeats to warn Rodrick if he was inside with them.

He was no more than three steps from the door when it opened and Morven appeared, pale and upset. Over her shoulder, a few feet inside the room, he saw what he'd feared. Rodrick, sitting slumped, staring at the floor where Rory lay. Before Morven called out his name, Drummond grabbed her arm and pulled her outside.

"He's got Rory," she hissed, as he pulled her out of sight beside the door. Rodrick hadn't charged out, so perhaps he hadn't seen Drummond.

"Why did he let ye go?" He kept his voice low as he folded

her into his embrace for a sweet moment, then stepped back and met her gaze.

"I'm to collect leaves for a poultice." She gestured for him to go around the corner of the cottage. "His shoulder wound has festered," she said as they moved away from the door. "His arm probably has, too. He's in bad shape, but he has a dirk in his hand, and Rory is unconscious." Her voice broke on the last word of her sentence.

Drummond cupped her face. "Stay out here, away from the door. Dinna try to come inside. I'll get Rodrick away from Rory."

"I'm sorry I told ye not to kill him," she said, first meeting his gaze, then looking aside.

"Are ye saying again that ye dinna want him dead?"

"Nay. I'm not." Her chin lifted and her eyes narrowed.

This was the fierce lass he loved. The realization shook him, but he set it aside until after he dealt with Rodrick and got Rory safely away. "Good. Ye'll never be safe as long as he's alive." He gave her a quick kiss, then slid around the corner, braced himself against the wall next to the door, and stole a glance through the open doorway. Rodrick had gotten up and was leaning against Morven's loom. He looked ill and weak, but Drummond knew how imminent danger could energize a man.

Rory worried him more. He lay on the floor between the doorway and where Rodrick stood. Drummond would have to pass him to get to Rodrick. If Rodrick reached him first, he would use Rory as a shield. Drummond could not let that happen. But Drummond could not move him out of the way without making both of them vulnerable to Rodrick's dirk.

He hefted his dirk, weighing its balance. It was a good weapon for close quarters, but fighting Rodrick inside the cottage put Rory at risk. Could he risk throwing it as he had done to kill a coney for their supper while they travelled? Nay.

If Rodrick moved suddenly, and he missed, Rory would still be in jeopardy.

Instead of charging in, he moved back around the cottage to Morven. "Call Rodrick," he told her. "Get him outside. I want him away from Rory."

She nodded, and he moved past her to go around the cottage and approach the door from the opposite side.

"Rodrick," she called softly. "I need yer help."

He didn't answer. Drummond peered around the opposite side of the cottage to the open front door, but Rodrick didn't come out.

"Rodrick!" Morven's voice rang out, louder and more insistent. "Come help me."

This time, he poked his head out of the door. "Quiet, woman. What do ye think ye are doing?"

"I canna get the plant I need out of the ground. I need yer strength to get to the roots."

Perfect, Drummond thought. She'd appealed to his vanity. Would it work?

Rodrick took a step outside, but ducked back in just as Drummond readied himself to rush him. When he reappeared, he held Rory against his good shoulder, Rory's head on his chest.

Damn. Drummond didn't dare attack Rodrick with Rory in his arms.

Rodrick made his way, haltingly, toward the corner of the cottage.

With Rodrick's back turned to him, Drummond saw his chance to get close. He moved as quietly as he could, but something gave him away. Before he reached them, Rodrick glanced around and saw him.

He lifted his blade against Rory's neck. "Ye again?"

"Aye. I thought I killed ye. Shall we see who survives this

meeting?" Drummond gestured at Rory. "Stop using the lad as a shield. Put him down and fight like a man."

"I'm not daft enough to fall for that. The lad stays with me. His mother, too. They're mine. My family."

"Nay. Ye dinna deserve them."

"I do. He's my so—"

Morven cracked him over the head with a rock. The word faded from his lips and his eyes widened in shock. Stunned, he turned, swiping around with his dirk, but Rory overbalanced him. He slid sideways, missing her. Morven's next blow missed him as Rory fell from Rodrick's grasp to the ground.

Drummond closed on Rodrick the moment Rory dropped to the ground, and he didn't miss. His blade bit deep into Rodrick's neck. Without another sound, Rodrick fell to his knees and collapsed, face down, next to his son.

Drummond held up a hand to prevent Morven from coming too close until he made sure Rodrick was truly dead. Once he was certain, he retrieved his dirk and plunged it into the soil to clean it, then looked up at her and nodded.

She rushed to Rory's side. "Help me get him inside. Rodrick must have hit him too hard. He's been like this far too long."

Drummond picked up the lad, carried him inside, and laid him on Morven's bed. He stepped back to let her examine her son, wishing suddenly that he had some of his siblings' healing talent. He'd do anything to ensure Rory was well. The lad deserved to live, and he couldn't imagine how Morven would go forward without him.

"How is he?"

She sighed and leaned back, then took his hand and guided it to Rory. "He has a lump on the back of his head, here."

Drummond touched it. An odd tingle in his fingertips surprised him, so faint at first, he thought he imagined it. It felt different than the tingle in his gut that seemed to have something to do with knowing where Morven and Rory were. Could he truly have a trace of the healing ability? If he did, it was nothing like his mother's or his siblings'. He didn't sense any power in it, but perhaps that grew over time, as his other ability had grown. This, at least, would have immediate benefit. If it was as real as he had begun to hope, he could help Rory. He left his hand in place on the lad's head and imagined the swelling going down, the injury healing. He might only be indulging in wishful thinking and could do nothing for the lad, but he wouldn't give up. Not until Morven pushed him aside. When the faint beginnings of a headache hit, he knew. His mother and siblings felt something from wounds they healed, though their ability was much stronger and better developed than this first hint of healing power in him.

Morven stood and fetched a cloth, poured cold water into a bowl and came back. "This will bring down the swelling."

It would. Perhaps faster than anything he could do—or perhaps both, together? But Morven wanted his help fetching water. He couldn't explain how he might have another way to heal Rory. Frustrated, Drummond helped her by changing the water each time she decreed that it had gotten too warm. After a while, she sent him to fetch a fresh bucket of cold water from the village well. On the way there, he realized the faint headache he'd noticed while touching Rory had faded away. Was Rory better, or had it been too long since Drummond touched his injury?

"Drummond Lathan! I thought ye and yer men left." Angus came up to him as he started back with the bucket.

"We did. I... forgot something. Ailbeart should be along soon, too. Ye should ken, I came back in time to find Rodrick in Morven's cottage. He'd attacked Rory and was holding them inside." He gestured with an open hand for Angus to join him. "I had to stop him."

Angus walked beside him back to Morven's. "Ah, I see," he

commented quietly as they neared Rodrick's body, lying in a pool of blood.

"He willna be a problem anymore." Drummond couldn't be sorry for that.

"And the lad?"

They entered the cottage. Rory was still in bed, but his eyes were open and Morven smiled. "He's awake."

"Good lad," Drummond told him, setting aside the bucket and dropping to his knees next to the bed. "How do ye feel?"

"Head hurts."

"I suppose so," Drummond agreed, "but it will be better soon." For good measure, he gently touched the lump, now much smaller, on the back of Rory's head. The strange tingle began immediately. Drummond kept his fingers in contact and thought, as he had done before, about the swelling going down and the wound healing.

Morven came back with another cold compress and gave it to Drummond. He laid it across Rory's forehead. "Thank ye," she told Drummond, then turned to her visitor. "Angus, Drummond told ye what happened?"

"Aye, lass. I'm glad Rory is all right."

"He will be. Can someone do something about..."

"Of course, lass. That will be gone before—ah, very soon."

"Thank ye."

"I should help ye," Drummond offered, though he didn't want to leave Rory's bedside, not if his touch truly helped the lad. "'Twas my doing." Angus knew it, but admitting it, saying the words, made his blood run cold. What would Angus do?

"Nay, ye stay here with Morven and Rory. I'll get some lads to help me."

Drummond nodded, relieved not to hear censure in Angus's voice, and not to have to deal any further with Rodrick. He couldn't do anything for the man. And he could, it seemed, help Rory. At the very least, the lad seemed calmer with his presence. Or was it his touch? When he got home, there were healers in his family who would know. He wished they could examine Rory, to be sure he was truly well. He'd been through so much.

Drummond barely noticed when Morven went with Angus. He kept his focus on Rory and the healing he believed he was doing to help him.

"Thank ye, Angus," Morven said as he stepped toward the door.

He paused there. "'Tis the only help from me ye'll accept. Now I ken why." He gave her a smile, glanced at Drummond and gave him a quick nod, then left them alone.

"The only help ye'd accept?"

"He offered to find me a husband. I told him I didna want one."

MORVEN'S DECLARATION made Drummond's heart sink. Had he wasted his time coming back for her? Nay, of course not. If he hadn't returned, she and Rory would still be in Rodrick's clutches, or worse. Drummond had no doubt if Rodrick had gotten his way, they would be gone and their life would not be what Morven wanted for herself or for Rory.

Morven continued to tend to Rory, sending Drummond several times for more cold water from the well. Finally, she set aside the cloth she'd been using and smiled at her son. "He's asleep," she announced softly and stood. "I'd best make us something for supper. Ye must be famished. I am. Rory will be, too, when he wakes."

"Angus told us when we arrived that we were welcome to food from the keep's kitchen. I'll fetch something from there and save ye the trouble."

Surprised pleasure lit Morven's eyes and her lips lifted for the first time since Rory woke up. "Thank ye. I appreciate the offer."

"He'll be all right, Morven," he told her when her gaze returned to her son.

"I canna help worrying."

"'Tis what mothers do." He smiled to soften the reminder of the conversation they'd had while hiding from Rodrick.

Drummond left the cottage to fetch their supper. Had taking care of Rory bonded them again? He'd hope for it, but after what she'd said to Angus, his hope was fading.

Morven appreciated his help today, but tomorrow, he'd be underfoot. He would not stay if she didn't want him there. If she hadn't learned enough about him by now, gotten to know him well enough, to want him by her side, helping her raise her son, and keeping them safe, then perhaps she never would.

In the morning, he'd set out for the Aerie with Ailbeart.

Supper was a quiet meal. They talked in low tones to keep from waking Rory, to no avail.

His eyes opened and his head turned toward them at the small table by the hearth. "Is that supper? I'm hungry."

Morven's hand went to her mouth, covering a cry, then she stood and helped him sit up. "I'm so glad to hear ye say that, lad. But first, tell me how ye feel. Does yer head still hurt?"

"A wee."

"Is yer belly upset?"

"Nay. 'Tis hungry is all."

She smiled, helped him stand, and ushered him to her place at the table. "Sit and eat, lad. Drummond brought us this stew from the keep's kitchen. 'Tis sure to help ye feel better."

She looked at Drummond over Rory's head. Tears shone in her eyes.

"Ye are a brave lad," Drummond told him, giving Morven time to get her emotions under control. "I'm glad to see ye out of that bed."

But what about his own emotions? This was a family he wanted to build from. Rory could not be his heir, but he'd be a sturdy older brother when the heir came along. If only Morven would see how he felt about her and give him that chance. But her gaze was on her son.

Rory nodded, but didn't stop eating to answer.

Drummond put aside the ache in his chest and forced a grin for Morven's sake. "All is well," he told her.

"Thanks to ye," she replied. "Thanks to ye."

WHEN RORY FINISHED HIS SUPPER, Morven felt more of the day's tension melt away. His appetite reassured her. He sat with her for a while, but before long, he went back to his pallet and quickly went to sleep. She'd keep an eye on him through the night, but Drummond was certain Rory was past the worst of his injury. She hadn't wanted to ask him what he remembered of the day. Bringing up bad memories would only lead to bad dreams. And he'd had too many of those of late. They could talk about it all tomorrow.

Tonight was for Drummond. They sat outside the cottage, side by side, quietly sipping the last of the ale she had on hand. Perhaps tomorrow she could prevail upon him to carry a cask to her from the keep. And bring more water from the well to fill her kettle and the pot she used for washing water.

She wanted him to stay, but she didn't think keeping him busy would fool him for long. He'd left her once, headed back to his responsibilities at the Lathan keep. She realized she didn't know what had brought him back to her in time to save them from Rodrick.

"Why did ye come back?" She asked so softly, she didn't think he heard her. But that changed when he took her hand in his and turned to face her.

"I came back for ye. I couldna leave ye. I thought I could, but I realized I didna wish to."

Her heart lifted at his admission. He'd come back for her. Maybe she hadn't lost the chance to have a life with this man.

He hesitated a moment, then admitted, "And I had a feeling we hadna seen the last of Rodrick."

"Do ye suffer these feelings often?"

"Nay, but I'm glad I had that one."

"I, too."

"I ken ye are safe now. He can never harm either of ye again. But that doesna change my mind about ye and Rory. I want ye to come back to the Aerie with me. He can foster there. Ye can do the work ye love. And I..."

He trailed off and cleared his throat. What was he trying to say?

"Ye what?"

"I can have more time with ye, to convince ye that we belong together. I canna get ye or Rory out of my mind, Morven. I want ye with me. Forever." He sighed, dropped her hand and looked away. "But I ken what ye told Angus. That ye dinna want him to find ye a husband. I ken ye feel that way now, but lass, if ye give me time, I can change yer mind."

Morven loved the desire, the longing in his words and in his eyes. No one had ever looked at her the same way. No one had ever saved her life—more than once. And Rory's. Drummond seemed to care for her son almost as much as she did. Could she do as he asked? Leave her home and make a new home among strangers? Let someone else have a hand in raising her son? Caring for her and protecting both of them?

"Drummond, I have a confession to make."

"Aye? Do ye need a priest? Can ye not wait until the Sabbath?"

She couldn't meet his gaze. Not yet. "I dinna need a priest for this confession. I told Angus I didna want him to find me a husband because I already know the man I want." Finally, she looked up. "The only man I want is ye."

Once she said it, once her truth was out, she felt light and hopeful and full of joy. From the look on Drummond's face, wide-eyed, his mouth falling open, then softening into a smile, she knew he felt the same.

He took her hands in his, his smile growing wider with each passing moment. "Does this mean ye will come with me? I willna ask ye to marry me. Not right away. Ye can have all the time ye need to settle into yer new life, and Rory's new life, at the Aerie. Unless ye want to be my bride, too?"

She grinned, knowing the impact of her next words would change both their lives forever. "I do."

19

D rummond's heart soared at Morven's simple words. *I do* was the sweetest phrase he'd ever heard. He couldn't help himself. He wrapped her in his arms, pulled her onto his lap, and kissed her. Not the gentle kiss he'd given her while they were on the run. This one was meant to stake his claim. To make her understand how dear she was, and how he longed to possess her.

He trailed kisses from her lips to her ear, then down her throat before he moved back to her mouth. Her arms went around him and her fingers tunneled into his hair, letting him know she wanted him, too.

"Morven," he whispered against her ear, making her name a plea, a prayer. "Do ye mean ye will marry me?"

"Aye, Drummond. I will. Tonight. Tomorrow. Here. At the Aerie. Whenever and wherever ye will."

"We can handfast if ye wish tonight, and marry in the kirk at the Aerie. If that pleases ye, milady."

"Milady?"

"Have ye forgotten I'm the heir to my father? I will be Laird someday, and ye will be my Lady."

"And Rory?"

"Rory will be my son, but he canna be my heir. Ye ken what that means?"

"More bairns, aye. A houseful, I hope."

His gaze lifted to the skies. "A houseful would suit me, aye." He wasn't sure who he was speaking to, but it became a fervent wish. He dropped his gaze back to Morven's. "But so would one or two. I want ye to be happy, love. We'll deal with bairns when the time comes."

Morven touched his face with warm fingertips.

He turned his head to kiss them, but she lifted them away.

"And to be sure, the Lady of the clan may still work at her loom?"

Ah, so she had conditions of her own. He should have expected this one. "Of course. Ye will always have yer work— yer art—to comfort ye. There are other duties as well, but ye will have years to learn them and all the assistance ye need from my mother and others in the clan. Ye can do this, Morven. Ye have shown me how strong ye are, how fiercely ye love yer son, how ye strive to do the best ye can. Ye are the best wife for me and Lady for my clan that I could hope to find. I have fallen in love with ye." His gaze lingered on hers. "I hope ye feel the same."

"I... I *have* fallen in love with ye, too, Drummond Lathan. Ye have my heart." Finally, she smiled.

"And ye mine." He kissed her again, softly this time, putting reverence and hope into every touch and every shared breath between them. "Always."

She leaned away from him again, uncertainty in the gaze she shifted away from him, then back to meet his. "I willna handfast with ye. Ye saw how it turned out for me the last time. To handfast again would be to invite evil fortune, and we have had more than enough of that. But I will go to the Aerie with ye, and marry ye in the kirk. Rory can be the big brother to any bairns we have, and support yer heir as a brother ought."

"Then that is what we will do."

"But that leaves the matter of moving the loom."

Drummond laughed and hugged her to him. "'Tis nay matter, milady. All we need are a few strong men to load a wagon, horses to pull it and the same at the Aerie to unload it and set it up." He curled a finger under her chin and lifted her face, so he could speak to her eyes. "I ken how important it is to ye. I willna leave it behind. Whatever ye need shall be done."

DRUMMOND WOULD HAVE PREFERRED to stay with Morven and Rory, but at Angus's insistence, he shared a chamber with Ailbeart in the keep, so he heard the uproar early the next morning. The thud of running feet on the hall outside his chamber and the roar of voices coming through his window woke him. He rolled out of bed and went to the window, afraid the raiders were attacking in broad daylight again.

What he saw made him wonder if he'd lost his mind.

The raiders were here, but they weren't attacking. He recognized several of them from his observation of their rough settlement when Rodrick held Morven and Rory. Lorne in the lead, they walked into the village as quietly and calmly as he, Morven and Rory had walked in only days ago, leading horses and the remaining livestock in their possession. What did they think they were doing?

"What is it?" Ailbeart's sleepy tone made him turn from the window.

"Ye'll have to see for yerself. Join me when ye can."

He pulled on his boots, grabbed his weapons, and ran downstairs to join Angus and his men outside the keep's door.

Angus glanced aside as Drummond joined him. "Are they who I think they are?"

"Aye. That blonde man is the leader, Lorne. I recognize others, but dinna ken their names."

"Well, if this isna the most interesting of developments, I dinna ken what could top it," Angus told him quietly. "Let's find out what they want."

Angus stepped forward and identified himself.

In turn, Lorne did the same. "We are what is left of the Moncreiffe insurrection of three years past. The leader was killed a few days ago. We are the ones who raided yer clan, at the behest of Rodrick Moncreiffe, with his knowledge of yer clan and crofts."

"We ken it," Angus said, and nodded for him to continue.

"We canna survive as we are. We come in peace, with all intent to make up for what we took from ye. We've come to join MacComas."

"Why not return to Moncreiffe? Surely the laird would forgive any who swore fealty."

"The Laird banished us for life. We canna go back there."

"And why should I risk taking ye in?"

"We owe ye. And we appeal to ye for Highland hospitality for the winter. We will swear to ye, and do whatever it takes to make amends."

Morven joined the throng that had gathered to listen. She looked pale and unhappy. He had no doubt she did not welcome this reminder of the trauma she and Rory had suffered. He hoped Rory was back in their cottage and not here to see this.

Angus studied the group.

They waited silently, most with downcast gazes, for his verdict. No doubt they knew if MacComas didn't take them in, they were doomed. Likely, they were right.

Lorne kept his gaze on Angus, stoic, but strong. Drummond

recalled that Lorne had tried to be the voice of reason advising Diarmad, but Rodrick had held the old chief in sway.

Angus barely moved his lips as he spoke to Drummond. "I was wrong. This got more interesting. What would ye recommend, Lathan?"

"I canna advise ye as my father might." He held up a hand as Angus opened his mouth to object. "But as someone who saw their settlement, saw their old leader killed, and saw that Lorne tried to keep Rodrick from succeeding in his power grab, I would advise giving them a chance. Of the two, Lorne seemed to have the better head on his shoulders. And ye ken as well as I that the women and bairns among them willna survive the winter."

"Nor most of the men, I'd wager," Angus agreed. "There are fewer of them than I thought there might be."

"I count thirty-five souls depending on ye to save their lives," Drummond told him. "Twenty-three men of an age to work, the rest women, with their own skills, I'm sure, or they wouldna have survived this long, and bairns. Och, and the lad, Bug. What did ye do with him?"

"He's been keeping Ilise company, believe it or not. He didna ken anything useful, and she took a liking to him. So..."

He paused to acknowledge Lady MacComas, who joined him and stood on his other side.

Drummond gave her a shallow bow, then raised an eye at the lad following her. "Bug?"

"His name is Knox," Ilise answered for him.

Bug... no, Knox, inclined his head, and met Drummond's gaze as if daring him to challenge his presence there.

Far be it from Drummond to do such a thing, and certainly not at this moment. Angus could handle the lad. And his friends—if they were his friends. The lad seemed in no hurry to join them. Only then did Drummond realize Ailbeart stood at his back.

Angus had straightened with the arrival of his wife. Now he addressed Lorne. "Ye are aware a MacComas man was killed during one of yer raids."

Lorne paled. Indeed he was, as were his people. They stirred and a murmur rose. Drummond could see hope fading from their eyes at Angus's pronouncement.

Angus held up a hand. "The man who committed the murder is dead. I hold none of ye responsible for that crime." He nodded to Lorne, who inclined his head.

"Thank ye, Laird MacComas. I am... we are grateful the stain of that act remains with Rodrick."

Angus nodded. "Now that is out of the way, be comforted. We will take ye in for the winter, but with conditions. Each of ye, from eldest to... almost youngest," he said, his gaze sweeping the group and pausing on a babe in arms, "will swear fealty to MacComas—to me and to this village—on pain of death if ye ever cause trouble such as yer leader caused at Moncreiffe. In recompense for the raids, ye will be put to work helping with the harvest, and any other tasks that must be done before the snows set in. Ye will be given warm places to sleep. Families will stay together. Single men will be housed together. Come spring, if all goes well and none of ye are the cause of more trouble, ye will be accepted and deemed full members of this clan." He turned to Ilise. "Does this arrangement meet with yer approval, my Lady?"

"It does, my Laird." She smiled at him, then addressed the gathered MacComas clan members watching this unfold. "We will make them welcome, feed and house them. In turn, they will help us. Together, we will thrive this winter. Let it be so."

A cheer went up at her words from the former raiders, many of whom shed tears and clung to each other. The gathered MacComas villagers were not quite as jubilant, but many smiled in welcome at the newcomers.

Morven remained silent and still.

Drummond knew why. And he knew leaving here would help her put the trauma of the last few days behind her. He stepped away from Angus and worked his way through the crowd to her. "I'm glad ye decided to come with me. I can see having them here troubles ye." He took her arm and walked with her back to her cottage.

"It does," she admitted, "but not for the reason ye might think. Kelso's cottage stands empty, and soon, my cottage will, as well. The sooner we can leave, the sooner those people will be able to have the homes they have dreamed of since Diarmad's rebellion made them outcast."

THE TRIP to the Aerie went faster than Drummond anticipated. Morven and Rory proved to be capable travelers, as they had been when on the trek back to their village from the raider's camp. Drummond insisted Rory sleep in the wagon with his mother's loom and their other belongings any time he wasn't riding with him or Morven on horseback. Their escort consisted of MacComas men and Ailbeart. Drummond hadn't wanted to take the time to send for men and wagons from Lathan. He could be home with Morven and Rory before a ghillie got to Lathan and made the return trip with a Lathan escort. He was eager to present his future bride and son to his family, and eager to join his father in preparing for the upcoming gathering.

Morven gasped when she first saw the Aerie, sitting on its high tor. The afternoon sunlight glinted in the diamond-paned window glass. Rory, as usual, had the most sagacious thing to say. "We're going up there? 'Tis very high."

Drummond laughed and assured him, "Aye, it is, but these horses can get us there. *Dinna fash.*"

"Mam?" Rory turned to his mother for confirmation.

She tore her gaze from their destination and studied her son.

His brow wrinkled in concern.

"Aye, son. Drummond wouldna tell ye so if 'twerena true."

That seemed to satisfy him.

They made the climb without incident. Once Drummond greeted his parents and the others who had gathered in the bailey as they climbed the tor, he made sure that Morven was settled in her own chamber at the Aerie, Rory with her for now, but eventually, he'd join the other lads his age in the nursery. Her precious loom was safely out of the weather before he made his way to his mother's herbal.

"Ah, at last," she said, waving him to a seat. "Is everyone well?"

"Aye, well. And tired. I brought a gift for ye from Morven." He held out the bundle of cloth. "She made this."

Aileanna took it and ran a hand across its surface. "'Tis exquisite, and beautifully made. Why did she not bring it to me herself?"

"She wanted it to be a gift from me to ye. But truly, 'tis her work, her heart, in the making of it, to thank ye for raising so well the man she loves. At least, that is how I recall she put it."

Aileanna's brow lifted. "I'll thank her when next I see her. Supper tonight?"

"I expect so. I dinna ken where we'll put her loom, but for now, the wagon carrying it is in a stall in the stable. Ye must think on where it makes sense for Morven to work before we set it up. She will not want to move it once 'tis ready for her to begin."

"Very well. I'll speak to Ferelith and get her advice. If both looms in the same space are too noisy or distracting, she'll be able to recommend an alternative."

"Thank ye, Mother."

She set the cloth aside. "Now, as for ye, my fine lad. What

did ye experience while ye were gone from us? When ye arrived, ye said only that something happened and ye needed to speak to me."

Drummond described his injuries, then turned to the awareness of Morven that had filled him when he came up from his fall down the cliff, and about sensing Rodrick's proximity to Morven's cottage. And later, the faint sensations he noticed when touching Rory and the mild headache he briefly had afterward.

"Well, better late than never," Aileanna said and took a seat next to him. She lifted a hand, her gaze on his and her head cocked, asking permission. "I'll see what's changed, but I'll also deal with any other damage ye sustained."

He nodded, and she touched his forehead, closed her eyes and stilled. Drummond closed his, too, the better to sense within himself. He didn't expect to feel his mother's touch reaching into him, and he didn't. But he did feel a quiet sense of confidence and wonder from her.

Time passed without his awareness. He knew that it had only by the change in the light coming in the herbal's window and the fact that his ribs and other damage no longer pained him. They'd been like that for an hour, maybe more.

"Mother, are ye well?"

"Aye." She took a breath. "Ye were battered, as ye said. Something else is different. Yer skill at finding things is unusually strong, but I think 'tis still tied to people ye ken. For now." She gave him an encouraging smile. "I believe it will grow and change. Ye have come to yer power very late."

"Change?" He felt a touch of the old fear he'd once had of his siblings' abilities, and how strange they seemed. His was stranger still, and nothing like any of theirs.

"As ye go, ye will learn control. Ye will learn to block it when ye havena need for it. I'll help ye, and the twins can, too, though Tavish is having a hard go lately. I may have to appeal to Ellie

MacKyrie for help with him. She's to be here for the lairds' gathering."

"He seemed fine before I left for the village."

"He hides it well, but dreams torment his sleep and some occur even during the day. I think 'tis a phase he must pass through, rather than true seeings. I've written to Ellie. I await her wisdom when she arrives."

"What about what I felt with Rory's injury?"

She picked up a sharp blade she used to mince herbs and dragged it across her forearm. Immediately, blood beaded up along the track.

"Mother!" Drummond looked aghast at what she'd done. All to prove a point to him?

"'Tis shallow. *Dinna fash*. Fix it, son."

He met her gaze and frowned. "Ye are serious?"

"Can ye think of a better test? Now touch my arm—nay, not the wound, but near it. Close yer eyes and reach into my arm. Feel the torn flesh and put it back together, the way it was meant to be."

He did as she bade and closed his eyes, but couldn't feel or see anything but the blackness behind his eyelids.

"Let it come," she murmured.

He sat still, breathing slowly, emptying his mind of everything but the two of them in this chamber and the wound Aileanna had inflicted on herself. He pictured the cut on her arm and urged her body's natural healing ability to speed up, to fill the gap and close the wound. Faint tingling in his fingertips gave him confidence that something was happening, but he didn't look. Only when he felt the irritation of a scratch like hers bloom on his own arm did he open his eyes. Her wound was closed. He stood and leaned over her arm, studying it.

Aileanna brushed away dried bits of blood, revealing perfect, unmarred skin. "Well done, Drummond. I'll make a healer out of ye yet."

"I'm going to be rather busy..."

"Of course. But ye should ken how to use this new skill. Ye canna anticipate when ye will need it." She smiled, then cocked her head. "I think 'tis likely ye saved Rory from worse than a headache. Getting hit as he was, at his young age, could have killed him."

"What?" A jolt of fear made the hair on Drummond's neck stand up.

"Ye said he slept for an unusually long time. That is a sign of deeper trouble. Whether ye ken it or not, ye healed that hurt, saved his mind and his life. If he bled deeper in his head, as I suspect he did, without what ye did, he would have died by now." She waved a hand as he sank, weak-kneed, onto a stool. "Still, I will feel better if ye bring him to me tomorrow. I will see for myself whether anything else needs tending.

"Should I get him now?"

"Nay, let the lad rest. If he has shown no signs of difficulty on the trip, tomorrow morning is soon enough."

"If ye are sure..."

"I am. Now, go on with ye and get some rest. Yer da will want to spend most of tomorrow with ye, preparing for the lairds' arrival in ten days."

"That, I ken how to do," he told her, leaned in and kissed her cheek, and stepped away. Then he turned back. "Did I really do that, or did ye?"

"I wouldna lie to ye, Drummond. Ye ken that. Ye did it."

He shook his head and left her, smiling.

20

After only two days, more quickly than she could have imagined, Morven began to feel at home. She had her own chamber, with a pallet for Rory, and she was meeting people and learning names with every meal. Drummond's mother had seen Rory that morning and pronounced him fully healed from the damage his father had done. She'd suggested, as a reward for his good behavior, that Drummond take him to the kennel to see the new litter one of the keep's mongrels had whelped two weeks before they arrived. Morven, thrilled to learn her son had taken no lasting harm, agreed. After all, who didn't love puppies? Her life had been turned upside down, too, even though the changes were all good, and nothing would please her more than to see new puppies—and see Rory laughing with them.

Rory was in heaven, greeting the dam with an outstretched hand for her to sniff, thereby gaining her permission for him to touch her puppies. Morven laughed as he sat down right in the kennel doorway, where the puppies could climb on him but not escape into the larger barn, and petted each until one of them fell asleep on his lap.

"Can I keep him?"

The longing in his expression stole her breath and reminded her of how desperately he'd searched for their missing dog last year. "'Tis up to the kennel master, and to yer soon-to-be father," she told him, hoping she wasn't putting Drummond in an impossible spot.

Rory gave Drummond his most enticing grin and held the puppy up for his inspection. "What do ye think, Da?"

Drummond shot her a look that told her just how hearing that word from Rory's mouth had hit him. Right in the heart. "I think he's a fine pup, and we should leave him with his dam for a few more weeks until he's weaned." When Rory's face fell, he quickly added, "Ye can see him every day, ye ken, and when he and the others are a little older, I'm sure they'll like to play with ye. But for now, I think they need a wee sleep." He nodded to the dozing puppy Rory held on his lap, then to the others who had returned to their dam and sprawled around her, some with fat little bellies exposed, snoring softly.

Rory took the hint, gently picked up his pup and placed it with the others. "*Dinna fash,*" he told it. "I'll be back to see ye again tomorrow."

"What will ye name him?" Morven wanted to see how far his creativity extended.

"I must ken him better," Rory said, in all seriousness. "He will tell me."

She raised an eyebrow at Drummond.

"I think he means the pup's personality, when he's a little older, will give Rory an idea of what he should be called."

"Ah, of course. Rory, that is an excellent plan." But would Rory recognize which one he'd decided was *his*?

Later, while Rory emulated the puppies and took a wee sleep, she and the Lathan weaver, Ferelith, set up her loom. Drummond, with Finn's help, had moved it into the airy room next door to Ferelith and her loom, in a low building along the outer wall of the bailey. Ferelith was her first friend here, other than Drummond and the men like Finn, who'd come with him to rid the village of the raiders. How ironic that the raiders had moved in, instead, and if all went well, they would become part of MacComas.

The looms were near enough for her and Ferelith to work together and consult, yet far enough apart to keep the noise of the weaving from being deafening if they worked at the same time. Even better, Morven's windows looked out on the bailey and the practice ground where Rory would spend much of his time. That is, when he wasn't working with the Lathan tutor to learn his letters and other skills—or visiting the puppies.

Over the next few days, Ferelith took charge of her when Drummond was busy with the Laird's business or on the practice ground honing his skills—or Rory's. He continued to teach her son the fundamentals that they had begun in the village. Thankfully, Rory was still young enough that he hadn't fallen too far behind his peers. And he enjoyed the attention as much as he enjoyed learning. Kelso had said Rory learned quickly. She'd always known he had a sharp mind. She was happy to see her opinion confirmed by both Drummond and Rory's tutor.

She had worried that Drummond's family would not accept her, or the idea of the heir marrying a woman with a son, but they were lovely to her and to Rory. Still, she was also beginning to suspect there was something different about the family. When Morven overheard two women talking about that very thing, she had all but fallen out of her open window so as not to miss anything they said as they crossed the bailey near her.

"Aileanna saved Marcail and her wee bairn. Without her healing touch, Marcail and her daughter would be dead."

Another woman said, "I ken that. And now my wee dog is sick. I wish Lianna was still here, but perhaps Eilidh could help."

Those, Morven knew, were Drummond's sisters. Lianna had an affinity for animals. She had married the MacDhai chief and moved away. Eilidh was Tavish's twin and apparently had the same healing talent as their mother. Aileanna had seen to Rory, making the information she sought even more important to Morven.

She went next door to Ferelith.

"I just overheard a conversation—mayhap ye did, too. Ye must tell me what it means." She repeated what she'd heard. "What exactly did those women mean by Aileanna's healing touch? I've heard bits and such here and there, but no one has explained..."

"Best ye ask Drummond, lass."

She planted her hands on her hips. "If 'tis such a problem, then I must ken what they were talking about before I speak to him, else how do I get him to explain it to me? Ye must tell me. What did those women mean?"

The weaver set aside her shuttle and stretched her back while she studied Morven, as if deciding whether she was worthy of the truth. Finally, she smiled and spoke. "Ye have heard of wise women—healers or those with the Sight, aye?"

"I have."

"Do ye ken these things are real?"

"I dinna ken. I've never met anyone with such abilities."

"Aye, ye have. Aileanna can heal with her touch. With her will. Injuries, illness, women suffering difficult deliveries and bairns that would otherwise die. Most of her children have some sort of gift like hers, to heal. Tavish is different. Drummond, too. He is the only one of his siblings lacking their gifts."

She wasn't so sure about that. "So the gifts passed to her daughters, but not to her sons, or not completely?"

"Nay, the youngest triplet with Drummond and Lianna, Jamie, is a healer like his mother. He's married away, as well. Likely he'll return for yer kirking."

Morven gulped. If there would be a wedding. After learning this, she wondered what she'd brought Rory to.

"Thank ye. I'll go talk to Drummond now."

"How could ye not tell me?"

Morven burst into his chamber just before the evening meal, where he'd gone to clean up after practicing at arms. Fortunately he was dressed, because he saw someone pass by in the hall before she closed the door behind her. Not that it would matter in two days. By then, they would be married in the kirk. But he didn't want any hint of scandal attached to her before then. Someone seeing him undressed, with her in his chamber, would cause problems.

Her accusatory tone captured Drummond's attention as much as her presence and her words themselves. "Tell ye what?" He asked her mildly, stalling, trying for time to think. But he knew better. He'd run out of time. Morven knew. Or thought she did. He hoped the truth, when she heard it, would not scare her away.

"That yer mother is a Wise Woman. A Healer with special abilities that go beyond herbs and such. So is Eilidh. 'Tis why she spends so much time with yer mother."

"She spends so much time with my mother because she is her apprentice."

Morven waved that away. "And Tavish and ye are different. How different are ye?"

Drummond heaved out a sigh. Here it came. Would she accept his family's abilities, or run screaming into the night? "Some would say Tavish is a Seer. He's not a good one. Not yet."

"And what about ye? What can ye do that ye havena told me?"

He shrugged. "Ye ken I've always been good at finding

things. People, too, especially since I met ye, after Rodrick's man knocked me off my horse and I fell down a cliff. I hit my head. Something... changed. Since the fall, I can see where people I ken are. I can also do a little of what my mother and sister do. I helped Rory, though I scarce knew it at the time. Mother thinks I saved his life."

Morven's hands flew to her mouth, and she choked on a gasp. "Ye saved him?"

"When ye had me touch the bump on his head, I felt something—faintly—akin to what my mother, brother, and sister have described. While ye fussed with cooling cloths, I thought about his hurts going away. It appears I was summoning what his body could do on its own to heal whatever was wrong. She says there was likely a deeper bleeding in his head that I stopped. It would have killed him by now, had I not been able to do the little I only imagined I did."

She collapsed back against the door, then sank to her haunches. Drummond went to her and knelt before her. "*Dinna fash*, Morven. Mother can see and do much more than I, and she says Rory is well. And I am the same man I've always been. Just with a little... something new. All my family has abilities, except for my da, of course. He has none, save to be who he is. My other two triplets, whom ye havena met, are both healers, though Lianna prefers animals to people. I grew up thinking I was the only one who didna inherit an ability, so being the heir had to be enough."

"Of course."

He couldn't tell if she meant her tone as sarcasm, or if she was in shock.

"All is well, Morven." He hoped he could make her see that.

"Could ye have helped Ilise? What about one of the others? Could someone go to MacComas and help her?"

"If she will agree to our help, certainly, we can try."

"Why did ye not tell me sooner?"

"How could I risk it? I couldna. Not until I kenned ye would accept me as I was. I dared not expose my family until ye met them, and I learned whether ye would like them. But with ye," he said and took her cold hands in his, shook them to make her look at him, and repeated, "with ye, I became more. And that makes me need ye even more than I kenned. As my talent matures, I need ye to keep me grounded, to help me remember who I am. Who I have always been. And someday when I become laird, I will need ye to keep me humble." He gave her a grin, but dropped it when she didn't respond in kind. "Can ye, Morven? Can ye help me?"

Finally, she nodded. "If ye promise me..."

"Anything, love."

"That ye will always be the man I fell in love with."

"I promise. Now, tell me this. Have ye seen anyone here afraid of my siblings, my mother or me?"

"Nay, of course not."

"What have ye seen, love?" She was staring at him, making him hope she wasn't about to run from him.

"Nothing I need fear, for myself or my son," she finally told him. "I see a man who saved us, over and over again. Yet, I see that same man needs *me*," she added and smiled. "I find I like that, very much."

Drummond chest expanded. He could breathe again.

"I see a strong clan of good people," she continued, "despite the strangeness that some have about them. That wee strangeness makes nay difference to me." She looked up and met his gaze with love in her eyes. "I see *ye*, Drummond. And ye are all I need."

MORVEN WOKE the morning of her wedding with a sense of unreality. She was going to marry Drummond Lathan today, and someday become the Lady of his clan. Lady of his mighty Aerie and all the lands this clan controlled, as far as she could see from the highest tower in the keep, all the way to her village, and more. She would be sister to his siblings, and responsible to keep safe the talents that made them unique and so very special.

Dear God, she wasn't sure she could do all that.

Could she marry Drummond? Certainly. She loved him. So did Rory. And Drummond loved them. Even if he were only a farmer like most of the men in her village, or a blacksmith, or... well, anything but heir to this clan, she would still marry him without hesitation.

So what had her heart beating frantically against her breast? She knew exactly what caused it. Fear. She was afraid she wasn't good enough. And would never learn what she needed to know to become good enough to measure up to his family.

But Drummond had promised to help her. That thought calmed her a little. Nay, a lot. She felt secure in his arms. She would not give him up for anything. Certainly not over her own insecurities. He'd told her she was strong and brave and fierce. Today was the day to use all those qualities to ready herself for her new role, for the wedding, and to become accustomed to being the center of attention. After that, the only thing that would remain was love.

She took a breath and smiled. Aye. Love would remain and would sustain them for the rest of their lives.

Suddenly she felt ready to get up and prepare for her day. And just in time. A knock on the door heralded the arrival of the serving girl assigned to help her.

"How are ye today, Lady...?"

Morven laughed. "Not sure what to call me? Nor am I. Morven will do for this morning. And I am fine. Ready for all that will happen." She sat up and threw aside the covers.

The lass smiled and held up a hand. "Wait a moment. There's a tub on the way up and a line of lads carrying buckets of hot water. Once they're gone, ye'll want to wash. I'll fetch something to break yer fast while ye do. Moina will bring yer gown, and we'll get ye dressed. I canna wait to see it. Moina is so clever with needle and thread."

Morven pulled up the covers, leaned back against her pillows and wrapped her arms around her knees, ready to enjoy the parade headed her way. "That sounds perfect. What about Rory?"

"Ah, and Rory will be readied as well. Ye will see him, soon."

The lass answered another knock at the door and gestured in the tub and small army of lads with buckets. As each poured his bucket into the tub, Morven thanked him, one after another. Soon, the tub was as full as she needed it to be, and the lads were gone. "I can take care of this," she told the lass. "If ye'll fetch some food and drink?"

"Ye dinna need me to wash yer hair?"

"Nay, lass. I've been doing it myself my entire life. Leave me be for a few minutes."

Once the girl left, Morven stripped out of her night rail, stepped into the steaming tub and sank into blissful heat. A dish of soap and cloths were on a bench at hand but first she leaned back to enjoy the luxury.

By the time the girl returned and announced herself, Morven was sitting by the fire in a robe, toweling her hair. "Ah, thank ye. I'm famished."

"Ye are not nervous milady?"

"Nay, lass. I'm joyful. And a little nervous. And hungry."

While she ate, the maid gently combed out her hair until it dried and shone. Then she began to style it, pinning it up with jeweled pins she took from a box she'd carried in the pocket of her apron and set on the table.

"Those are lovely," Morven said, picking one from the box and turning it over in her hand. "Sapphires?"

"Aye, Lady. They belong to Lady Aileanna, but she offered them to ye for yer special day."

"How very kind of her."

Moina arrived, a gorgeous blue silk gown draped over her arm. "Ah, good, ye are ready for yer dress," she said. "Lass, her hair is lovely. Ye did well."

"Thank ye Moina. Shall I stay and help ye?"

"Can ye check on Rory first?" Morven hadn't seen or spoken to him all morning, and she missed him.

"Of course."

The girl left and Moina spread the dress out on the bed. Also on her arm was a filmy silk chemise. Morven joined her and pressed it between her finger and thumb, enjoying the cool slide of the fabric. "This is exquisite." She reached for a seam and marveled at the tiny, delicate stitches. "Did ye do this?"

Moina nodded. "Aye, milady. I have always enjoyed the fine work."

"Ye must. Ye are a master of it."

"Try it on, and let's see if I need to adjust it."

Morven removed her robe, then shivered as the cool fabric slipped over her head and down her body.

"Aye, that'll do," Moina commented and picked up the dress. As she moved it, the deep sapphire blue changed, every ripple absorbing and reflecting the morning sunlight streaming in the window differently, like the shimmering surface of a deep loch.

"'Tis beautiful," Morven said, breathless. Wide white edging finished the bell sleeves and folded back from her hands. That was made of silk as well, soft as any fabric she'd ever felt or hoped to weave. Moina helped her don it.

"I'm pleased ye like it," Moina told her. "Ach, I forgot the slippers that go with the dress. A moment only, milady. I'll return." She bustled out, giving Morven time to marvel at the dress she had created.

"Mam, ye look like a princess!" Rory's voice started her, and she turned to find him standing in the doorway, mouth open and eyes wide.

"Thank ye, son. Ye look handsome, indeed," she answered. "Come in. Let me see." He wore a wee kilt in a plaid she recognized as the Lathans', topped by a white shirt and a short jacket in the same blue as her dress.

"Thank ye, Mother," he said, sounding very grown up. "Do ye ken this is Drummond's tartan?"

"I do. What do ye think of wearing it?"

"Now that I have a good father, I'm happy. We belong here."

She brushed a stray hair out of his face and smiled as he squirmed. "Aye, we do. I'm happy, too."

Moina came back in, holding two jewel-encrusted slippers. "Here ye are, lass. These should fit ye, but try them on to be sure."

Morven took a breath. This was all too much. But she did as the dressmaker bade. "They're perfect. Thank ye."

"Dinna thank me. Thank the cobbler, and yer soon-to-be husband. Well," she added, looking Morven up and down. She held up a hand, one finger pointed down and drew a circle.

Morven turned around as she directed.

"My work here is done," Moina announced.

"And just in time," Aileanna said from the doorway. "Lass, ye are a vision. Moina, ye have worked another of yer miracles in that dress, and the jacket for the lad."

"Thank ye," Morven and Moina said at the same time. "There were enough scraps from the dress to make something to suit young Rory," Moina added.

Moina had crafted Aileanna's dress from the candlelight over dark green fabric Morven gifted her. "Ye look beautiful," Morven told her. "While it was still on my loom, Drummond said ye would like that weave and those colors. I'm glad he was right."

"I do, and I'm pleased Moina was able to finish this dress in time for yer wedding. 'Tis the best use I could imagine for this beautiful cloth." Aileanna smiled, then looked at Rory as Moina slipped out of the room. "Are ye ready to see yer mother to the kirk, lad?"

"Aye, Lady, I am."

"Very well." She looked up at Morven and gestured toward the door. "Shall we?"

Morven's knees went weak. "Aye, we shall," she said, as much to bolster her own confidence as to answer Drummond's mother. She straightened her spine, took the hand Rory offered her, and followed Aileanna out of the keep and around the bailey to the kirk.

Drummond stood by the door, dressed much the same as Rory. The deliberate similarity charmed Morven. She had no doubt he'd requested it to make Rory feel included. The priest stood with Drummond, as did his father, the laird, and his brother Tavish and sister Eilidh. Two more, who by their looks were obviously the siblings she had yet to meet, also stood with Drummond, waiting for her. Given the speed at which this wedding was occurring—to have it done well before the gathering of the treaty lairds, as she had heard others refer to the upcoming event—the two other triplets with Drummond, Jamie and Lianna, must have arrived just this morning, or she would have met them before now.

Morven gave them a nod of greeting as she approached, then turned her attention to Drummond.

He came down the steps to her and took her hand. "Breathtaking. I kenned ye would be. And Rory! How grand ye look."

"I look like ye." He glanced at Drummond's brothers and his eyes widened. "And them, too."

Drummond planted his hands on his hips and shifted from foot to foot. "And don't we all look grand, lad?"

Rory grinned at that. "Aye, we do."

"I'm glad ye agree. Now, will ye go stand with the priest while I have a word with yer mother?"

Rory thought for a moment. "Ye willna make her cry, will ye?"

Morven, laughing behind her hand at Drummond and Rory's posturing, quickly cut it off and fought not to let it become a sob. Her dear, sweet lad!

Drummond shook his head. "Nay, I willna," he said, his tone solemn and earnest at the same time. "I promise."

Satisfied, Rory went away, followed by Aileanna, leaving them as alone as they could be in the midst of the crowd of Lathans gathered to see them wed.

Drummond took her hand. "Ye are the most beautiful sight I've ever seen," he told her, then lifted her hand to his lips. "I love ye. I wanted to tell ye that before we get started."

"I love ye, too, Drummond, or I wouldna be here. Ye ken that."

"I do," he said, turned her and walked by her side toward the priest. "Everyone canna fit in the kirk, so most of this will be done on the steps. We'll go inside only for the last prayers."

Morven nodded in time for them to reach the steps and pause. Drummond's parents and Rory stood to one side of them, his siblings on the other. She forgot them as the priest began speaking and remained conscious only of the warmth of Drummond's hand holding hers and the heat of his body beside hers. She heard him answer the priest, and she managed to answer as well, when he turned his words and his questions to her.

Rory appeared and handed something to Drummond, then stepped back.

Drummond slipped a ring on her finger, and she gasped at

the beautiful blue sapphire set in gold that now adorned her hand.

The priest declared them man and wife.

Her heart swelled and happy tears pricked her eyes as Drummond bent to kiss her, and the assembled clan cheered.

The final prayers in the kirk with Drummond's family—hers, too, now—passed in a happy blur. Then it was done, and they left the kirk to the cheers of their people.

21

Drummond had never known feelings this big. This deep. He'd watched his brother, Jamie at his wedding and heard all about Lianna's, though he hadn't been able to attend. He felt happy for them, but nothing like this. Simply sitting with his new wife by the fire in his chamber—now his and Morven's—made his heart full to bursting with love, contentment, even hope. The most beautiful, brilliant, fierce, loving woman he'd ever known was his. It all had happened so fast, he could scarce believe it.

"I never expected a trip to the edges of Lathan territory, a trip I didna want to make, would end here, with ye."

"After bumping into each other—twice—outside Angus's keep, perhaps it was inevitable."

"Ye sound like Tavish," Drummond said, and chuckled. "He would see the hand of fate in everything we went through."

She took a sip of the fine French wine he'd brought to his chamber from the *ceilidh* still underway in the great hall. "That is good," she said after savoring a sip. "Thank ye." She gifted him with the smile he'd come to cherish. "Fate may have had something to do with bringing ye to us, but if it did, it had very human agents. Yer da could have sent anyone else."

"And ye could have had a very different life at the end of the handfasting." What if he had talked his father out of sending him with Angus? He never would have met her, and she'd be in Rodrick's clutches. The thought gave him chills. He banished it.

She set her glass aside. "I dinna want to think about that any longer. That part of my life is over. I have a new life here with ye. And I want it to start now."

She stood, crossed the narrow space between them and sank onto his lap. "Tell me ye want that, too."

Instead of using words, he used his hands and lips, his tongue and teeth, to arouse and delight her. She answered his ardor with her own. Something passed between them as they learned each other's needs, something Drummond could only sense as a connection, an awareness, of all that was Morven. The beat of her heart, the breath in her body, the arousal making her cling to him.

Did his rudimentary healing talent cause it? He would explore that possibility later. For now, he didn't need answers. All he needed was her. "I love ye," he whispered in her ear, and murmured it again as he kissed his way down her throat to the upper swell of her breasts. "I want ye more than ye ken."

Morven slipped from his lap, took his hand and urged him up. When he stood, she began taking his wedding finery from him, first his kilt pin, then his belt. She slid the plaid crossing his shoulder down his arm to join the rest of the fabric on the floor at his feet, then helped him remove his boots. Clad only in his thigh-length leine, he took her hands in his and kissed her, building their passion with every stroke of his tongue. Then he loosened her dress and pulled the jeweled pins from her hair, all that he could find quickly. When the bright mass tumbled down her back, loose pins fell with it.

"Those were lent to me," Morven warned. "I must not lose them."

"We'll find them later." He pulled her dress over her head, then paused, overwhelmed by the beauty of her body, visible through her nearly sheer silk chemise. "Ye are so lovely." He said it reverently, but in truth, his blood heated at the sight of her. "'Tis all I can do to keep from tossing ye on the bed. But we'll take all the time ye need."

"I am not a virgin, Drummond. Ye dinna have to coddle me."

"What if I wish to?"

That seemed to charm her. She relaxed against him. "It may have been seven years since I've done this, but I think I still remember how. Does that bother ye? That I have a child? That I'm not untouched?"

"Do I look like it bothers me?" Drummond traced her cheek with a gentle finger. "I'm glad ye are exactly as ye are. Ye have given me a fine son, and I hope for another and more. But for now, I hope only to please ye and make ye mine, and to be the husband ye want and need me to be, and father to Rory and any other children we have. I want ye, lass. I love ye. I married ye so we could spend our lives together. So ye can be by my side when my turn comes to be laird. So ye can help me defend this keep and make a good life for our people. Ye are all I've ever wanted, and so much more than I ever imagined I could have."

A sheen of tears filled her gaze as it lingered on his face. "I'm so glad ye found me," she said and turned her head to kiss his fingers. Then she grinned, lifted his shirt and stripped it over his head. "Now let me look at ye."

"Only if I can look at ye as well."

She glanced down. Her face bloomed with color. "I dinna believe this chemise hides much at all."

He smirked. "It doesna, but I want ye out of it. I willna force ye, Morven. When ye are ready, when ye say *aye*, and only then."

"*Aye*, my love. I trust ye to take good care of me. 'Tis who ye are."

"And who ye are, as well."

AS DRUMMOND LIFTED the chemise over her head and tossed it aside, Morven shivered with anticipation. She had never felt like this, never been admired like this, never felt loved and cared for like this. Since the disaster of her handfasting, she'd thought she would never again enjoy a man's attention, nor *deserve* to enjoy a man's attention. Especially not a husband's affection.

Without knowing it, Drummond proved her wrong.

He swept her off her feet and carried her to their bed, laid her gently on it, and stood back, just looking at her.

She looked back.

She loved the way his eyes darkened as his gaze roved over her body. When he knelt above her, his scent filled her nose and made her long for the taste of his kiss. She enjoyed the color and texture of his hair as she pulled his head down to her. As he kissed her, she ran her hands over the ridged muscles and the taut, firm skin covering his shoulders and back, marveling at his strength. His body was so powerful, yet he handled her with such delicacy, such care. His touch warmed and excited her as he explored her body.

"Morven, how I love ye. I never kenned I could feel this way."

The timbre of his voice as he said her name heated her blood. The sweet words he whispered in her ear brought up emotions she'd forgotten she was capable of. Being with him made her feel like a lass again—a lass with her first lover, full of anxiety and arousal, excitement and need.

And most of all, the way he looked at her made her bold. She slid her hands further down. The taut muscles of his ass flexed under her fingers as he shifted more fully over her, as though he wanted to devour her, to absorb her through his skin, to hold her and never let her go. His manhood pressed against the curls at the top of her thighs, long, heavy, and so very hot.

"I love ye, too, with all of my heart," she murmured. "And all of my body. Take me, husband," she demanded. "I need ye, now." She tried with every touch of her hand, kiss of her mouth, and yearning gaze in her eyes to let him feel how much she loved him. She was ready to be his.

"With pleasure, milady." Drummond filled her thoughts as he filled her body with heat and pressure. She imagined the blood pulsing molten through his veins. She reveled in his arousal as it stretched and filled her, throbbing inside her, the taut muscles under her hands driving the rhythm of his thrusts, pushing them to completion, and the rapturous release of the hot seed he spilled into her body. She'd never felt so *intimate* with another person, not even when she carried her unborn child within her.

In the final breathless moment Drummond gave her, when she felt suspended between *now* and *forever*, she was sure they'd created the future they dreamed of, and that this bond between them would grow stronger, more joyful, and more intimate with each joining. Perhaps this night, they'd even made the heir he would someday need. They would enjoy loving each other until they did, and never stop until they had the houseful they wanted.

As she held him, listening to his breathing slow and deepen, she vowed her life began anew with him this night. She would do all she could to be the wife and partner he needed.

Light snow was falling as Morven, Drummond, Eilidh, and their escort entered the MacComas village. Though Morven had been away only two months, somehow, everything looked different. Fresher, peaceful. Was it the snow now dusting the ground and frosting the evergreens with white? Or the fact that the raiders had been absorbed into the village, the raids were long over, and the men behind them were dead and buried, no longer a threat to the village or to her and her son?

"How does it feel to be back?" Drummond asked as he helped her dismount and set her gently on the ground.

"More... strange... than I expected. Why I thought 'twould be the same, I canna say. I supposed only that it would appear as it did the day we left for the Aerie."

Eilidh joined them. "Let's go in. 'Tis freezing out here. This is nay place to reminisce. Ye couldha done that the whole way here."

Morven grinned at her, glad of the distraction to shake the sense of... nervousness... from her flesh. Eilidh was usually so quiet, so reserved, that her outburst surprised Morven. Judging by Drummond's raised eyebrows, she'd surprised him, too.

"Eager to get to work, are ye?" Drummond teased.

"Ye said Lady Ilise agreed to see us. Why wait?"

The keep's door opened to reveal Angus. "What are ye doin' standin' out in the snow? Come in!"

"Thank ye," Eilidh remarked, and headed for the doorway. "Someone here has sense."

"That is Chief MacComas to ye," Drummond told her, following with Morven.

"Angus will do," he said, waving her past him into the relative warmth of the keep's lowest floor. "Ye'd be the healer our Morven wrote about to my wife?"

"I am," Eilidh agreed.

Angus nodded. "Good. Ilise needs ye." He turned to greet Drummond and Morven. "'Tis been a wee," he told them after seeing them inside. He glanced outside. "Yer men can bed down here in the lower hall," he told them and waved the others inside. "Good to see ye again, Eduard," he added as the first of eight men filed in. "Let's go upstairs. Ye'll be tired and hungry. Ilise is up there, waiting to care for ye."

"She's better?" Morven hadn't seen Ilise attempt to climb to the keep's upper floors in months.

"Nay," Angus shook his head, his gaze downcast. "She's much the same. I carried her up. Dinna tell her I told ye." He led them upstairs to the great hall, where Ilise sat by the hearth, doing needlework.

"Morven!" She dropped her work into the basket at her side and put her hands on the chair arms as if about to rise.

"Dinna get up," Morven said, rushing to her and bending down to wrap her in a hug. "Angus is going to show us to our chambers, then we'll share a meal with ye before anything else."

"Very well. And thank ye for the beautiful cloth ye sent. I canna wait for ye to see the dress made from it."

"I look forward to seeing ye in it," Morven told her with a smile. And standing, walking easily, even dancing with her husband. Morven prayed Eilidh could make it all happen for her.

"Let's get ye settled," Angus said, interrupting them. "The meal will be served soon."

"What do ye think?" Drummond asked, once they were alone in their chamber and the servants had brought up their trunk. "Does she seem the same?"

Morven shrugged. "'Tis only been two months, so perhaps. She's sitting warm by the fire, and excited to see us, so that would make her seem more lively, which might mean she's gotten worse. I canna tell."

"We'll find out soon. Once Eilidh eats and has a chance to rest, she'll want to begin."

"She should wait until tomorrow. We just arrived from a long, cold ride."

"Eilidh will decide." Drummond stroked her face. Ye ken she wants my help. Ye should rest while I do that."

Morven leaned her cheek into his warm palm. "As long as ye rest, too."

A knock on the door interrupted them. "Milord, milady, the chief sent me to fetch ye to supper."

They exchanged a glance and a grin. Drummond opened the door, thanked the serving lass, and escorted Morven downstairs. Eilidh was already there, speaking with Ilise. Drummond raised his brow at her, and she responded with a quick shake of her head.

Morven worried that meant Eilidh had determined she could not help Ilise. But she pasted on a smile, greeted the MacComas Lady and took her seat.

A moment later, she stared in shock as the woman who'd warned her to run from Rodrick came out with another other lass, bearing their food.

Her eyes widened when she noticed Morven.

Morven waited until she set down her burden and turned to go, then stood and took her aside. "Who are ye? Why did ye warn me to escape?"

"I? No one ye need care about."

"Then why did ye do it? Ye didna ken me. Ye risked much if I told him what ye said."

The woman sighed and pursed her lips. "I was his wife. His second wife, after ye. I bore him two daughters. Not the son he craved."

"Dear God," Morven breathed, knowing what she had to be about to say.

"When he learned a lad lived with ye, he set everything in

motion, and sealed my fate and my daughters', as well. Yers, too."

Morven fought the urge to take her hand. What had this woman been through? "Where are yer daughters?"

"They are cared for in the nursery with the clan's other young lads and lasses."

"I'm glad of that." She glanced at the table, where Eilidh continued to distract Ilise. But Drummond was watching her over Angus's shoulder. The chief hadn't yet looked around to see what she was doing. "Do they ken who ye were?" Morven asked softly. "Who ye wed?"

"Nay, and I'd appreciate if ye didna tell them. The others who came with us will say naught. I dinna wish for my lasses to be stained—"

Morven held up a hand. "I understand and willna say anything. But if there is anything I can do to help ye, ye will ask me. What is yer name?"

"'Tis Arabella. Thank ye. Ye are most kind."

"As were ye. We suffered much the same."

"No longer," she answered, with a glance toward Drummond.

"Dinna give up hope. There are many good men here at MacComas. Yer future can be better than yer past."

Arabella nodded. "It already is." She smiled and headed back toward the kitchen.

Morven took a breath, hoping to calm her pounding heart before she returned to her seat.

Drummond leaned close after she settled by him and whispered, "Ye ken her?"

"I do. She warned me to escape," she replied softly, "when she didna have to say anything. She was Rodrick's wife and has two daughters by him. Rory has half-sisters."

"What can we do for them?"

"She seems happy here, but I told her to send word to me if she needed anything."

As the meal was ending, Eilidh requested some brandy or wine and poured a glass for Ilise. "Drink this, milady." Once she finished it, Eilidh helped Ilise to her feet. "Brother?"

Drummond nodded and turned to Morven. "That is my cue. She's ready."

"I'll come with ye."

"Nay, go to yer rest. I dinna ken how long this will take, and there will be naught for ye to see or to do to help yer friend."

Hours passed. Morven paced their chamber, then lay down, trying to compose herself, but too restless and concerned about Ilise to sleep.

Finally, the door opened and Drummond staggered in.

"How is she?" Morven asked and sat up. "How are ye?" she added once she got a good look at her husband. Dark circles rimmed his eyes. He hadn't looked so exhausted since the day they finally walked into the village after their trek through the mountains.

Drummond sat on the edge of the bed, pulled off his boots, and stretched out beside her. "She is fine. Eilidh, too, or as well as can be expected after treating Ilise's injury. Yer friend will walk without pain from now until she falls off another horse."

"What did ye do?"

"Eilidh did most of it. I lent her strength when she needed it. We finished nigh an hour ago."

"An hour? What have ye been doing since then?"

"Eating. Drinking. Letting Ilise's pain fade from us. I had some, but nothing like Eilidh's. Healing takes a lot out of the healer. I'm sorry. I'd tell ye more, but now, I need to sleep." He closed his eyes, and in moments, emitted a soft snore.

What had they done? Morven fell back on her pillow, suddenly exhausted, too. The next she knew, daylight streamed in around the window covering. Drummond still slept.

Tomorrow was the Martinmas celebration. Today, she was eager to visit Ilise, and to get answers. She dressed and left the chamber quietly. In the great hall, clan members were breaking their fast, serving girls in attendance, but she didn't see Arabella. Angus came in as her food was being put in front of her. She stood and went to him. "How is she?"

"Still asleep, but…" He trailed off and his gaze slid sideways, as if deep in thought. "She seemed softer, more relaxed, resting easier. Does that make sense?"

"Aye, if she nay longer suffers pain, it does."

"Well, we'll let her sleep. Her maid is nearby. I'll have her send for ye when she wakes."

"Thank ye."

Another hour passed before Ilise summoned her to her chamber. Morven couldn't believe what she found when she entered. Ilise was up and moving around with ease.

"Morven! I'm so glad ye are here. Can ye believe this?" She held out her arms and spun slowly around.

"'Tis wonderful, Ilise!"

"I'll wear my new dress tomorrow night and dance with my husband. Won't he be surprised!"

"He'll be thrilled," Morven told her. "As will everyone who sees ye."

"Eilidh told me to take it slow, and no riding horses until the spring. I canna wait."

"Best ye do," Eilidh said, coming into the chamber. "Or ye will undo all the good I did ye."

Ilise's eyes went wide. "I will?"

"Only if ye do something daft. Ye are still healing, so I beg ye to have a care how much ye walk and move about for the next sennight."

"Ye mean I canna dance at the Martinmas celebration?" Ilise's face fell, and Morven's heart broke for her.

"Of course ye can," Eilidh told her. "With Angus, and slowly." Eilidh grinned. "I think ye'll both enjoy that more than a lively country dance."

Ilise brightened. "I, too. Thank ye, Eilidh. I dinna ken how ye did this, but I'll be forever grateful."

Eilidh nodded and looked away, but while she did so, she also rubbed her lower back.

Morven started to ask if she was well, but Angus came in, Drummond on his heels. She'd talk to Eilidh—or Drummond —later.

The next evening's *ceilidh* exceeded everyone's expectations. The hall filled with MacComas and the former raider folk. Laughter rang out above the music, and after the sumptuous meal to celebrate the harvest, men pushed back the tables to clear the floor for dancing. Angus led Ilise out and the music stayed soft and slow as he led her around the floor, holding her tenderly in his massive arms.

"'Tis a dream come true for her," Morven told Drummond, sitting next to her, and Eilidh, on his other side.

"How are ye?" Eilidh asked her. "'Tis yer longest separation from Rory, aye?"

Morven watched her friend dance for a moment while she thought how to answer Drummond's sister. "I find it liberating," she finally said. "I ken he's well cared for at the Aerie by people who love him. I miss him, of course, but not as desperately as I thought I might."

"'Tis because ye are with me," Drummond teased.

"And me," Eilidh added with a shy grin.

"Aye," Morven said, and smiled at them. "I finally have the large family I always dreamed of." She took Drummond's hand and placed it on her waist. "Soon, ours will be even larger."

"Morven! Do ye mean it?"

"Of course. I wouldna jest about something that means so much to both of us."

"I never kenned Martinmas was a time when wishes came

true," he told her and kissed her soundly, then grinned with delight. "I love ye more than I can say."

"Mine came true when ye married me," Morven told him, and leaned in for another kiss.

On his other side, Eilidh groaned. "I hope I'm never as starry-eyed as the two of ye."

Drummond broke the kiss and met Morven's loving gaze with his own. Then they turned to his younger sister. Together they told her, "Ye will be."

EPILOGUE
THREE YEARS LATER

M orven scooped up wee Aillig before he could reach the
table where Drummond and Rory bent over a chess
board. A large mongrel dog dozed at Rory's feet. Aillig might
have meant to climb on Cuilean. But she expected she'd
prevented the wee scamp from upsetting the game. She
returned to her chair, holding him, protesting, on her lap.

Aillig, at two summers in age, could be counted on to wreak
havoc with great intensity and enjoyment, as any two-year-old
lad would do. She hoped she could survive the next year while
he outgrew this stage. So far, he lacked his father's even temper
and years of experience, but Drummond's heir already showed
plenty of the singularity of purpose that made his father
respected in the Lathan clan. Though Drummond had yet to
succeed Toran as Lathan Laird, and they both hoped that event
was still many years in the future, over time, Drummond had
taken on many of the responsibilities Toran used to carry alone.

To say Drummond and Rory were playing chess was a wee
exaggeration. Drummond was teaching their eldest son the
game, certain that it would appeal to Rory's innate facility with
strategy and tactics. Morven knew what Drummond was up to.

If Aillig remained as impetuous when grown as he was as a wean, he would need a steady, analytical advisor at his side. Someone whom he loved and respected, but also trusted not to become a rival for the position he would hold.

Drummond had big plans for her son. Their son. Both of their sons. Morven was unceasingly proud of both lads, and of the family they had created.

"So *that* is what I have been doing wrong," Rory commented after Drummond explained the pattern in a series of moves they had practiced. "I see it now. Thank ye, Da."

"Ye did well, Rory. And never fear, there is much more to learn. I'll show ye another strategy tomorrow evening." He glanced at Morven, his gaze sweetly adoring at first, then going molten. "I see yer mother is ready to put Aillig to bed. 'Tis nearly time for ye to get some sleep as well. Bhaltair expects ye at arms practice in the morning."

Rory sighed and stood, obedient.

Cuilean heaved to his feet and leaned into the lad. A wolfhound somewhere in his heritage gave him his rough coat, but his sire and dam had been smaller dogs, so full-grown, Cuilean's nose only came up to Rory's waist—for now. Morven thought he'd grow to be tall, like his father and her.

"I'd rather spend more time with grandmother in her herbal," Rory said as he stroked Cuilean's head. "She is teaching me to make some of her healing poultices."

Morven stood with Aillig on her hip. "As if there were a lack of healers in this clan?"

Rory grinned and colored. But his fingers clenched in Cuilean's rough hair. He would rather learn than fight, but he needed to be able to do both, and he knew it as well as she and Drummond did. "Ye can spend some time with her after yer morning training, not instead of it," she told him. "Now get ready for bed while I wrestle this wee one into submission." She shifted Aillig on her hip and took him off to the chamber he and Rory shared, opposite the sitting room from hers and Drummond's.

They'd moved to this larger suite of rooms after the wedding, but she was beginning to think they would soon need more chambers. If their youngest continued to be as active as he grew, Rory would need his own space rather than share with Aillig. And if they were blessed with more bairns—well, they'd deal with that as it happened. Besides the dormitory for the older lads, the keep boasted a nursery for infants and young weans, but Morven preferred to have her bairns nearby. For now.

By the time she had their sons settled, Cuilean dozing on the floor between their beds, Drummond had cleared away the chess set. He sat by the hearth with two glasses of wine on the wee table between their chairs.

"Did Aillig go to sleep for ye?" He handed her one of the glasses, touched his to hers in a silent toast, then they both took a sip.

"Better than I feared. I'll be glad when he is a little older and more settled."

"Ye dinna want to wish away the time we have with him when he is so small."

"I ken it. 'Tis precious. He is precious, but he's also more tiring than Rory was at that age." She took another sip, leaned against the back of the padded chair and sighed in appreciation. "'Tis good of yer mother to tutor Rory."

"Do ye think he gave her a choice?"

Morven chuckled at that. "He *is* insatiably curious. An excellent quality in an advisor to the Laird."

Drummond nodded. "We must consider his needs, love. If ever a lad was meant to attend university, Rory is that lad."

"I ken it. As much as I hate for him to go away, he must eventually. But he will also return."

"Aye. Aillig will need him. And ye need him, too."

"Not as much as I used to. We have Aillig. And I have ye to love me, and to love. I'm glad we have these years before ye must succeed yer father. Yer time willna be yer own, come that day."

"For now, it is. At least some of it is. And I have an idea for how we should use some of it right now." That molten, heavy-lidded gaze was back. She knew it well and loved to see it in Drummond's eyes.

"Bring yer wine. We'll finish it in bed," she suggested. "Afterward."

Drummond took her hand and pulled her to her feet and into his arms. Then he grinned and asked, "Do ye really want wine for breakfast?"

AUTHOR'S NOTE

Look for Book 4 in my Highland Talents Heritage series, *Highland Dreamer*, Tavish Lathan's story, in November 2022, and Book 5, *Highland Echo*, Eilidh Lathan's story, in April 2023.

HIGHLAND DREAMER
(Highland Talents Heritage Book 4)

Tavish Lathan sees the future in his dreams. Because he lacks a full command of the talent he inherited from his mother, his predictions don't always come to pass. So when death clouds the destiny he foresees for a beautiful visitor to the Lathan keep, Tavish prays this foreshadowing will be one of his unfulfilled visions.

After her seer's sense warns of danger, Yvaine's begs her parents to allow her to accompany them to a gathering of clan chiefs at the Aerie. Her father has his share of enemies, and her powers of prophecy are often less than reliable, so her only hope of seeing the threat in time to protect him is to remain close at hand.

Tavish's visions fail to predict the ardent feelings he

develops when he meets the doomed lass. His efforts to protect Yvaine from her fate cause her to misunderstand his intentions. She believes that he is part of a conspiracy to kill her father. When the real danger appears, can they trust each other—and their burgeoning abilities—enough to keep their dreams of death from coming true?

HIGHLAND ECHO
(Highland Talents Heritage Book 5)

Eilidh Lathan is bound to the Aerie by two things—the echo in her blood of her mother's healing talent, and her love for one man. But he is unaware that he has claimed her heart. If only she had the courage to tell him—and he felt the same.

Bhaltair Lathan's intimidating stature makes him an ideal chief guard for the clan. But when it comes to Eilidh, the braw man does his best to be gentle. No matter that he treats her like spun glass, Bhaltair believes that she will never see him as a lover, but will forever view him as a warrior to be feared.

When Eilidh is assaulted by a visiting guardsman and left bruised and shaken, she's mortified that Bhaltair is the one who saves her from a worse fate. Having seen her at her weakest, Bhaltair wants to hunt down her attacker, but fears losing any chance of gaining her heart if he surrenders to his vengeful fury. Can the timid healer and the clan's most fearsome warrior find a love that will bind them forever?

ALSO BY WILLA BLAIR

His Highland Heart

His Highland Rose

His Highland Heart

His Highland Love

His Highland Bride

Highland Talents

Heart of Stone

Highland Healer

Highland Seer

Highland Troth

The Healer's Gift

When Highland Lightning Strikes

Highland Talents Legacy

Highland Prodigy

Highland Memories

Highland Reckoning

Sweetie Pie (A Candy Hearts Novella)

Waiting for the Laird

When You Find Love

ABOUT THE AUTHOR

Willa Blair is an award-wining Amazon and Barnes & Noble #1 bestselling author of Scottish historical, light paranormal and contemporary romance filled with men in kilts, psi talents, and plenty of spice. Her books have won numerous accolades, including the Marlene, the Merritt, National Readers' Choice Award Finalist, Reader's Crown finalist, InD'Tale Magazine's RONE Award Honorable Mention, and NightOwl Reviews Top Picks. She loves scouting new settings for books, and thinks being an author is the best job she's ever had.

Willa loves hearing from readers!
Contact her:
www.willablair.com
authorwillablair@gmail.com

Sign up for my Newsletter
Find links to the rest of my books